Sand Island Diaries

by

Lael R. Neill

Sand Island Diaries

Cover Art by *Debbie Taylor*

The Wild Rose Press, Inc.
PO Box 708
Adams Basin, NY 14410-0708
Visit us at www.thewildrosepress.com

Publishing History
First Mainstream Historical Rose Edition, 2014
Print ISBN 978-1-62830-595-1
Digital ISBN 978-1-62830-596-8

Published in the United States of America

All the love scenes in every penny dreadful she had ever read flashed through her mind as Paul reached out and softly drew her toward him. She knew where this would lead and she was oh, so ready for it!

His hands explored her back as though memorizing the feel of her. She came easily into his embrace, her arms going behind his waist. Letting herself drift toward him, she tipped her face up and closed her eyes, inviting his kiss. His long arms enveloped her, and she pressed herself against the front of his Red Serge, immersed in his warmth and the masculine scent surrounding him. She felt his height dominating her, possessing her, and she let herself go into the moment. When at last their lips touched, she knew how a skyrocket felt when it exploded at the peak of flight. She yielded herself to him completely, body and soul, her whole being gone into the softness of his lips and his somewhat harsh Mountie mustache. Lightning flashed within her, turning her to liquid warmth inside. She did not exactly understand what she wanted, but it certainly did include him, and a lot more than just this one kiss. Her hand crept up over the back of his neck, pressing him against her, deepening the kiss. When his tongue caressed her upper lip, she was certain she would collapse from his sheer nearness.

They parted at last, breathless and shaken by the depth of passion that had passed between them. She backed away and looked up at Paul, seeing his fair skin ruddy with excitement. Then, unable to bear his gaze, she closed her eyes and felt those wonderfully expressive lips against her forehead. In that instant she went from a girl poised on the brink of life to a woman fallen headlong in love.

Dedication

To the memory of my mother, Eva Heath,
who liked happy endings

Acknowledgements

With gratitude to the members of
the Writers' Guild of Bastrop, Texas,
for all their encouragement and support.

Chapter 1

Elizabeth Talbot watched herself in one of the many mirrors of the upper-class modiste's fitting room. As the seamstress fastened the row of tiny cloth-covered buttons up the back of her gown, Elizabeth reached up to her fashionable pile of mahogany curls, trying to ease a hairpin digging into her scalp.

"Elizabeth, dear, *do* quit fidgeting, *please*! You'll drive the poor woman to distraction," her mother complained.

"Oh, Aunt Rose, it won't be but a moment. I know the gown fits perfectly. This is just a final check," Jenny Weston's tone was soothing, and Elizabeth looked at her older cousin. *Jenny's going to be the most beautiful bride ever. She's so small and slender, with that lovely hair. Even though our mothers were sisters, aside from the Brisbane brown eyes we really don't look a thing alike. I'm surprised she chose me as her Maid of Honor, but then, her best friend Caroline is obviously expecting, and that wouldn't do at all. I know I'm not her first choice, but I'll do my best for her...*

"I'm certainly glad you chose a subdued color, Jenny," Rose continued, interrupting Elizabeth's thoughts. "Anyone can wear deep gold, and that style will flatter Elizabeth. She's so big and tall she simply can't wear certain cuts. And I would not recommend any sort of heel whatsoever." Elizabeth had heard that

1

so often it should have rolled off like water from a duck's back, but her mother's carping criticism still stung. *It's true. I'm too tall, and I'm Junoesque, like all the women in Father's family.* She wanted to voice her protests aloud, but she had been cut to pieces so many times she knew better than to try.

"Cousin Jen, you said you're certain it's all right for me to wear heels," she half-asked, her confidence shaken by her mother's remarks.

"Of course. I told you, Shane's best man is six feet three in stocking feet. You could wear stilts if you wanted to."

"And when is the groom's party arriving, then?" Rose inquired.

"The train will be in at four-something this afternoon."

"They're all staying at... Where? The Waldorf, isn't it?"

"Yes, they are. I wish they could have stayed at Parkfield too. It's not like we don't have room, but the bride's and groom's parties staying under the same roof would raise a few eyebrows. It's odd to me, though, being back in my childhood bedroom."

"I'd have thought you'd be starving to see home again. New York, after all, is..."

"New York," Jenny interrupted. "If I wanted to live here, Aunt Rose, I never would have gone to Canada in the first place."

"But I've heard that the little hamlet where you live is so...*backward!*"

"It's true there's no electricity in the country outside of River Bend yet, but supposedly that will be coming next summer. Uncle Richard's house does have running water and a full bathroom, and kerosene lamps aren't all that bad."

"I understand there are no automobiles, though."

Jenny laughed merrily. "No, thank heaven. Not yet. They'll come soon enough, I know, and I imagine Uncle Richard will have the very first one." Elizabeth watched her mother and her cousin in a mirror, glad to keep a low profile and stay out of her mother's line of fire.

The seamstress knelt on the hard floor, a ruler in her left hand, checking the hem length. "Would you please turn to your left a little, ma'am?" she asked, tugging gently on the skirt. Elizabeth looked down at her, surprised. She had forgotten the birdlike little woman was even there. Obediently she rotated a quarter turn and found another mirror in which to watch her cousin and her mother.

"So, this best man of Inspector Adair's? What did you say his name was?" Rose had asked the same question at least five times since their luncheon.

"Sergeant Paul Weller. He's twenty-six years old, tall, and blond, and his family owns a large lumber mill in River Bend."

"A little old to be paired with Elizabeth, don't you think?"

"Not at all. It wasn't long ago, you remember, the ideal bridegroom was supposed to be eight years older than his bride. That rule of thumb makes Shane a little young for me. He's only five years my senior."

"Well, I certainly hope this friend of yours knows how to dance. That's one thing Elizabeth does decently." Elizabeth had heard that one often enough too, but her heart still sank to her toes.

"He dances quite well, Aunt Rose. So does Shane, for all that. And do you think it's polite to be discussing Elizabeth as though she weren't here? She's not a child any longer." Elizabeth had seen that before too. Her cousin Jenny, a physician, had a way of cutting through to the heart of a matter and had no compunctions about doing so when she felt it necessary.

"No, I suppose not, Jenny. She did come out last year, after all," Rose agreed with a grudging sigh.

"There, ma'am. All done. Does it meet with your satisfaction?" the seamstress asked the bride-to-be. Elizabeth walked a few steps and turned before the mirrors.

"It's perfect," Jenny said before Rose could open her mouth, but she got her two cents' worth in anyway.

"But what if those heels make you taller than some of the men in the groom's party?"

"Be proud of it," Jenny responded. "I doubt that will be a problem. They're all rather on the tall side. I think the Royal Northwest Mounted Police must have a minimum height."

"I can't wait to see those romantic red uniforms," Elizabeth said, turning to her cousin.

"They're striking, all right," Jenny agreed.

"Will they be wearing them at the rehearsal, then?"

"I imagine so—at least their daily uniforms. Shane doesn't even own proper civilian clothes. But wait until you see the dress uniform. It's really stunning." Jenny gave Elizabeth a wicked private wink that made the younger woman's cheeks flush.

Elizabeth stood patiently while the seamstress unbuttoned the closure and eased the volume of whispering satin off over her head. Then she sat down and changed her shoes before letting the woman aid her with her clothes.

"Then, aside from the hem, is there any other alteration you want me to make, ma'am?" the seamstress asked Jenny.

"No, definitely not. It's perfect just as it is. You've done a lovely job on all my bridesmaids' gowns." Jenny's charming, dimpled smile drew an old-fashioned curtsey.

"I'm glad to be of service, then, ma'am."

"Well, we'd best return to Parkfield," Rose said, seeming to grow an inch or two with pride. *Mother so likes to brag about being the guest of the famous Doctor John Weston. And actually I'm happy we're visiting there now, too. I've so looked forward to seeing Cousin Jen again and having a nice long intimate visit. I'll always remember the hijinks we got up to there, especially at Christmas, sleeping in the ballroom, hiding in the attic, and playing pranks on everyone. But that was when we were children. As Jen pointed out, I'm not a child, no longer to be seen and not heard. I'm a lady of prominent social standing and good breeding. It's time I began living up to it.* She tied the bow at the neck of her cream silk shirtwaist and stood up, then took a moment to settle the shirtwaist down over her fashionably narrow tulip skirt.

"Elizabeth, dear, please don't slouch. No matter how tall you are, stand up."

"I wasn't slouching, Mother," she replied in a deliberately bored monotone. Rose glared at her daughter, but in the presence of the niece who had changed from a pretty, charming little girl into a beautiful, outspoken lady, she kept her mouth shut.

A junior employee of the modiste carried Elizabeth's bridesmaid gown, packed in a huge box and a mountain of tissue, out to John Weston's new Packard touring car. Wilson, the driver, dug himself out from behind the wheel and ushered the ladies into the vehicle, carefully closing the doors once they were seated.

"Where to, Miz Jenny?" he asked as he reclaimed his driver's seat. He had been a lifelong Brisbane family retainer who moved to New York with Jenny's mother; his voice still held the honeyed vowels of his Virginia roots.

"We need to go home. Uncle Richard and his horde will be arriving for dinner around seven, and of course we ladies must have time to get ready."

"Yes, ma'am." He nodded, stomping on the electric starter of the hulking Packard. Elizabeth had heard John Weston proudly proclaiming that he had purchased the newest and greatest; it was one of the first models that did not need to be cranked. After waiting for a carter's wagon to pass, he pulled out into the street.

In spite of her studied cool, a little frisson of anticipation ran down Elizabeth's spine. She had picked out an especially lovely outfit for the rehearsal on Saturday and another for dinner tonight, and secretly she wanted to show her mother she was neither awkward, ungainly, nor unladylike.

After threading their way through New York traffic for perhaps half an hour, they approached Parkfield. Elizabeth had been gazing idly out the open window of the touring car. The Weston family mansion never ceased to amaze her. In front, Ionic columns soared up to the roof, supporting balconies on the upper floors and sheltering a huge veranda on which many parties had been given during mild spring and summer evenings. Wilson turned down the side drive to the *porte cochère*, where he halted the big car with a squeak of brakes. He gave the ladies a hand out, then carried Elizabeth's dress box inside.

Rose bustled into the big side foyer, ordering one of the servants to take Elizabeth's gown to her room and see it properly hung up so it would not wrinkle. Eleven-year-old Clara, who had been practicing on the concert grand piano in the formal parlor, scooted off the bench and ran through the marble-tiled hallway to greet her mother and sister. Elizabeth gave her a grizzly bear hug with a growl, and she squirmed and giggled.

"Elizabeth, you know I don't encourage that kind of hoydenish behavior," Rose snapped. "It's well and good with Robbie, but Clara must be brought up as a lady."

"Father does it," Elizabeth riposted.

"Your father is the head of his household. It is his privilege to do as he chooses." Rose's tone was stiff.

"Elizabeth, this is such a lovely day, and we have almost three hours until dinner. Would you go walk the maze with me?" Jenny asked.

"Oh, may I come with you? I love that maze, but I'm not allowed to go in alone!" Clara asked, bouncing on her toes. A charming and delicate girl with blond-streaked hair and dark Brisbane eyes, she already showed the promise of the true beauty to come.

"Of course you may, as long as it's all right with your mother. And I don't see why you're not allowed in the maze alone. If someone gets lost, all we need to do is go to the ballroom balcony and direct them out. It's how we all learned to navigate it."

"That was well and good for you, Jenny, growing up in Parkfield. I don't want Clara frightened," Rose interjected.

"She won't be frightened with us. Now let's go, while the light is good."

"Let me get Barkley. He'll love the maze!" Clara ran off after her plush dog.

In the gentle spring day all the outside doors and most of the windows were open, to air the huge mansion. Clara took Elizabeth's hand as they walked through the side door and toward the garden. But as they approached the maze, temptation was too much. She dropped her sister's hand and held up her toy dog.

"There's a cat in the maze! Barkley can smell it! He's going to chase it! Woof! Woof!" She dived in and promptly turned the wrong way.

"Clara! Come back here! You'll get lost!" Elizabeth called.

"Oh, let her go. That's a dead end," Jenny said reassuringly. A moment or so later, Clara reappeared.

"What happened to the cat?" Elizabeth asked.

"Oh, it got away. It went through a hole under the bushes. Barkley can chase it later." Jenny turned to the right, and Clara skipped on ahead.

"Somebody told me this maze is copied from some famous place in Britain. Was it Hampton Court Palace?" Elizabeth asked as they strolled down the raked gravel path.

"No. Bromwich Hall. It's not huge, as mazes go, but it's complex and takes a long time to get to the center. We can turn around any time you'd like."

"No. I'd just like to walk a while. Cousin Jen, tell me, what's it like to be in love?"

Jenny sighed. "Love is... Well, it's when the other person's happiness and welfare mean more to you than your own. And if you ever have to ask yourself whether or not you're in love, the answer is no. Love requires you to be committed to your relationship. You don't just let go of it the minute he does or says something you don't like."

"Does it just happen, then?"

"You're full of tough questions this afternoon, aren't you?"

"You don't have to answer, you know." She tried not to take her cousin's reply as yet another rejection, but hurt always lay just below the surface.

"Elizabeth, I'm not Aunt Rose. I'll answer anything you ask, to the best of my ability, but believe me, being a doctor doesn't make me an expert on anything except the human body. I suppose love does just happen sometimes, but in my case it took a while."

"I don't suppose it'll ever happen for me." In her heart of hearts she heard her mother telling the world how tall, awkward, and unattractive she was.

"Bet, you're only twenty years old. You haven't even gotten your toes wet yet. Don't believe everything Aunt Rose tells you. Thousands of tall women have very happy marriages. And secretly I've always envied how graceful you are. You carry yourself like the ballerina you trained to be when you were younger. Me, I'm a Shetland pony who has to trot along just to keep up."

"*You* envy *me*?" Elizabeth echoed, incredulous.

"Yes, I do. And you're not fat at all. You have a

lovely full bosom, a slender waist, nice hips, and long legs. I'll bet anything that, of all my bridesmaids, you'll look the best in that dress. That's why I chose the pattern." Elizabeth felt herself blush and, as an afternoon breeze cooled her face, she changed the subject.

"What's your gown like?"

"Oh, my. Well, it's a slightly ivory satin because I really don't look all that well in ice white. The top has lace over it, elbow-length sleeves, and a neckline cut to the shape of Grandmother's diamond-and-pearl necklace."

"And the skirt?"

"It's like a tulip skirt with a short train and a split up the front. It's gorgeous and I love it."

They were interrupted when Clara woofed and went running off again.

"Clara, turn left. The other side is another dead end," Jenny called.

"She's so pretty, and Robbie is so smart. Where does that leave me?" Elizabeth sighed.

"That sounds like more of Aunt Rose's nonsense. What would you like to be?"

"Well, a wife and a mother, of course. But what you do is so wonderful, Jen. You help people get well. I can't think of anything more noble."

"Well, you could be a part of that, too. Have you ever thought of becoming a nurse?"

"Oh, dear, Mother wouldn't stand for that! When you went to medical school I talked to her about it, and she told me all nurses are, well, ladies of low morals."

"Is that what she thinks of me? If so, I'll sort her out in short order!" Jenny exclaimed.

"N...no. She never said that about doctors. Just nurses. Though she did say if you associated with such low people you'd eventually come around to acting like them."

"Well, she's wrong. All the nurses I have known are fine, upstanding ladies."

"Still, she says it's not suitable for someone of our social standing to do manual labor."

"Nursing isn't really manual labor. It's as professional as what I do. Oh, of course, there's a certain amount of routine work to it, but I'm not too proud to do that myself."

"I could think about it, I guess." But she knew thinking about it would be all she could do. Her mother would roll over her like a loaded freight wagon if she so much as breathed a word.

They made it to the center of the maze and sat a while on the marble benches, listening to the fountain and chatting. The spring sun reached in only gently, the fountain purled and splashed, and the air hung heavy with the sharp, green, slightly musky scent of the privet around them. Then Clara announced Barkley had found his cat again, and the three started back out.

"We're lost in the maze! Lost in the maze! We'll never find our way out! We'll be here forever! We're lost in the maze!" Clara chanted, throwing her arms out dramatically and spinning around until her skirt belled out under her pinafore.

"We are not lost, Clara. Cousin Jen knows it like the back of her hand," Elizabeth said.

"Well, Clara, do you remember what to do if you were really lost?" Jenny asked.

"You said just yell and scream until somebody

went up there and told me which way to turn." She pointed at the ballroom balcony on the third floor.

"That's exactly right. And I'll bet you wouldn't be scared, either, would you?"

Clara shook her head. "No. I know I'd find my way out somehow. Barkley could lead me. If I told him to, he would sniff out where we've been." Elizabeth followed Jenny as they wended their way out. When they had finally reached the edge and the long path leading past the end of the hedges, they heard a coach pull up beneath the *porte cochère*.

"Oh! They're here!" Jenny exclaimed. She tore down the final gallery with Elizabeth and Clara in pursuit. Though Elizabeth's long legs made her a fast runner, the hem of her hobble underskirt became a real handicap after the first step or two. She barely kept up with her smaller cousin, who pivoted around the last corner of the maze and headed to the side of the house where a large hired coach had just finished disgorging its load of passengers. Elizabeth recognized Jenny's Uncle Richard, but the other six men all wore identical red tunics. She stopped as Jenny ran into the arms of one of the red-clad men, who gave her a quick, discreet kiss. She backed away from him, her hands intertwined with his and laughter on her countenance. Whatever they said was lost in the mighty organ pealing in Elizabeth's heart. *They're so in love! I never saw anything so wonderful in my entire life!* Automatically she reached for Clara's hand as her little sister started to run for Jenny.

"No, Clara. Give her a chance to say hello," she said.

"But, Bet, she already *kissed* him!" The light,

childish voice floated over the whole scene and froze everyone in their tracks.

The tall, rangy officer closest to Elizabeth turned around. She looked up and her whole world narrowed to sparkling summer-blue eyes and a smile that could have lit the darkest winter night. *Up?* she wondered. *I'm actually looking up?* Even at five-eight plus two-inch heels, she came barely to the tip of his nose. Time slowed as he removed his tan Stetson, revealing crisply curling blond hair. Then she realized her heart had taken off at such a pace that it buzzed inside her chest.

"Bet, I believe introductions are in order," Jenny said. She led her fiancé by the hand as she came over to them. "Elizabeth, this is Sergeant Paul Weller. He is Shane's partner and his best man. Paul, meet my cousin, Miss Elizabeth Talbot, and her younger sister Clara."

"My pleasure, Misses Talbot." Paul reached toward her. Numbly she let go of Clara and gave her hand to Paul. He took it and bowed very properly; his fingers were warm and strong.

"Charmed, Sergeant Weller." *Oh, how gauche! Charmed. It sounds like some thirteen-year-old on her first day of debutante school. He must think I'm such a moron.* But Clara diverted his attention with a giggling curtsey, and Jenny introduced Shane.

Indisputably handsome, her cousin's fiancé had a fair Irish complexion, and jet black hair. His greeting had been punctiliously polite, but despite his exceptional looks and suave charm Elizabeth found herself stuck in the moment when she had first looked up and lost herself in Paul Weller's crystal blue eyes. The rest of the introductions flowed past her like the

Hudson in full spate. Finally, almost as an afterthought, she hugged Jenny's Uncle Richard.

Eventually the guests sorted themselves out and started for the side entrance hall.

"Miss Talbot?" a voice said nearly in her ear. She turned abruptly and saw Paul had offered his arm.

"Thank you, Sergeant Weller," she responded, thinking how unutterably stiff she sounded. Her breath nearly stopped when her fingers encountered the warm sleeve of his Red Serge. Then her heart, which had barely quieted, took off again, thundering until she was certain everyone in the entire party could hear it. She kept her touch light. The rule was a gentleman should not feel a lady's hand unless she meant him to, and certainly not when they had just met. *Thank heaven for all the lessons in formal etiquette. At least I didn't make a total fool of myself for the third time.*

"I do hope we're partnered at dinner," Paul opined as he ushered her through the door and into the side hall.

"I don't think Aunt Martha has worked out a formal seating plan for tonight."

"I'm glad. Perhaps I might persuade her that we need to sit together so we can become acquainted. After all, we are the bridal party's primary attendants." She managed to smile up at him.

"I'd like that very much." Those marvelous eyes beamed down at her once again, and his smile went straight to the center of her being and melted something there.

After a polite interval during which the myriad introductions were concluded, Jenny's father, John Weston, herded the men into the library, while the ladies retired to dress for dinner. Elizabeth had been deliberately given the beautifully appointed blue bedroom adjacent to Jenny's own. It welcomed her with the quiet peace she had sought all day. She removed her shirtwaist and then stepped out of the slender tulip skirt, carefully hanging both in the elaborate parquetry armoire. Then, stripped down to her corset and camisole, she managed a quick but refreshing sponge bath, patted lavender talc into her underarms, and put on fresh underthings. She reached for her petticoat, but was distracted by her image in the cheval glass. Adjusting the glass so she could see her feet as well as her head, she ran through the five basic ballet positions. It was something she did often, since it relaxed her and made her accept her height. A gentle demi-plié followed. As she set herself for a sauté, a soft knock came at her door. She made a grab for the petticoat, dropped it over her head, and tied the waist.

"Yes?" she called.

"Bet? It's me. May I come in?"

"Of course, Jen. But be careful. I'm not decent."

With a soft giggle Jenny, enveloped in a voluminous antique silk shawl, opened the door only as far as she needed to and edged in. "I'm not really decent either. I wondered if you'd help me with my buttons."

"If you'll help me with mine."

"Fair's fair, then." She unwound the shawl and turned so Elizabeth could do up the back of her gown. Its silvery pearlescent watered silk shimmered as she moved.

"That dress is lovely, Jen. Inspector Adair is going to take one look at you and fall in love all over again."

"I don't think Shane puts much store in that kind of thing," Jenny responded with an airy gesture of dismissal. *That attitude is well and good for her. She has her man. What about the rest of us?* "But I saw Paul escort you into the house. What do you think of him?"

Elizabeth touched the center of her chest as though to keep her heart in place. "We've just met. He seems congenial, and he's certainly a gentleman, but I can't draw any conclusions yet." The look Jenny gave her said she took the bland statement with a whole spoonful of salt. Curiosity crawled around just beneath Elizabeth's skin, and her cousin knew her well enough to sense it.

"I'll help you with your dress and tell you a little bit about Paul. How's that?"

"If you want to." It was hard to dissemble before the cousin who knew her so well, but after eons of practice with her mother, she had developed the talent. She shook out her dress and Jenny held it up, easing it over Elizabeth's elaborate coiffure.

"I like the material, Elizabeth. It's so soft, and forest green is a good color for you."

"Mother keeps harping on colors that won't make me look sallow."

"Oh, phooey. Your complexion isn't sallow any more than mine is." While Elizabeth slid her sleeves into place, Jenny straightened the waist of the dress, took up a small button hook, and started on the buttons with their tiny loops. "Anyway, about Paul. I liked him from the first moment we met. He's always smiling, always has something good to say. He's patient and kind and considerate and would give you the shirt off his back. But never underrate him or take him for granted. He's shrewd, intelligent, and anything but shallow. And only a fool would provoke him. I saw how easily he handled Philip Hildebrand when Father tried to make me come back to New York last August."

"He sounds admirable," she said, feeling the small pulls and tugs as her cousin did up the back of her dress.

"Oh, he has his flaws. We all do. His spelling is one of them. Shane is forever telling me he has to rewrite all of Paul's reports."

"I can't spell all that well either," Elizabeth said with a shrug. "But I'm good at mathematics. That drives Mother to distraction, too, because it's not feminine."

"Aunt Rose is easily distracted. I hope you don't take her histrionics too seriously. And in all confidence, I'm better at math than spelling too."

Elizabeth appreciated her cousin's attempt to cheer her, but sighed nevertheless. "It's sometimes difficult to ignore Mother when you have to live with her day in and day out. But in her defense, she is one of the most generous people you could ever hope to meet."

"Don't get me wrong. I love Aunt Rose, but sometimes I wish I could just tell her to shut her mouth. There. You're all buttoned up." Elizabeth felt a pat at the back of her shoulder.

"Thank you. Without your help I'd certainly have mussed my hair."

"Then let's go on downstairs. They'll be calling us for dinner soon."

Elizabeth followed Jenny down the hallway to the grand staircase. The intricately carved Carrera marble spindles and the elaborate balustrades crowning them curved in a wide, graceful arc to the foyer below. She smiled inwardly, remembering all the times they had incurred parental wrath by sliding down the smooth sweep of polished stone. In spite of herself, she giggled aloud. Jenny turned around and looked up at her from two steps below.

"What's funny, Bet?" she asked.

"I was just remembering Mother scolding us for sliding down the balustrade. She kept telling us we'd fall over the edge and smash our heads on the floor."

"We're the fifth generation here at Parkfield, and I never heard of anyone falling from the stairs, or the gallery either, for that matter." Jenny gestured to the long rail on either side of the head of the stairs.

"No ghosts?" Elizabeth asked lightly.

"Not that I know of. But some of those early Westons whose portraits are all over the place certainly look capable of haunting a house." Elizabeth laughed merrily.

As they reached the bottom of the stairs, John Weston ushered his herd of gentlemen out of the library. Shane looked around, spied Jenny, and smiled broadly.

"What were you two laughing about, then?" he asked, making eye contact with Elizabeth.

"We were just discussing the possibility Parkfield might be haunted," Jenny responded.

"Some of those dubious ancestors of ours could certainly be lingering in dark corners," Richard agreed. "There were indeed some grand rogues among us. If I were in their shoes, I'd be in no rush to go to meet my final reward either."

John slapped his brother lightly on the shoulder. "I've lived here all my life and I've never seen or heard anything of the kind."

"That's because you're a scientist, John. Everything has to be cut and dried, impaled on a pin or stained on a slide, proven empirically beyond a shadow of a doubt, and committed to paper. You've no romance about you."

"Not now. I'm hungry enough to eat a whole horse raw. Let's go see what Mrs. Hall has offered up to us, shall we?" He herded his charges back down the hallway, to the formal dining room. Elizabeth trailed behind Jenny until she realized Paul was at her elbow. She encountered the marvelous blue eyes again as he held out his arm to her.

"Miss Talbot?" he asked.

"Thank you, Sergeant Weller." She took his arm very properly, using her free hand to corral her skirt. Feeling very daring indeed, she lifted her hem just enough to grant a glimpse of trim ankles between evening pumps and the seafoam lace bordering her petticoat.

What John had referred to as "Mrs. Hall's offering" turned out to be roast pork with potato dumplings, but since she was indeed seated next to Paul, it could have been chopped hay for all Elizabeth noticed. The usual brilliant Weston table conversation swirled around her unheeded. Finally she turned to Paul.

"So, Sergeant Weller, how do you find New York?"

Paul gave half a shrug. "A bit like Ottawa, I think. It's a large city but certainly not overwhelming. Actually, I've been here before."

"Oh?"

"Yes. I've come with my father when he was here on business. At one time he had hopes I'd follow in his footsteps and take over the family lumber mill, but I'm afraid I disappointed him. All I ever wanted to do since I was a child was join the Northwest Mounted."

Oh, I could fill an encyclopedia with how it feels to disappoint one's parents. "Has he reconciled himself to your choice, then?" Elizabeth asked.

"I think he still holds out hope I'll get this out of my system someday, but yes, we're on good terms."

"That's fortunate. Uncle John and Cousin Jenny almost tore each other limb from limb before they worked out their differences."

"I saw a good bit of that first-hand, especially after the August Curse set in."

"August Curse?" she prompted.

Paul smiled nostalgically. "Strange things always seem to happen to us in August. We've come to call it the August Curse. It began when I was just a constable and rode rounds with Shane for the first time. I didn't have a good hill horse like I do now. It panicked in a narrow place, fell over a steep bank, landed on me, and broke my leg. He had to shoot the horse because its back was broken, and then we had a very difficult time getting out of the woods. The next year we had to swim to an island in the middle of a lake to get away from a forest fire and were stranded there five days. We've had escaped convicts and been ambushed by moonshiners and even had a murder, and it all seems to happen in August."

"Then there was last August."

"I don't even want to think of last August," he

replied, his expression going suddenly grim. "Seeing Shane get kicked in the head was the worst experience of my whole life. But then, it led to Jenny reconciling with her father, and Shane eventually recovered completely. If all's well that ends well, I'd say this is ending very well indeed."

"Quite so," she agreed, looking at him and taking in a smile that made her warm all over.

"I've never seen Shane so happy. But he and Jenny had their rocky beginning. I think they roundly detested each other at first. I stayed very far away from that situation until I saw how it would play out."

"Jenny's beautiful, isn't she, Sergeant Weller?"

"Of course she is. Your family produces lovely ladies, Miss Talbot." Elizabeth felt a flush creep across the tops of her cheekbones and she looked down at the dissected pork roast on her plate.

"You flatter me, sir."

"I have every intention of flattering you. But fortunately in this case I have the best of both worlds. I'm able to be flattering with complete sincerity." She was at a loss for a reply, but in the end Jenny saved her.

"Bet, we've just had a wonderful idea," Jenny said, leaning forward slightly and raising her voice across the table.

"Oh? What's that?"

"Of course the rehearsal will take up Saturday, but no one seems to have any plans for tomorrow. Why don't we go riding in the park? You and Paul can take Polly and Dancer, and I'll borrow Caroline's horses for Shane and me. If anyone else wants to go, there are plenty of other horses at Aunt Eleanor's riding school."

Before her mother could object, Elizabeth flashed a

bright smile. "That sounds absolutely wonderful, Jen. I'd love it. How about you, Sergeant Weller?"

"I'm looking forward to it already."

"Have you ever ridden a five-gaited horse? Dancer is an American Saddlebred. He was my late uncle's dressage horse," Jenny continued.

"As a matter of fact, I've shown," Paul replied.

"Well, Dancer is an equine elder statesman and sometimes crotchety, but I know you're up to it. And you've ridden Polly before, Bet."

"Polly is always a perfect lady."

"Then you and Paul take the horses from here. Wilson can drive Shane and me to Caroline's, take everyone else to the riding school, and we'll meet at the park."

"I can scarcely wait, Jen!" Elizabeth clasped her hands and gave an excited little bounce in her chair.

"Then I know we'll all have a grand time." Jenny looked to Shane for concurrence and received it immediately.

In spite of the long day, Elizabeth barely slept that night. The anticipation of the riding party intruded the moment she closed her eyes. Consequently, she awoke the moment the sun came through the gap in her drapes. Well ahead of the wake-up call she dressed in her fawn summer riding habit, and when the maid came to open the curtains, she already sat at her vanity table doing her hair. She had just put the last of the pins in place when Jenny knocked at her door.

"Ready for breakfast, Bet?" she caroled.

"Come in, Jen. Yes, I'm ready. I've been ready since last night."

Jenny let herself into the room. She wore a riding

habit similar to Elizabeth's but in light antique rose. "I know you have. Actually, I have too. Tomorrow will be too much waiting around doing boring things."

"It's your own wedding, you got to try on that lovely dress you told me all about, and you think you'll be *bored*? I'd be on top of the world."

"I will be Sunday. Tomorrow I have to wear new shoes, and I know my feet are going to hurt."

Elizabeth giggled behind her hand. "Oh, Jen! But on Sunday I hope you'll be wearing shoes that won't pinch."

"I am. The same white glove pumps I wore when I came out. They're well broken in and so comfortable I could dance all night in them."

"You may have to."

"Well...not *all* night." Jenny's cheeks flushed at the daring comment, and Elizabeth reddened an instant later.

"Oh, Jen, I'm so happy for you. You and Shane are so much in love."

"Yes, we are. It's the beginning of a new life, and I can't imagine it'll be any easier than my life has been so far. It'll just be different, and Shane and I will face it together."

"That's the important thing. Together. Now tell me, Jen, does the back of my hair look all right?" Between the triptych mirror in its carved frame and the equally elaborate silver-backed hand mirror, Elizabeth had a good view of her hair, but Jenny checked it over anyway, tucking in a hairpin here and there.

"There. You're fit for an audience with the Sultan of Timbuktoo. Now let's go to breakfast. Shane and Paul should be here in an hour or so." Elizabeth put down her mirror, gathered her hat and gloves, and followed Jenny down the grand staircase.

Breakfast was served in the family dining room, since there were only eight adults. Jenny unabashedly put ketchup on her scrambled eggs. Elizabeth caught her mother's glance of disapproval—she had often opined ketchup was lowbrow—and defiantly reached for the bottle after Jenny was finished with it. Under her mother's scowl she generously drenched her eggs. The first bite tasted delicious.

"So, Jen, tell me again—where are we supposed to meet you?" Elizabeth asked at length.

"The boathouse. We may get there before you do, since Wilson is driving us to the Bynums' and you two will be riding all the way. You do remember where the boathouse is, don't you?"

"Oh, yes. You and I have ridden in the park so often I know it like the back of my hand. We won't get lost."

"You're certain?" Rose asked.

"Yes, Mother. I know where I'm going, and I do have a good sense of direction."

"I certainly hope so." Her voice dripped doubt.

"Aunt Rose, it's easy to find this place from Central Park. All you do is orient yourself to the north and turn right. Park Avenue is the third street. And finding north is easy. The streets on three sides of the park are labeled south, west, and north. You don't cross any of them. You want to cross Fifth Avenue, Madison, and then you come to Park. I could find my way there and back when I was half Clara's age."

"Well, I hope she never has to. The very thought of Elizabeth riding out there alone, unchaperoned..."

Jenny rolled her eyes. "Elizabeth will *not* be unchaperoned, Aunt Rose. I will be with her as soon as we get the horses from Caroline, and Central Park is a very large, public place. It would take a great deal of determination to get into mischief there. Now please, Aunt Rose, don't spoil breakfast."

"Hear, hear," Rose's sister Eleanor echoed, anointing her own eggs with ketchup. When she set the bottle down, John reached for it and doused his own plate.

"May I, John, if you're finished?" Richard asked. John handed him the ketchup bottle, and from there it went to the hands of Rose's husband Tal, their son Robbie, then John and Richard's sister Martha. Eventually everyone's plate except Rose's bore red smears, and Rose subsided into indignant silence.

About half way through breakfast the butler escorted Shane and Paul into the dining room. John rose to greet them.

"Good morning, gentlemen! Will you have breakfast with us?"

"We've already eaten, thank you," Shane responded.

"Coffee, then?"

Shane pulled an odd face and looked at Paul, which made Jenny laugh aloud. "They're Canadians, Father," she reminded him.

"We've tea, haven't we, Mart?" Richard asked his sister.

"Of course. I'll call for it." She picked up the little silver bell next to her plate and rang it with a precise twist of her wrist. It brought the serving maid immediately, and within a few minutes Shane and Paul had their tea.

"So, gentlemen, how is the weather this morning? Any more rain?" John asked.

"It's cool and clear. It looks like yesterday's storm blew itself out and it'll warm up later. It's a fine morning for a ride," Paul responded, glancing at Elizabeth. A pleasant little shiver ran down her back and she hid it by looking modestly at her plate. Precisely she broke off a bite of toast, put a bit of plum jelly on it, and conveyed it to her mouth with debutante delicacy.

In another few minutes everyone had finished. Martha signaled the end of the meal by rising and calling for the staff to clear the table. Instantly everyone began milling about and several conversations ran at once. Jenny sought out Paul.

"Why don't you and Elizabeth go to the stable? It's out back behind the privet maze. Wilson will have the horses ready, and when he gets the two of you mounted he can drive the rest of us to get our horses. Elizabeth knows where we're going to meet up."

"Fair enough," Paul replied. "Miss Talbot?" He offered her his arm, and she looked up into his smile. A flush of warmth ran through her entire body, starting at her toes and growing more intense the further up it went.

They exited through the *porte cochère* door and she led him through the garden. The early morning dew magnified the somewhat sharp musk of privet, overlaid with sweetness from the banks of tea roses that competed with each other as to which could bloom most heavily.

"It really is a lovely day. You weren't

exaggerating," she said as they turned down the path toward the stable.

"It's still cool. But of course it's colder in Elk Gap. We're so much farther north."

"I imagine it's beautiful country, if everything Cousin Jen says is true."

"Lovely. It's mostly big, rolling hills and deep woods. Some of the country is a bit rough, and so are some of the people, but I wouldn't trade it for anywhere in the world."

"It makes me wish I could see it all."

"Perhaps you could visit Jenny and Shane someday. If so, I promise you a better place to ride than a city park."

"Don't disparage Central Park. It'll surprise you."

"It may be I'll stand corrected."

"We'll see, won't we?" she countered with an easy laugh. Then they rounded the back of the maze and came to the stable yard. Wilson waited there with the two horses.

"Miz Elizabeth," he said with a nod and a kindly smile. "Polly's ready for you, ma'am." He led a beautiful mahogany bay Morgan mare up to her and handed her the reins. The mare was muscular and short-coupled, with a clean, graceful neck and a delicate face. Wilson interlocked his fingers to give Elizabeth a leg up, and Paul automatically took the reins until she mounted. Morgans, being fine harness horses, are not small; Polly's size suited Elizabeth's tall grace well. Then Wilson untied the big chestnut American Saddlebred from a hitching ring on the side of the stable wall.

"Sergeant Weller, this is Dancer. Do you know

about Saddlebreds?" Wilson asked.

"Yes, I do. They have a fifth gait called a rack. It's been a while since I've ridden one, though." While Paul spoke he allowed Dancer to become accustomed to his scent and his touch.

"Dancer belonged to Aunt Eleanor's late husband. She has a whole roomful of equitation trophies he won," Elizabeth volunteered.

"He's certainly a handsome old gentleman," Paul agreed, patting the gelding's satiny neck. While Wilson held the reins, Paul mounted easily, then kicked his foot out of the iron so Wilson could adjust the leathers for his long legs.

"You're tall, Sergeant," Wilson remarked with a rasping laugh.

"So they tell me."

"How does this feel?"

Paul slipped his boot in the iron and tested the left stirrup. "It seems to be about right."

"Good, because it's as far as they go." He walked around in front of Dancer and adjusted the right stirrup. Then he gave the horse a light pat on the rump. "You're ready, then, Miss Elizabeth. Enjoy yourselves."

"Thank you, Wilson," Elizabeth said, thinking her voice sounded detached. She had been paying such close attention to Paul the privet maze could have gone up in flames and she would not have noticed.

"Which way, Miss Talbot?" Paul asked.

Once again she had to look up at him, and warm weakness washed through the pit of her stomach. "Just follow me," she responded. She touched Polly with her heel and started out through the stable yard to the alley behind. Then, as Paul came up beside her, she cranked up her courage and looked into his eyes.

"I'd like it very much if you'd call me Elizabeth."

He smiled broadly. "I'll admit that makes me very happy."

"Then I'm glad." She looked down momentarily, and then her gaze swung back to Paul, sitting the handsome old gelding with easy grace.

"So how far is it to the park?"

"Only three blocks. But we need to be a little careful of Dancer. He really doesn't like automobiles. However, this early on a Saturday there probably won't be many."

"I know quite a bit more about motor-shy horses than I wish I did," he said darkly.

"Inspector Adair's accident?" she prompted.

He nodded slowly, his sudden gravity tugging at her heart. "I thought I was watching my best friend die right in front of me." He reset his grip on Dancer's reins as if to distract himself, and Elizabeth waited him out quietly. "The thing of it was, it was my horse that panicked when the touring car backfired across the street, and that totally surprised me because she's not gun-shy. She threw a first-class tantrum and kicked Shane's horse right in the middle of his chest. He reared up and struck Shane in the head. I don't think Midnight would have done anything worse than cock an ear if it hadn't been for Brandy."

"Does that make you feel you're responsible?"

"In a way. But then, neither horse has had much exposure to automobiles. There aren't any in Elk Gap yet. You have to go to River Bend, and they're not common there either. Plus, most times when Shane and I go to River Bend we take the train."

"You can't blame yourself, Paul. From what I understand, you were occupied at the time."

"Occupied. Yes, that's a polite way of putting it. I was trying my very best to pick a fight with Jenny's father and that insufferable fat popinjay he brought with him. I was provoking them as hard as I could, hoping one of them would give me the slightest cause to arrest everyone and keep her from getting on that train. If all else failed, I was prepared to run Jenny in for practicing medicine without a license. Of course it would have been a spurious charge and I would have run a great risk of receiving a reprimand for it, but it would have disrupted her father's intention to make her go to New York, and maybe in the interim we could have come up with another plan."

"You would have arrested Jenny? Oh, my goodness! Did you ever tell her that?" Elizabeth's eyes went wide with delighted surprise.

"Yes, much later, after Shane was on the road to recovery. We had a good laugh over it. She said if she had realized what I was doing she would have slapped me silly and given me a sound reason to arrest her."

Elizabeth laughed delightedly. "The thought of Jen assaulting a police officer! That's just too much! I mean, she can be unconventional, but..."

"Oh, I've no doubt she'd have done it, and it probably would have hurt like everything. She's a great example of the adage against judging books by their covers."

"She had to be as tough as nails to leave her family behind to go to medical school. And then it nearly broke her heart when she couldn't find anywhere to practice. I had hoped Uncle John would relent and invite her to join Northtown, but by the time she finished her residency they weren't even speaking."

"Well, perhaps, as my mother says, the Good Lord had other plans. She's found her niche in Elk Gap. We'd needed another doctor there for years."

Their conversation had carried them three blocks, to 86th Street below the reservoir, and there Dancer proved Elizabeth right. A delivery truck rattled past and he humped his back and sidled toward Polly. Instantly Paul had the reins firmly down and was talking gently to the old horse. After a moment the animal settled, mouthing his bit, but still they waited carefully for traffic to clear before they crossed the street.

"He really doesn't like motors, does he?" Paul asked rhetorically. "But Polly acted like the lorry wasn't even there." Elizabeth caught his British term and was once again reminded he was Canadian.

"Polly is trained within a hair of her life. Aunt Eleanor shows her in combined harness and equitation classes. Besides, Morgans are cold-blooded horses."

"Oh! She's a Morgan. That really does explain it."

"Yes. If someone held a gun to my head and told me I had to raise horses, I'd pick Morgans. They're not temperamental at all, they're beautiful, intelligent, strong, and can go on all day. What kind of horse do you have?"

"Brandy's an Irish thoroughbred. My parents gave her to me after I lost my horse on rounds that time. She's a good hill horse, tough as they come, but she can be hard-headed and she does act up on me occasionally. I think she just has to keep me in my place." They continued at a sedate walk down the path shadowing East Drive, passing the Great Lawn and heading toward the Ramble.

Paul's flashy Red Serge attracted every pair of eyes in the vicinity. The attention made Elizabeth doubly careful of her posture on the dark bay mare. Inwardly she hoped Jenny and Shane would take their time. She felt herself the target of no small envy, riding with Paul, and wanted to revel in every single minute. However, her moment in the sun proved all too brief. As they approached the Ramble, the shrilling of police whistles and the racket of men shouting interrupted their idyll. She spotted two New York police officers chasing a fleeing figure off to their left. To Paul it was like a bell to an old fire horse. He smacked Dancer's rump with the reins and Elizabeth heeled Polly into a hard gallop to keep up. They arrived just as the fugitive disappeared into the copse. Paul brought Dancer to a plowing stop and jumped off.

"It's no use goin' in there. We've lost him good," one officer said to the other in a lilting Irish brogue.

"Perhaps I can help you," Paul volunteered. "Is this where he ran in?"

"Aye, Sergeant. Them's his tracks."

"Well, with those old boots he may as well have left his signature." Paul squatted down and examined the prints, then started through the widely spaced stand of trees.

"Be careful in there, Sergeant," the other officer cautioned. "He's hidin' in them woods and he's dangerous. He just robbed a shopkeeper, and the man said he had a bloody great knife." Elizabeth looked at the officers and her heart seized in her chest, then took off, pounding. However, Paul remained unfazed.

"Paul..." She heard her voice coming out breathy

and an octave high.

"Don't worry. I'll be careful. I've faced down far worse than a fugitive with a knife." He rose, leading Dancer, following a trail Elizabeth could not see. She tagged well behind, not wanting to miss anything but nevertheless staying out of the way. She had no idea what he found to follow amid the welter of footprints in the damp ground. Suddenly a figure bolted from behind a tree and ran at an angle to their right. Paul leaped into the saddle, and in an instant he was galloping in pursuit.

With the two patrolmen on foot behind Paul, the miscreant's only course of action was to flee into the open and hope to elude his pursuers somehow. Elizabeth urged Polly up next to Dancer, cantering hard as they overtook the fugitive. Quickly Paul threw a rough knot into his reins. He leaned down and his arm went around the suspect's neck. Elizabeth muffled a cry as a knife flashed in the man's right hand. Paul grabbed his wrist and brought the arm up sharply behind him.

"Elizabeth! Get my reins!" he barked. She reached out for Dancer's reins and slowed both horses.

"Ow! Ow! You're breakin' me arm!" the man screamed, kicking and twisting in Paul's grasp as the red-clad arms lifted him off his feet.

"If you don't stop fighting me I'll break your damn neck!"

"All right! Leggo! Yer killin' me!" Paul eased the pressure around the man's throat, holding him instead by his right wrist and his jacket collar. Elizabeth marveled at the strength that had allowed Paul to drag a grown man half way across Dancer's saddle.

The foot patrolmen caught up momentarily. Paul dropped the prisoner to the ground and the officers piled on and handcuffed him, not bothering to be gentle.

"Come on. An' it's off to see Black Maria for you!" one officer said, giving the prisoner a rough shove. As he marched the man back the way they had come, the taller of the two—Elizabeth saw he also wore sergeant's stripes on his sleeve—turned to Paul.

"I never seen the likes of that in all my life, Sergeant. You got 'im right an' proper. Why, you tracked 'im down like you was a bloody red indjun! Then allow me to introduce meself. I'm Sergeant James O'Leary, NYPD. Who might you be?" Paul dismounted, meeting the hand Sergeant O'Leary held out.

"Sergeant Paul Weller, River Bend, Ontario Detachment, Royal Northwest Mounted Police. Pleased to make your acquaintance, Sergeant."

"My pleasure entirely. They say you Mounties always get your man, but this time you really went that second mile! You got ours!" He laughed and slapped his hand against his leg. "I'm grateful to you, Sergeant. But how could you follow 'is tracks like that?"

"River Bend is a rural area. Most of my work is done in the woods. I had to learn to track."

"What are you doin' clear down 'ere in New York, then?"

"I came down for my partner's wedding. If you need some sort of statement, I'm at the Waldorf until Monday morning."

All three heads turned simultaneously as Jenny and Shane cantered toward them across the Ramble. Shane pulled up his sorrel gelding and Jenny reined to a stop a moment later.

"Paul?" Shane asked in an undertone, suddenly diffident, as though he had interrupted something.

"Inspector, this is Sergeant James O'Leary, New York Police Department. Sergeant, this is my superior officer, Inspector Shane Adair, Royal Northwest Mounted Police."

"Lord love us!" Sergeant O'Leary exclaimed, meeting Shane's hand. "They got Irish cops in Canada too!"

As the three men conferred with each other, Elizabeth met Jenny's eyes across the intervening distance and gave her a small gesture saying everything was under control. Jenny walked her gray gelding around to her cousin.

"What happened, Bet?" she asked.

"A robber went running across the Ramble with two police officers after him. Paul tracked him through the brush, and when he made a break for it, Paul ran him down." Elizabeth tried hard to conceal the pride making heart soar.

"So it's Paul now, is it?" Jenny asked, cocking an eyebrow. Elizabeth felt herself flush.

"Yes, it is. I find him…pleasant company."

"I do too. In fact, I always have." A few moments later Shane and Paul rejoined the interrupted party.

"Well, that was today's excitement, and it's not even August yet. Shall we continue with our ride?" Shane suggested. By common consent Jenny led, since she knew the area better than anyone else did. That left Elizabeth and Paul tagging behind, paying much more attention to each other than to the lovely day or the freshness of the spring greenery about them.

****

So close to the summer solstice, morning came early. Paul, tense with anticipation, had only dozed since midnight, while in the next bed Shane slept the innocent sleep of the unsuspecting. Finally, with false dawn beginning to stir in the east, Paul could wait no longer. He eased from his bed and drew his clothes on, slowly and quietly. When he had his belt half way fastened, Shane turned over. His gray eyes momentarily flashed colorless in the half-dark.

"Go back to sleep. I gotta piss," Paul grumped, hoping he sounded convincing. Shane acquiesced, turning over languidly and pulling the covers half way across his face. Paul eased out the door, leaving it slightly ajar rather than risk the noisy latch. He knew Shane for a heavy sleeper, but he did not want to push his luck.

Outside in the hallway he joined Bob Shepherd, Laurence Bernard, and Theo Bane, a classmate of Shane's from the Academy. Jenny's bridesmaids stood a short distance away, sleepy-eyed but tittering behind their hands. Bea Brisbane, Elizabeth's cousin, had masterminded their plot but had no problem enlisting Elizabeth and Jenny's identical twin second cousins, Grace and Hope Weston.

Everyone looked from Paul to Bob.

"Ready?" Bob breathed. Paul nodded, slipping the door open. Three Mounties crept in behind him. Shane sat up with a yelp, but it came too late.

"What in hell..." he exclaimed as Paul tackled him and drove him backward into his pillows.

"You're getting kidnapped. Now shut up and give in." Paul expected the struggle that left the bed a tumbled tangle of sheets and blankets. While Shane might have been the stronger of the two, Paul's height gave him the advantage of leverage, and he capitalized on the element of surprise. He managed to spread-eagle Shane's arms and pin his wrists a bare instant before Laurence jumped on the bed and sat on his friend's legs. Theo tied a blindfold over Shane's eyes, and then the bilingual cursing match started. Because they were in a hotel all three kept their voices down, but Bob broke in anyway.

"Watch the language. There are ladies present," he warned.

"Ladies?" Shane echoed, his voice going upward in a shocked glissando.

"That's why I told you to wear skivvies to bed," Paul laughed.

"What's going on?" Shane finally managed.

"I already told you. You're being kidnapped."

Bob trotted out his best no-nonsense police-officer tone. "If you don't cooperate, we'll put you in handcuffs."

As Paul let go, Shane's hands came up in surrender. "Are you going to let me get dressed? Since there are ladies present, I mean?"

"All right. Get dressed. But the blindfold stays." The voice was Bea's from the doorway as she closed the door to allow the bridegroom his modesty.

Paul handed Shane his clothes a garment at a time, indulgently correcting the shirt buttons when his partner could not get them straight by feel. Then he stuffed Shane's feet into his boots and led him out into the hallway.

"Who all is here?" Shane asked, being sporting enough not to touch his blindfold.

"Everybody but Jenny," Bea responded.

"So you're kidnapping me and not her?"

"That's the fun of it," bubbly Grace said with a giggle.

"Letting her sweat when we go missing," Hope finished. Paul ventured a glance across them to Elizabeth. She looked so perfectly coiffed and neatly dressed he wondered if she had even gone to bed. She caught his gaze and her private smile drew him back to the previous day and their ride in the park. He allowed himself to go into the distraction so deeply he forgot to steer Shane, who veered off to the side and bumped into him.

"Hey! Not fair!" Shane protested. "Either somebody lead me or let me take this blindfold off!"

Bob reached out and tucked Shane's hand into the bend of his own elbow. "There. Hang onto me. I'm the only one who's not flirting."

"I'm engaged, so let's don't flirt with each other." Hope took his other arm, and Bob nodded gallantly toward her.

"All right, Shane. Steps," Bob said as they approached the staircase. He carefully took the first step and Shane tentatively followed him. A few moments later they arrived in the lobby. Paul looked around, relieved it was still deserted at the early hour. He had harbored more than a few fears someone might take the abduction seriously.

Outside they piled into a large hired coach; nine people made a tight fit. With a daring laugh Bea settled herself on Laurence's lap. Paul felt a moment of hope, but Elizabeth dashed it by wedging herself into an eight-inch space between his leg and the side of the carriage. Nevertheless, when he draped his arm across the back of the bench seat she cuddled willingly against his side.

"Where are we going?" Shane asked as the carriage pulled out into the street.

"You're not supposed to know," Bea informed him. "That's the point of a kidnapping."

"I suppose we could let him take off the blindfold if we pull the curtains," Grace suggested.

"That's all right by me," Elizabeth agreed.

Shane slipped the blindfold off, knuckled his eyes, and tried to smooth the sleep-rumpled hair he had not had a chance to comb. "So what are you doing this to me for?" he asked.

"It's better than a chivaree," Laurence responded, shrugging as well as he could with Bea draped all over him.

"Besides, it's a great chance to spend time with you," Paul said privately, his lips close to Elizabeth's ear.

"I don't mind that one little bit." Unconsciously her soft Virginia drawl deepened and she relaxed against him.

"You're sure we'll be back in time for the rehearsal dinner?" Grace asked at length.

"Of course we will. We're only going to Liberty Island, not China," Bea reassured her.

"So we're going to see the statue?" Shane asked.

"We thought it would make a good outing."

"How far is it?"

"Oh, no, you don't, partner. Besides, you have such a good sense of direction I'm sure you could find your way back by yourself," Paul put in.

"That only works for me in the woods. Yesterday I was as lost as a goose. I'd probably have wound up in Mexico if Jenny hadn't been there to navigate."

Eventually the teamster pulled the carriage to a halt. They untangled themselves, and when Paul stepped out and turned to give Elizabeth his hand, they were on a pier. The distinctive but strange scent of salt water and creosote swirled about him, and he felt the unaccustomed touch of a damp estuarine breeze.

"See over there?" Elizabeth pointed roughly westward across the river, where the Statue of Liberty stood on her pedestal.

"That's where we're going?"

"Mm-hmm. We thought it would be something interesting for you Canadians."

"Definitely," Laurence agreed, looking down at Bea. Paul regarded his friend and had the definite impression he gladly would have followed Bea to Outer Mongolia or perhaps the far side of the moon. Then he had to admit he was just as smitten with Elizabeth. The only difference was that with Laurence, out of sight immediately became out of mind. Paul knew he was not so lucky. When he boarded the train to go back to Elk Gap, he would leave a piece of himself behind.

After a quick breakfast from a vendor's cart, they boarded an ancient water taxi. Shane balked at boarding the rundown old boat. "You know, I've never been in anything bigger than a canoe," he said, obviously distrusting the rickety craft.

"Me either," Theo agreed.

"Well, don't worry about it. We're not going far enough for anybody to get seasick."

"Grace, you would have to mention that, wouldn't

you?" Hope shot her sister a dirty look.

"You're just jealous," Grace sniffed.

"Well, I'm going below. If I don't watch the water, I get along better."

"All of you need to go below," the grizzled skipper informed them. "The deck isn't big enough for anybody to ride topside."

Paul descended the short ladder three steps at a time and reached up to steady Elizabeth. She thanked him, and when he looked into her Brisbane brown eyes, so like Jenny's, a rush of warmth suffused him. He had to agree he knew how Shane felt.

The party arranged themselves on the two benches in what passed for a salon belowdecks. A few minutes later they felt the skipper engage the clutch. The sidewheel started with a protesting creak, and the boat made its way from the pier and out into the smooth water. Immediately Paul noticed an alarming thumping vibration coming from the sidewheel mechanism. With his knowledge of mills, he knew something had gone amiss, probably long ago, and would be neglected until it broke. Hopefully it would not break today.

"Since we're at sea, shouldn't we maybe sing a sea chanty?" Grace suggested, looking at her sister, who had begun to turn a decisive shade of green.

"You'll really make me ill if you do that," Hope grumbled. Next to Paul, Elizabeth began humming *Shenandoah,* then singing softly. Eventually Bea slipped under Elizabeth's melody with her rich alto, and finally Paul joined the trio. The lyrical rise and fall of the song did seem to soothe Hope, who finally summoned up nerve to look out the window and watch as their water taxi threaded its way through the boat traffic.

The trip passed all too quickly for Paul, who relished every moment next to Elizabeth. Soon the boat glided up to a pier and the shabby deckhand leaped ashore with a line. Expertly he wrapped it figure-eight fashion around an iron cleat, securing the bow. A moment later the stern line followed. Then their skipper poked his head in.

"All ashore what's goin' ashore. And remember we depart at two, smartish. Anyone wot's not here gets left behind." Unbelievably, his lips moved but the pipe welded between them did not.

Elizabeth rose and smoothed her skirt, then took Paul's proffered arm. He relished a fleeting glimpse of her ankle as she preceded him up the short stairway to the deck. The light June breeze toyed with a wayward lock of hair at the nape of her neck, and he had an almost irresistible urge to corral it and tuck it back into the mass of glossy curls cascading down from the crown of her head. He became so caught up in the play of light and shadow in her walnut hair that when he looked up, the sheer bulk of the famous Statue of Liberty made him flinch.

With Hope's incipient seasickness banished, the group of young people chatted and laughed their way to the base of the great statue. The poem on its plaque could have been in Hindi for all Paul comprehended, and he fairly floated up the stairs to the observation deck in the crown. Granted, New York lay magnificently before them, but he found himself too taken by the line of Elizabeth's cheek and her fragrant warmth next to him to notice anything else.

Taking the gnarled old skipper seriously, they

made it back to the pier ten minutes before two. They watched as the lone deckhand tied up the *River Witch* and ushered a fresh batch of passengers off.

The skipper did not waste a minute herding Bob Shepherd and his gaggle of wedding attendants back on board. Once again below, they arranged themselves as they had during the trip over.

"I'll bet Jenny's sweating blood by now." Bea giggled.

"I'd love to be a fly on the wall. Our good doctor is so much the cool lady," Hope agreed.

"You don't think she'll be angry?" Grace asked. "I'd hate for that to happen."

"I doubt it. Jenny's a good sport, and we all have such a history of playing pranks on each other." Elizabeth, who probably knew Jenny better than anyone else, tried to reassure Grace no real harm would be done.

The deckhand cast off the lines and jumped aboard as he had a thousand times. A shuddering, grinding thump vibrated through the old boat as the skipper engaged the clutch and the sidewheel began to turn. Paul felt Elizabeth's eyes asking him an unspoken question.

"I have enough experience with Father's sawmill that I don't like that either," he murmured.

"And the tide's running pretty good. It looked close to high slack when we got off. It's had enough time to pick up some speed."

"I don't know a thing about the ocean. What does that mean?"

"It's ebbing, so it's running in the same direction as the river: out to sea. The moon is also full, so the high tides are higher and the lows are lower, meaning more water, moving faster. It's called a spring tide."

"Oh. So it sounds like if we got into trouble we might stay that way."

"You could say that," Elizabeth agreed quietly. He could only hope the old boat made it safely back to Manhattan before whatever limped along in its battered insides broke altogether. Unable to do anything about their questionable transportation, he surreptitiously took her hand and settled in to wait. However, his hope was in vain. Somewhere around the middle of the estuary a loud bang, followed by a tearing shudder, shook the boat, and they were suddenly dead in the water. Involuntarily Paul's arm went around Elizabeth's shoulders and he pulled her against his side. One of the other girls let out a surprised yip.

"What in hell..." Bob's oath trailed off.

"I've been listening to the drive mechanism since we left Manhattan. Something broke. You notice the wheel stopped," Paul responded.

"Then we're drifting, and the tide's going out," Elizabeth said.

"What does that mean?" Bob asked her.

"The tide and the river are going in the same direction right now. We're being carried out to sea."

"Oh, goodness! Is that dangerous?" Bea retreated closer to Laurence.

"Not really, except we're out here in shipping traffic and we can't steer," Elizabeth explained.

"So what can they do about it?" Grace asked nervously.

"We'll just have to wait and see what the captain decides. After all, it's not like we're sinking." She accompanied it with a nonchalant shrug. Paul's estimation of her went up another notch. He noticed, though, that she kept an eye on whatever transpired outside. Taking a cue from her, he watched the harbor traffic, wishing he understood what he was seeing.

"What are you watching?" he asked quietly.

"How fast we're drifting. We're really moving along at a pretty good clip."

"And we're supposed to be at the church at four?"

"I'm trying not to think about that," she responded. "Playing a trick on Jenny is one thing; frightening everybody half to death when we turn up missing is another altogether."

"Including you?"

She shook her head. "No, I'm not scared. I won't be unless the skipper tells us this tub is taking on water. Then I might be a little on edge." She measured out perhaps half an inch between a thumb and forefinger.

"I think I need to find out what's going on." The take-charge statement came from Bob Shepherd. He nodded at Shane, who acknowledged the silent order and rose as Bob did. They stepped over the feet in the aisle and made their way up to the deck, leaving the others staring after them. Up until now, Paul had resisted the temptation to look at his watch, but now he fished it out of his pocket. It read two forty-five. He showed it to Elizabeth, and her eyes questioned him.

"Maybe Bea's idea of a prank wasn't all that good," she murmured under her breath.

"We're not dead yet," he whispered back.

"Jenny hasn't got hold of us, either." The wit in her reply felt as dry as a desert morning.

"Miss Talbot, you are an amazing woman," he

said, noting a delicate blush rising in her cheeks.

"I fail to see what's amazing about not panicking before the fact."

"Everyone else is hanging on by their fingernails, but you're acting like you do this every day of your life."

"I probably do have a little more experience around the water than the rest of us," she agreed. Suddenly a shot shattered the quiet. Nearly everybody flinched, and Paul was instantly on alert, his hand going to the sidearm that he did not find.

"What was that?" Grace asked dumbly.

"An emergency signal," Elizabeth informed everyone. "Maybe someone will help us now."

"I certainly hope so." Hope sighed. "We've been stuck out here just about long enough."

"We really are getting a ways down the river," Elizabeth agreed. "We'll be out to sea pretty soon."

"Oh, dear," Bea said, her tone tongue-in-cheek. In Paul's opinion she was having much too good a time cuddling next to Laurence, who lapped up the attention like a cat on cream. But he could also see Hope had taken her seriously.

"That's dangerous, isn't it?" She looked toward Elizabeth, who in the last half hour had emerged as the natural leader.

"Not really. Inconvenient, maybe, but not that dangerous. Eventually we'll get found and we'll get back to shore."

"But Jenny is going to pitch a ring-tailed conniption fit, and I really don't blame her."

"Yes, that's a distinct possibility," Paul agreed. "I'm beginning to regret agreeing with this hare-brained scheme." He pitched his voice low enough that Bea, who had masterminded the whole thing, could not hear him.

"We all agreed, Paul. She'll have to kill all of us." Elizabeth's hand sneaked under his, softly warm.

"Can we sing? I'm getting scared." Hope's voice sounded timorous, making Paul appreciate Elizabeth all the more.

"I have just the song," Bea announced. "It was all the rage at the summer camp my brother went to last year." Without waiting for confirmation, she launched into "Drunken Sailor." The simple tune proved easy for Paul to grasp, as did the repetitive nature of the lyrics.

"What do we do with a drunken sailor,
What do we do with a drunken sailor,
What do we do with a drunken sailor,
Early in the morning?
Put him in the bilge and make him drink it,
Put him in the bilge and make him drink it,
Put him in the bilge and make him drink it,
Early in the morning."

They went through four more horrible punishments, including shave his belly with a rusty razor, before Bob and Shane returned. The two picked their way toward their former seats, stepping around the feet crowded into the narrow aisle. Paul looked up at Shane, asking him an unworded question.

"Well, ladies and gentlemen, we are safe," Bob announced. "After the distress signal some kind of little boat pulled up beside us. It was too small to take everybody back to Manhattan, but they said they'd send a tug out to tow us in. It may take a while, though."

"Will we make it back in time?" Paul asked.

"That's anyone's guess. If we do, it's going to be tight," Shane said.

"Well, I'm sorry we got you into this mess."

Shane shook his head. "Sometimes things just happen." He sighed, dropping down next to Paul.

"Even when it's not August." That drew a wry grin from Shane.

The song started up again, with a vengeance. Paul joined in, trying to stay in the spirit of the day even though it had degenerated into chaos.

Eventually their salvation did arrive, in the form of a tug as battered and decrepit as the boat that had let them down in the first place. It took the sidewheeler under tow and began to steam phlegmatically back toward Manhattan. With maddening slowness it nudged its charge up to the pier, and the group finally debarked. Paul's pocket watch told him they had only half an hour to make it to the church.

"Hadn't we better get a cab?" Bea suggested.

"We could go somewhere and telephone the house," Elizabeth countered. "Look. Isn't that a police station over there?" She pointed down the street beyond the cab stands.

"I'm sure they'll let us use their telephone. Professional courtesy and all that," Bob said, obviously ready to use his rank for a little more pull.

"Could that be Sergeant O'Leary's station?" Paul wondered aloud.

"The officer we met in Central Park? One could hope," Shane said.

"Well, we're only wasting time standing here," Elizabeth said, touching Paul's sleeve.

"You're right."

"Let's go, then," Bob said, obviously realizing they looked to him to take the initiative. He led off down the street, leading his gaggle of red uniforms and their respective young ladies. They walked up the steps and into the lobby of the police station. It surprised Paul to see Sergeant O'Leary behind the desk. He rose and held his hand out as they approached, seemingly unfazed at the crowd that suddenly materialized in his station.

"Sergeant Weller! To what do we owe the honor of your visit?" he asked, smiling broadly.

"Hello, Sergeant O'Leary. I'm afraid we've hit a snag in our plans and we need to use a telephone. You see, we're due at a wedding rehearsal in slightly under half an hour. I don't think we're going to make it."

"Is that your wedding he's talking about?" he asked Shane.

"Yes, I'm afraid so. You see, they thought they'd play a prank, and they kidnapped me. We went to see the Statue of Liberty, and on the way back the boat broke down. It's taken us nearly two hours to make it back to Manhattan."

"And where and when is your rehearsal?"

"It's at Park Avenue Methodist Church at four," Elizabeth informed him.

"That's a ways to cover in half an hour."

"That's why I wanted to use the telephone. I can at least call the bride's home and let her know we're on our way."

"I've got a better idea than that. Let's just get everyone there on time, shall we?"

"And how do you propose to do that? It's some distance to the church."

"I have an idea. Black Maria is big enough for all

of you, and it has a siren. You are about to get a very exciting ride to your church. It's the least I can do, since you caught our robber, Sergeant Weller. And besides, I need something to liven up my desk shift."

"Black Maria?" Elizabeth echoed, laughing. "Can you imagine what everyone is going to think when we arrive at the church in that thing? Mother will absolutely have apoplexy!"

"And what fun that will be!" Bea crowed.

"Come with me, then. It's out back, and it's just been cleaned up. Otherwise I wouldn't even think of letting ladies ride in it." He clapped his billed cap on his unruly red hair and led them back through a hallway flanked by offices. Here and there a curious face poked out and promptly retreated again, with the exception of two who at their superior's beckoning fell in behind the wedding party. *Sergeant O'Leary must manage with an iron hand.*

A moment later they were outside, where the infamous prisoner transport wagon waited, the horses standing sleepily in their traces. The two officers Sergeant O'Leary had picked out took their places in the driver and shotgun seats, the one on the left preparing to man the crank handle of the siren. The sergeant unlocked the back doors and swung them back, revealing the interior of the Black Maria with its plain wood benches equipped with rings meant to hold manacles. The interior smelled of bleach, hinting that in times past it had smelled of much worse.

Paul waited beside Shane, giving a hand up to each of the girls, Elizabeth last. Then he swung in and sat next to her. The sergeant made as if to close the doors behind them, then paused.

"So, Inspector Adair, it's your wedding they're here to celebrate?" he asked.

"Yes. It's tomorrow."

"Then accept my congratulations and best wishes for every happiness."

"Thank you, Sergeant," Shane responded, returning Sergeant O'Leary's salute. The doors closed decisively behind them and the driver smacked his horses with the reins. The wagon lurched to an abrupt start as the officer next to the driver wound the siren up into a wail. Paul braced a hand against the back corner and tried to shield Elizabeth from the worst of the jostling. He could tell from the shrieks and giggles around him the others were trying to do the same thing with varying degrees of success. Then Bea's voice broke through the cacophony.

"What do we do with a drunken sailor,
What do we do with a drunken sailor,
What do we do with a drunken sailor,
Early in the morning?
Keel haul him 'til he's sober,
Keel haul him 'til he's sober,
Keel haul him 'til he's sober,
Early in the morning."

The rest joined her with grim determination as Black Maria flew through the streets, siren shrilling.

Because the windows were mere ventilation slits, nobody knew where they were or how much ground they had covered. But eventually the siren ran down and the driver pulled the horses up. The singers were just into a verse that began "Put him in bed with the captain's daughter." The daring lyrics rang out, and this time even Shane sang, if his horrid monotone could be called singing. He made it sound like the drunken sailor was alive and well and with them. They finished with a raucous "That's what we do with a drunken sailor" just as the back doors of Black Maria swung open. They all piled out in time to see Jenny's family spilling out of the church doors and down the stairs. Shane stepped down first, and Jenny trotted over to him.

"The explanation for all of this is bound to be good," she said, laughing at the ridiculous scene before her. He caught her hand as Paul turned and lifted Elizabeth down. For a moment she came close enough her light lavender cologne enveloped him, shutting out the world. But then Clara interrupted his train of thought, running to her sister for a hug.

"Where have you been?" she asked. "Mama has been beside herself."

"I'll say I've been beside myself! And I'm not the only one!" Rose charged up to the party like an enraged buffalo. "And I heard that hideous song you people were singing. I can see why the police brought you here. It's fortunate they didn't arrest the lot of you!"

"Oh, no, ma'am. They weren't under arrest. Our sergeant had us bring them here like it was an emergency, so to speak. He wanted to make certain his friends got to where they were goin' in time, since their boat got stuck in the river," the driver said, breaking into Rose's tirade.

"Their boat got stuck in the river?" she echoed as though the officer were speaking in tongues.

"All's well that ends well, Aunt Rose," Jenny broke in, taking Shane's arm. "Now let's go in. We have only five minutes until the rehearsal starts. I'm certain we'll hear the whole story in due time."

"But nobody's dressed..."

"I don't see a single naked person here," John Weston said crisply, moving to his daughter's side. He took her free hand. "Now, since it'll be my privilege to give my daughter away, I say let's get on with the show."

"Miss Elizabeth?" Paul gallantly offered Elizabeth his arm. But the tension of the afternoon had caught up with everyone. She looked up at him and burst into laughter, which the rest of the bridesmaids caught. The rest of the day bade fair to be as quirky and unexpected as the beginning had been, and he, for one, looked forward to it.

Chapter 2

Sunday dawned with a poignant excitement pricking at Elizabeth like a horde of tiny needles under her skin. They endured a long, leisurely, and somewhat late breakfast which no one felt like eating, and then the process of getting ready began. Jenny, who was so willowy she rarely wore a corset, crammed herself into one and sneaked into Elizabeth's room for help with her laces. Then, two hours before the service, giggly, giddy, and impeccably coiffed, they left for the church. While Elizabeth wore her bridesmaid's dress in the touring car, Jenny sat engulfed in a tea dress of antique rose and sage green. She was uncharacteristically silent during the ride and sat chewing her lips. Elizabeth could not believe the cool, unflappable cousin she worshiped was actually nervous.

The silence persisted until they were inside the bride's room of the old Park Avenue Methodist Church. With all four bridesmaids gathered around, plus Jenny's aunts and her best friend, Eleanor and Martha ceremoniously unfolded the wedding gown and dropped it over her head. While Eleanor Hanley cooed and Rose Talbot fussed, ever-practical Martha Weston took a button hook to the seemingly endless row of pearl buttons up the back. Elizabeth almost could not watch. The dress was so beautiful tears threatened her eyes. While the skirt was not full, the elaborately gathered satin draped in graceful folds to the floor. The short sleeves, overlaid with pearl-embroidered lace, came barely to Jenny's elbows, and a panel in the front winked and glimmered with pearls and rhinestones.

While Martha fluffed the side drapes and the court train, Eleanor took out the magnificent diamond-and-pearl necklace Jenny's Grandmother Weston had given her for her eighteenth birthday. Platinum-and-diamond slides held up three strands of matching graduated pearls in four deep scallops. These draped gracefully around a huge central teardrop pearl with a diamond cap. Smaller identical teardrop earrings complemented the ensemble; Jenny had elected not to wear the ring or the tortoiseshell comb with its big pearl drop. While Jenny worked the earrings through her earlobes, Martha fastened the necklace. Acting in the stead of the bride's mother, it was up to Eleanor to set the headdress on Jenny's tawny, curling mane and drape the veil over her face. As Elizabeth watched Aunt Eleanor manipulating the antique veil under which five generations of Weston brides had been given away, she gulped, feeling the pressure of tears against her lower lids. Automatically she felt up her left sleeve for the gossamer silk handkerchief she had secreted there. *You will not cry, you cretin. You'll spoil your dress and make a total fool of yourself.* She bit her lip until the pain distracted her.

Paul stood next to Shane in the seclusion of a side hallway behind the door to the right of the communion rail. Shane looked like he had withdrawn somewhere into the obscure reaches of his mind. His expressionless eyes gazed unfocused into the indefinite distance somewhere above the floor. Paul tried to relax, letting his mind roam backward over his relationship with his best friend. To begin with, Shane, infinitely patient, had taken a green recruit barely twenty years old and taught him woodsmanship, marksmanship, and the tact and skill to handle people and bring them around to his point of view.

Knowing him has changed me so much. I had some very skewed ideas of what it meant to be a police officer. Shane disabused me of those in short order. Then he proceeded to make a woodsman of me. I'll never have his skill in the woods, though. It's in his blood, from his voyageur grandfather and his Iroquois grandmother. I don't know why he held the secret of his mixed blood from me for so long—not that I didn't figure it out. Nobody could be that fluent in any Aboriginal language unless he grew up with it, and he moves so easily among those people. Even though the North Village people are used to me, they're always on their guard when I'm around. Not that I don't feel the same way, even after six years.

We've been a good many miles together, and I daresay he's learned nearly as much from me as I from him. He was a wild street brawler and he rode like an Indian when we met; I at least turned him into a decent boxer and a better rider.

Then Jenny happened. That's the only way I can describe it. She was an event in both our lives, as sudden and brilliant as lightning. From the first moment, Shane lost his heart to her. I would have aspired to her myself but for that. I couldn't trespass on my best friend's territory. Because of her he came out of himself and owned his Iroquois blood, and then he nearly died. All it took was one inattentive moment and two panicked horses, and he was in the hospital in

River Bend, fighting for his life. When Jenny and her father managed to save him, in doing so they reconciled their differences. They say all's well that ends well. And when he puts that ring on her finger, all will have ended well indeed. Or, rather, all is beginning well indeed.

Then his thoughts took another turn. *Elizabeth.* He had known her exactly four days, a four-day eternity sending him in an entirely new direction, spinning off into some arcane lunar orbit from which he knew he would never descend. His family moved in the higher social circles of River Bend, a respectably large city, but Elizabeth stood out against the crowd of small town debutantes there like a blooded Arabian in a herd of dairy cows. Even the way she moved—her unconscious, studied grace—went through his blood like liquid fire. He thought of her as without flaw, from the walnut mass of her carefully coiffed hair to the slim ankles he had admired while they were riding. And for once, next to her, he was not conscious of his own height. He usually felt as though he could accidentally step on smaller girls, but Elizabeth came comfortably to his cheekbones.

His mind roamed back over the day they had spent riding in Central Park. He had watched her with the intensity of a desert enjoying a rainstorm, soaking in every detail of her, from her foot in the stirrup to the expertise of her hands on the reins to the grace with which she carried herself. Then the dust-up with the robber proved to him she had courage and intelligence to back up her lovely exterior, a heady combination he had never encountered before. If his heart had been hers from the moment they met, she possessed him even more completely now.

In the sanctuary, the organist began the prelude. Paul continued to stand at parade rest until a friend of Jenny's, whom he had met only once and whose name he did not remember, came and told them it was time to enter.

In the hallway, the bridesmaids and ushers had assembled quietly. When Paul and Shane were in their places by the altar rail, Elizabeth positioned herself behind the maids of honor and groomsmen, and they paired up and started to process in, spacing themselves two pews apart as they had rehearsed. She felt her stomach tighten as her turn came. Holding her bouquet very precisely in front of her waist, she stepped into the aisle and matched her pace to the line of attendants ahead of her. In her imagination she could see the ring bearer behind her and then Clara, who had practiced strewing rose petals as though the fate of the world depended on her.

The organist cut his prelude short, leaving a pause while he reset his stops. Then the mighty strains of the old, familiar wedding march pealed out. The bride was on her way.

On the arm of her father, Jenny floated between the pews with their huge white-and-gold bows and bouquets of white roses, every inch of the spectacular gown glittering and glowing. The early evening sun slanting through the stained glass windows painted the sanctuary with patches of warm color, seemingly stitched together with the vibrant tones of the throaty pipe organ. The effect was such complete happiness that for the second time Elizabeth felt tears threaten. This time she pinched the web of her left thumb hard with the fingers of her other hand, the gesture concealed by her lace-trimmed nosegay. Then John formally gave Jenny away and she ascended the steps to stand between Elizabeth and Shane. Through the antique lace Elizabeth could see her cousin's dark eyes sparkling.

The minister picked up his book and began to intone the familiar, lovely old words of the wedding ceremony, but Elizabeth stopped hearing him after "Dearly beloved." Instead she immersed herself in the beauty of the scene, knowing deep inside herself this elegant pageant would never be reenacted for her.

She looked down the line of the groom's attendants, standing crisply at attention in their glowing red tunics. She could just see Paul's pale hair beyond Shane, who faced the minister. She hung on the man's every word while the light from the multicolored windows painted pastels across the pristine white of the bride's bouquet of roses and orange blossoms.

A classmate of Jenny's sang, accompanied by her mother on a harp. The delicate notes wound themselves around Elizabeth's heart and made the tears threaten again. This time she concentrated on Paul. From time to time she caught the merest glimpse of his profile: high forehead, sternly disciplined hair, straight nose, determined chin with a hint of cleft, square jaw line. She tried to commit his features to memory with the intent of sketching him later.

She heard Jenny and Shane exchange their vows, and then the minister took the ring from young David Brisbane and blessed it. Jenny turned to Elizabeth and handed over her bouquet, and Shane slipped the heavily ornate set of rings onto Jenny's finger, declaring, "Jennifer Catherine, with this ring I thee wed." A moment later, the minister pronounced them man and wife. Shane turned back the froth of lace veiling his bride, and, with a poignant gesture only Elizabeth could see, caressed Jenny's cheek with his left hand before finding her shoulder. He leaned down and their lips met briefly, but with such love and consummate gentleness that Elizabeth's tears won out, if only briefly. One made it half way down her right cheek and the other splashed on the pavé heart below the hollow of her throat.

To the heroically soaring strains of the famous Mendelssohn recessional, Jenny and Shane led down the aisle. When nearly all the Weston and Brisbane cousins had already gone outside, with pockets full of rice to shower the wedding couple, Jenny paused on the top of the stairs, waiting for her attendants to assemble below her. Then, to cheers from everyone gathered around, she gave her bouquet a large, underhand toss. However, throwing had never been Jenny's strong suit and it did not go far. Although Elizabeth suspected Jenny had targeted her, she stepped out of the way, and the blessing of the next to wed went to a slightly older second cousin, Laura Brisbane. She appeared delighted. *That's logical. After all, her engagement was announced last month.*

By the time the newlyweds made it into the ponderous Packard, rice had peppered Shane's dark hair until it looked like he had run through a snowstorm, and Elizabeth had caught enough of the overspray that when she and Paul climbed into the second coach, he paused to fluff it out of her curls.

"Well, what did you think?" he asked.

"The whole ceremony was so beautiful. I don't think I'll ever see anything like that again if I live to be a hundred."

"Oh, I don't know. You have your own to look forward to, after all."

She felt her cheeks flush and looked down. "I don't think so," she whispered, with what seemed like a dark premonition of her future.

Whatever reply Paul had in mind was cut short when the rest of the officers and two bridesmaids crammed themselves into the coach. The giggling girls forced Elizabeth very close to Paul, who laid his arm across the seat behind her and invited her next to him. Feeling quite daring indeed, she cuddled against his side and felt his cheek brush her temple when the coach hit a bump.

The reception was at the Waldorf, coincidentally where the groom's party was staying. The amount of time it had taken to festoon the whole of one banquet room and the ballroom with roses, bells, and voluminous satin bows, all in white and gold, did not bear thinking about. The bright Northwest Mounted Red Serges and the rich gowns of the ladies offset the otherwise unrelieved black of men in evening dress.

Elizabeth drew enjoyment out of every moment of dinner in listening to the fascinating conversation among the group of Mounties. She half regretted when the meal was over, but the dancing would be the high point of the evening for her. She drew on her gloves, took a small button hook from her bag, then paused to watch Paul. He put on his left glove, buttoned it, then fastened the right one and started to wiggle his hand in.

"Not that way, silly," she said with a soft laugh. "You'll pull the buttons off or stretch your glove beyond recognition. Here. Let me help you." He

61

unbuttoned the glove, pushed his hand in, and held it out to her palm up. Deftly she worked up the buttons, then fastened her own.

"Thank you," he said almost shyly. "Buttoning the second glove is like working with blankets on your fingers."

"Don't you have a button hook?"

"No. Not one that small."

With a smile she reached up, slipped the little silver trinket into his left breast pocket, and gave it a pat. "You do now."

"But I can't take yours…"

"Oh, piffle. It was a favor from some trifling party or other I attended years ago. Keep it. I have many others."

"Then I'll call it a keepsake and treasure it forever."

"Until you lose it somewhere."

He shook his head. "No. I'll keep it always to remember this lovely evening."

"It has been lovely, hasn't it? And the dancing is coming up. It's always my favorite part."

Just then the orchestra began to play. Jenny took the floor with her father. Every inch of her sparkled and glimmered under the ballroom lights. Shane had no one to dance with, so after a proper interval John handed Jenny off to him. To the strains of Jenny's favorite "Emperor Waltz," Shane led out, the short train of her gown flowing delicately behind them. The sheer beauty of the scene had Elizabeth almost in tears yet again.

"They look so happy," she said, glancing up at Paul.

"They do, don't they? Especially Shane. He's so,

well, contained, if you will. Even after six years I can't always read him. I never would have believed he'd have his heart on his sleeve like that."

"Now's a safe time for it."

"I daresay, after all those two have been through."

"Adversity is the tempering fire, they say."

"If so, they ought to be able to face anything from now until doomsday. So, Elizabeth, shall we dance so everyone else can?" He held out his arm to her, leading her out past the tables and onto the dance floor. She came easily into his arms, noting yet again she had to look up to meet his eyes. Once he had figured out her long stride could match his, he opened up a little more and let the strong, swinging rhythm carry them along. From that moment on, she sailed on a cloud in a way she had never before been granted in her entire life.

Afterward she found it hard to believe the night passed at the same speed as any other night of her life. Too soon the orchestra struck up "Auld Lang Syne." She danced as close to Paul as she dared, closing her eyes to concentrate on his nearness, feeling his warmth and smelling the heady combination of clean wool and virile male. When the last note died she was in no hurry to move away from him, and let her hand stray from his shoulder tab to the crook of his elbow. He looked down at her with a smile.

"Elizabeth, may I correspond with you?" he asked.

A huge wave of warmth rushed up from the pit of her stomach and she feared her cheeks would take fire. "Certainly."

"And your address?"

"In two days we'll be going to our summer house. It's Brookhaven Cottage, Sand Island, Massachusetts."

"Brookhaven Cottage, Sand Island, Massachusetts," he repeated, graving it into his memory.

"I presume yours is just Elk Gap, Ontario, the same way I write to Jenny."

"It'll get there fine that way, and it's probably faster than being proper and sending it through Royal Northwest in River Bend."

"All right. If I don't hear from you in a fortnight or so, I'll write and remind you of my address."

"I couldn't forget something that important," he responded. By now the dancers had begun to move from the floor, the bridal couple had disappeared, and families were sorting themselves out to go home. She felt a curious mixture of elation and disappointment.

"I see my parents making signals. It's time to leave, though I so wish it weren't." She sighed.

"I know. I feel the same way. Well, then, Elizabeth, it's time for farewell. But we'll see each other again, I promise, and I'll write as soon as the train gets in."

"Goodbye, Paul. It's been a lovely few days."

"It has been that, and more. I'll remember it always." He patted his breast pocket for emphasis. She had nearly forgotten the button hook.

"Oh, that! Well, I'll never forget this evening either, button hooks or no."

He looked over at the corner of the ballroom where the rest of his friends had gathered around Bob Shepherd. At the moment no one seemed to be watching them. He caught her hand and whisked her into a niche where the draperies shielded them from view. All the love scenes in every penny dreadful she had ever read flashed through her mind as Paul reached out, one hand coming behind her waist, and softly drew her toward him. She knew where this would lead and she was oh, so ready for it!

His hands explored her back as though memorizing the feel of her. She came easily into his embrace, her arms going behind his waist. Letting herself drift toward him, she tipped her face up and closed her eyes, inviting his kiss. His long arms enveloped her, and she pressed herself against the front of his Red Serge, immersed in his warmth and the masculine scent surrounding him. She felt his height dominating her, possessing her, and she let herself go into the moment. When at last their lips touched, she knew how a skyrocket felt when it exploded at the peak of flight. She yielded herself to him completely, body and soul, her whole being gone into the softness of his lips and his somewhat harsh Mountie mustache. Lightning flashed within her, turning her to liquid warmth inside. She did not exactly understand what she wanted, but it certainly did include him, and a lot more than just this one kiss. Her hand crept up over the back of his neck, pressing him against her, deepening the kiss. When his tongue caressed her upper lip, she was certain she would collapse from his sheer nearness.

They parted at last, breathless and shaken by the depth of passion that had passed between them. She backed away and looked up at Paul, seeing his fair skin ruddy with excitement. Then, unable to bear his gaze, she closed her eyes and felt those wonderfully expressive lips against her forehead. In that instant she went from a girl poised on the brink of life to a woman fallen headlong in love.

Their stolen moment more than spent, they left their hideaway by mutual consent. She glanced at her parents and then back at him. To her surprise he caught her hand, bowed, and kissed it, as cool as though nothing at all had passed between them, then disappeared through the thinning crowd. The soft touch sank through her glove and lingered on the back of her hand as though he had branded her his own forever.

Chapter 3

The ancestral Talbot summer house at Sand Island had been opened and cleaned by the time the family arrived. Rose went into a flurry Elizabeth knew from experience would last several days, directing the servants who had first packed and now unloaded the family's various bags and trunks. Elizabeth always looked forward to this chaos with delicious anticipation. It meant a whole summer free of lessons, manners, and rules—except when she was in her mother's presence. There the Great God Decorum would reign forever with his iron fist.

She watched from the porch as Clara kicked off her shoes and stockings and ran barefoot down the sandy cove toward the water. A bird in the air could not feel that free, she considered, watching her little sister spinning in circles, holding Barkley high overhead. Then Clara broke off and ran along the tide line, kicking up sandy spray that would certainly earn her a scolding for muddying the hem of her dress.

Elizabeth anticipated being sent off to mind her sister's safety around the water, but to her relief Robbie stepped into the breach. He left his own shoes and stockings on the weathered wood steps leading down to the sandy cove and walked out after her. Elizabeth wasted no time in disappearing to her second-floor bedroom, ostensibly to unpack her belongings.

Her small room, like the other upstairs bedrooms, hugged the slope of the roof. Behind the outside walls and running the length of the building, a long storage cubby reached to the eaves. Until now she had never risked more than a tentative peek inside the spooky darkness, but boredom is often the mother of adventure. She opened the door all the way and dropped to all fours, sticking her head into the lightless space.

After her eyes adjusted, she could see a tricycle, an ancient hobby horse, and some amorphous shapes that looked like boxes. A decent-sized but very old camel-back trunk sat within reach to her right. Impulsively she grabbed it by a stiffly dry leather handle and backed out, dragging it with her.

Once she had it out in the light, she saw the top lay thick with dust. She took the face cloth from her washstand, dampened it slightly, and cleaned the top and sides of the trunk. She did not know if it could be her imagination, but the moment she touched the leather, a tingling shot up her arm. Then she realized her hand rested on embossed initials: ERT. She repeated them slowly to herself, then realization dawned. It had to have belonged to her great-grandmother, Eliza Talbot. They shared their middle name, Regina. Her father had told her the story a hundred times, laughing as he did so. *I was to have been named for her, but Mother thought the name Eliza was hopelessly old-fashioned and out of date. So she gave me an even older name. My father even called me "Queenie" when I was younger, until Mother made him stop—in front of her, that is.*

Her hands paused on the trunk lid as she thought of the great-grandmother she had never known. *She lived to a respectable old age and passed only two months before I was born. That gave Mother the chance to renege on her promise to name me after her.*

The lacquered brass hinges had not corroded in the salty air. They reflected the light from the windows, as shiny as the day they had been made. She unsnapped the hasps and drew a deep breath, feeling a tingle of anticipation tighten her belly. Then she involuntarily closed her eyes and carefully raised the lid. It swung up smoothly, and she encountered a layer of old newspaper carefully tucked over the trunk's contents. She saw the date: September 2, 1886. *Eight years before I was born. She was eighty-four then. It must have been one of her last summers at Sand Island.* Carefully Elizabeth lifted the newspaper off, almost afraid of what she might find. But she came across only tissue paper covering a light summer shawl of naturally colored fine-spun lamb's wool, folded about a packet of tobacco to keep the moths away. It had evidently worked, because, between it and the tight seal of the trunk, the shawl, an enchanting froth of knitted lace with large peacock-tail motifs, looked virtually new. It came to a sharp V in the back and, when she flipped it about her shoulders, the tails fell properly below her waist. *But then, everyone has told me my great-grandmother was not a small woman. Father says she was the source of the Talbot height.*

Elizabeth folded the shawl and laid it on the foot of her bed. A plain woven straw hat with a large sunshade brim came out next. An embroidered scarf had been tacked around the crown by way of a hatband, with more newspaper crumpled inside the crown to prevent it from being crushed. She resisted trying it on, since her dressing table and tall mirror stood on the other side of the room. It joined the shawl on the bed.

Then she looked back into the trunk and gasped. The next item down could only be described as a fairy fantasy, an elaborately sprigged summer gown—or more properly a skirt and shirtwaist—of ivory lawn so delicate it looked like frost on a windowpane. The jewelry neckline had a shallow, rounded collar edged with lace merging into a waterfall down the front, concealing lovely buttons of real freshwater pearl. More lace decorated the three-quarter handkerchief sleeves and also made a flaring panel down the front of the skirt, dividing into long curves eventually edging the hem. The same small embroidered flowers of matching ivory sprigging the shirtwaist also repeated themselves on the skirt. The two side closures lay concealed beneath a wide sash meant to tie in a fluffy bow at the back. She reverently refolded each garment and laid them on her bed, and to her surprise, below them she found a complete set of matching lawn underthings, including an embroidered lace-front camisole and a tucked petticoat edged with lace meant to be glimpsed delicately below the hem of the skirt.

Then she encountered a satin scarf wrapped around an indefinite collection of small items. When she laid it on the floor before her and gently undid the folds, she found a string of graduated crystal beads and a silver bracelet with the initials "ERM" on a little heart charm. It gave her a moment's pause, until she remembered her great-grandmother's maiden name had been Morgan. It looked like a Christmas or a birthday gift suitable for a girl in her early teens. Lastly she picked up a breathtaking gold locket, a large filigree oval, delicately incised, with a huge rose-cut diamond set into a flower motif on the front. The chain had a clever closure she had never seen before, a small heart at each end and a clip-fastened slide that adjusted it to the desired length, leaving the hearts to dangle charmingly down the wearer's back. This was no young girl's bauble, but a precious piece of jewelry that would only be given by a serious beau to a young woman of an age and status to receive it.

Elizabeth turned the locket over in her hand. The back bore a pattern similar to the front, but was flat instead of convex. The freshness of the carving said the locket had not been worn much. Then she undid the catch and it opened in her palm, revealing on the right side a precisely executed miniature portrait on ivory, of a young man with flowing dark hair, kind eyes, and a warm half-smile on decidedly sensuous lips. Opposite it, under glass, rested a curled lock of deep brown-black hair. This definitely was not her great-grandfather, who, according to two portraits hung in Talbot House, had been blond and fine of feature. Suddenly the great-grandmother she had just missed knowing became a real woman, youthful in her turn, and in love. But who was this young man with the face of a Romantic poet? What had he meant to Eliza Morgan? How had their romance ended? For it had to have been a romance. No one would give a gift this magnificent casually.

On an impulse she undid the closure and fastened the locket around her neck, then worked it down inside the high collar of her blouse. It felt cool at first, but when she maneuvered it inside her camisole it became a comforting, warm weight between her breasts. *Oh, Nana! Father always told me you wanted a great-*

granddaughter, since Uncle Thomas has only sons. You knew Mother was expecting, but you never had a chance to know me. How I wish I could talk to you now! How I wish I could hear of your life when you were my age, of the man who gave you this locket, and what became of your love. Elizabeth touched the hard shape beneath her clothing. *Was your heart broken? Was his? What intervened, family or fate?*

She turned back to the trunk and removed the tissue that had lain beneath the clothing. The bottom layer of contents consisted of books packed with their spines facing upward. First she drew out a volume of the poetry of Emily Brontë, followed by matching volumes of Keats, Byron, and Robert Browning. But the next one, a generic bound journal without inscription on its cover, drew a curious frown.

One thing the family knew about Eliza Morgan Talbot was that throughout her life she had been a meticulous diarist. Her journals took up an entire shelf in the family's library and presented a lively and fascinating account of her life from the age of twenty-two, when she gave birth to her first child, up until her mid-eighties, when failing eyesight made her lay aside her hitherto prolific pen. Within the volumes lay an intimate portrait of gracious, genteel antebellum Virginia, the economic chaos leading to the Southern secession, and the hideous years of the Civil War and the Reconstruction, including an account of the shock the nation felt at Lincoln's assassination. But it had long been opined by Mother Talbot that her mother-in-law's journaling must have begun well before her marriage, and someday someone would discover the lost diaries of her early years. This book did resemble the rest of the journals. Could it possibly be…

She took up the first volume. With trembling hands she opened the front cover and the flyleaf, and on the title page an ornate script read, "Eliza Regina Morgan, Her Journal, 1824-1825." Hurriedly she set the book on her lap and picked up the next one. A similar inscription dated the journal from 1826 to 1827. The next volume began in 1828. Elizabeth scooped up all three books and held them against her heart. There it was! The missing story of her great-grandmother's early life! It seemed as if Elizabeth's wish had been heard—the grandmother her father had called Nana actually reached forward through time to hold out a hand to her oldest great-granddaughter. Elizabeth's eyes filled with tears, and she fumbled in her skirt pocket for a handkerchief.

Her life had made her cautious. She knew at that moment the last thing she would do would be to run to her parents with news of her discovery. The trunk, the clothing, and the girlish jewelry, yes. But not the diaries, and certainly not the gold locket. They would be her secret for the present, her link with the ancestress she had barely missed knowing. She would read the diaries first, then give them to her father when the time was right.

She left the poetry books on her nightstand, tucked the three precious journals under her pillow, then sat on the bed and closed her eyes, visualizing herself wearing the lovely outfit. Of course, the pantalets were simply much too outdated, but the rest would be just right for summer here.

But this was not the time to sit daydreaming. Mother would be calling them down to lunch soon. The jewelry went into a drawer in the bonnet-box highboy. She would give Clara the bracelet, to keep her from complaining to Mother, and keep the rest. She hung the garments in her armoire, set the hat on the top shelf, placed the shawl in a drawer in the bureau, and lastly scooted the trunk back to its place under the eaves. Then with a sigh she tackled the first of her own three trunks.

Not until she went to bed could she open the first of the diaries and begin to know the great-grandmother who had such influence on the family even yet. Finally, in her nightdress with her curling Brisbane hair up in rags, she stuffed three pillows behind her back, turned her old-fashioned bullseye kerosene lamp down as low as she could comfortably stand it, took up the book, and began to read.

May 16, 1821

We are at Sand Island very early this year, so early that there was no time to send ahead to have the house readied for us. When we arrived (Mother, the twins— Charles Junior and Rob—Mary, and me, along with Nanny Pearl, Cicero, and Penelope) the furniture was shrouded in dust sheets, all the linens needed turning out, the floors swept, and the counters and shelves wiped down. But it is said that many hands make light work, so we all lent ours, until by evening we had the house more or less in order, and we retired after a light, yet satisfying supper.

The reason for our unseasonable removal from Virginia is also the reason that I must start my journaling over again. Just over a fortnight ago the big house at Brookhaven was struck by lightning and badly damaged in the resulting fire. The rooms given over to

Mary and me were among those totally destroyed. I lost all my possessions except for my jewelry box, which I managed to snatch from my vanity table as Father pulled me from the room. I did not have time to unlock my writing desk and retrieve my journals, so my last five years' entries were totally destroyed. Fortunately the storm was so severe that we were awake when it happened, and Father was able to marshal all the field hands to remove our valuables and to form a bucket brigade that eventually quenched the fire and saved the greater part of the house.

We passed the next few nights in the big tobacco barn. It was not at all unpleasant, but it was not seemly for ladies to remain there, either, so even though we could have stayed with our neighbors, Father and Mother made the decision that she would take us to Sand Island early, leaving Father and Philip behind to superintend the rebuilding of the big house. Of course the twins lamented long and hard that they were being exiled while brother Phillip stayed with Father, but Phillip is twenty-one and of age, while Father deemed the twins, at fourteen years old and prone to mischief, too young to be anything but a nuisance to him.

Mother could have taken on as though the world had come to an end. I know far too many ladies who do just that. Even my best friend Tabitha Kendall laments a lost button as though someone near and dear to her had passed on. But Mother is steel inside, and she has a way of seeing a bright side to everything, even when it may not be so evident to those about her. She turned our train journey into a grand shopping trip from which we all returned with sparkling new wardrobes, and Mary and I arrived at Sand Island feeling very grand indeed.

It may seem odd that we brought Cicero and Penelope with us. Normally we get by with only Nanny Pearl, and a cook who also helps her with the house. Penelope, as head cook at Brookhaven, always remained behind with her husband, our butler Cicero, to manage the big house while we summered in the cooler climes of Massachusetts. But a butler in a house under repair is of little use, and besides, Cicero is nearing sixty, and I believe Father wanted to spare him from feeling as though he needed to help with the heavy work. Father depends very much upon Cicero in the day-to-day running of the big house and has often said he would trust him with our lives. Besides, Cicero is a humble man who in his youth was a carpenter, and is not above turning his hands to manual labor should it be needed. Already he has mended the front steps and installed a new screen door in the kitchen.

Both Cicero and Penelope were born at Brookhaven and served Grandfather Morgan before his death. Of course they were freed by Grandfather's will, but they have elected to stay with our family as salaried servants. Nanny Pearl, on the other hand, is a year older than Mother and was given to her at her birth to be maid and companion, and when we came along, it was natural that she become our mammy. She is a spare woman, very black of complexion, a continuous wellspring of hugs and wise sayings. But there is a dark side to Nanny Pearl. She does not speak like a slave, at least around white folk, but in an eyeblink she can sink deep into the rapid patter of Gullah that sounds like hail on a tin roof and give herself over so completely to pagan superstitions and primitive African lore that she can make one's hair stand on end. What is even more chilling is that I think she believes all of it. Her own mother, an ancient African freedwoman living not far from Brookhaven, spent a great part of her life in the swamps of Louisiana and brought all kinds of strange and forbidden beliefs with her. When I am in the presence of Mama Lou I always feel that I am looking straight into the heart of something primal, timeless, perhaps even tinged with evil, that must be handled with utmost care.

In the same vein, all of us—my brothers, my sister, and I—have our own people, given to us by custom at our births, but only Nanny Pearl comes to Sand Island with us. There simply is no room for anyone else. Our family, being on the large side, fills the simple house to overflowing. Father often speaks of adding onto it but has yet to do anything about it.

Naturally I miss my dearest Pansy, and she always sees me off with tears in her eyes. In turn I always promise to try to take her with me, but we both know we will have to endure our separation until I return in September.

When Elizabeth awoke the next morning, the ivory handkerchief dress called to her. She washed up, combed her hair and gathered it back with a bow, then donned her underthings and the lace-edged petticoat. She hesitated before deciding this was, after all, Sand Island. She would wear her great-grandmother's dress if she chose to. Her justification, should her mother question her, was she was going out to Lighthouse Point to do some plein air sketching. The old lighthouse would provide a perfect excuse, and she could potter about the tide pools to her heart's content, as she had done when she was Clara's age.

She donned the underthings and shirtwaist first. It buttoned easily, and the years-old wrinkles had all but hung out of it overnight. The skirt also made a surprising fit, fastening at the smaller of the two sets of buttons with a little to spare. She tied the sash, then craned her head around to check her appearance in the tall cheval glass. She had to admit the effect pleased her very much. The froth of lace on the shirtwaist emphasized the bust her cousin Jenny had admitted envying, while it flattered her small, fashionably corseted waist.

Only belatedly did she remember the locket. She took it from its hiding place, but since there was no way the blouse would conceal it, she buried it in the bottom of her box of drawing supplies. Then she took the box and her great-grandmother's straw hat and descended the stairs to face the ordeal of breakfast.

It was her father who noticed her first. "My, Bet, you look lovely this morning! Where did you find those clothes?" he boomed heartily. His face looked flushed, and his customary early-morning constitutional along the beach had left him in high spirits. Her mother turned to look, and her mouth set itself into a grim line, but she would never contradict her husband in front of the family.

"I ran across an old trunk belonging to your grandmother. It was in the cubby under the eaves. This was evidently her outfit at one time."

"Yes, she was the tall one in the family. It fits you quite nicely."

"But it's so dated," Rose complained.

Elizabeth's reply was an airy shrug. "I don't intend

to go visiting in it, Mother. It's comfortable in the heat, and I'm only going to walk down to Lighthouse Point and do some sketching. It's not like anyone who matters will see me."

"I hope not. And I also hope you don't have one of those penny dreadfuls in with your pencils."

"For heaven's sake, Rose! We're only young once, and after all, this is Sand Island, not New York City. If she wants to play dress-up and read trashy fiction, let her. I, for one, think she looks devastating in that outfit." He seated his wife at the table, then plunked down emphatically in the head chair and eyed Robbie, waiting for him to pull out Elizabeth's chair for her. Grudgingly Robbie seated his elder sister.

Grace over and food before them, Elizabeth watched everyone else eat. For some reason her stomach was tight, as though with the premonition of a great adventure ahead. She managed a cup of black coffee and most of one piece of toast, and when she finally excused herself, she felt as free as Clara had looked the day before.

The Talbot summer home lay in the crook of a sandy cove facing generally south to southeast, sheltered by a long headland and defined at the northern end by Lighthouse Point and the old light that had guided sailors away from the sandbars for some two hundred years. The lighthouse tower had been rebuilt once, to raise it to its present height and add a clockwork beacon, and just before the outbreak of the Civil War a keeper's cottage had been built of matching stonework. At one point the tower had borne stripes, whose remnants could be seen on close inspection, but now it was solid white, accented with smart red trim and black ironwork. Elizabeth took the path to the lighthouse grounds, over to a small sand beach not frequented because the approach was rocky and rough. However, it afforded a lovely vista of the lighthouse and the lonely, restless Atlantic that was, for once, rather calm.

She found herself a convenient rock, sat down, and took off her shoes. Her stockings followed, and after stuffing them down into one shoe, she tested the temperature of the sand. It felt just as warm and welcoming as it had always been every other summer of her life. She tipped the brim of her hat down against the low morning sun, then opened her sketch box and assembled the portable easel that fit in brackets under the lid. The glimmer of the gold locket she had stashed beneath the sketch pad caught her eye, and she drew it out, holding it up so the sun caught the large diamond. Once again she wondered about the young man portrayed in the miniature inside, and about the great-grandmother she knew only from her journal entries. She clipped the chain about her neck, then adjusted the slide so the locket hung just above the margin of her collar. The gold lay like a soft and nearly living thing against her skin, and for just a moment she felt as lovely as she had in her bridesmaid's gown, when she had danced the night away in the arms of the handsome young Mountie with a sunny smile and summer-blue eyes.

At first she truly tried to sketch the lighthouse, but after much doctoring with an eraser and a bit more fiddling, it turned into a representation of Paul which did not satisfy her in the least. Her art talent was only moderate; she longed for Shane's graphic gift that allowing him to spend only an hour executing two very professional wax pastel studies of Barkley for Clara's birthday. One had shown a baffled and startled young hound face to face with a furiously barking Gray squirrel, while in the next he stood with one forepaw curved up to his breast and the other on a deadfall, baying at a full moon caught in the spooky branches of a winter-bare tree. They had immediately become Clara's prized possessions, next to Barkley himself, to the point she had brought them with her and hung them in her bedroom. Even in her best moments, Elizabeth came nowhere near Shane's ability.

She realized her rendering of Paul bore very little resemblance to the handsome officer she thought of nearly every other moment of her waking life. With a sigh she turned over another sheet on her sketch pad and went back to the lighthouse. At least she could draw straight lines. But the paper in her hand mocked her. There was simply no lighthouse in it. She sighed again and abandoned her easel for the call of the isolated pools emerging on the ebbing tide. She touched her toes to the receding water, letting the sun-warmed wavelets lap over them and turning her mind loose to roam. Not surprisingly, it immediately went back to the Waldorf ballroom, and she danced in Paul's arms again. She moved away from the exposed rocks and dreamily began to dance. At first it was a solo waltz to the music in her head, which seemed to bear some relationship to "The Beautiful Blue Danube." She rose up demi-pointe, her bare feet leaving dimples in the warm sand. Then it turned into free-form ballet, a *pas de deux* with an imaginary partner. She pirouetted and jumped, extending her whole body, bending and rising again as her feet carried her around the small sandy cove. At one point, in the midst of a *grand jeté,* her hat blew off, but she ignored it, merely reaching back to free her hair from its ribbon, which she then held in her left hand. It became an extension of her body, no heavier nor less limber than the summer breeze itself. And when she found she could actually dance *en pointe* in the sand, she fairly flew, letting the ribbon lead, her lace-embellished skirt and petticoat swirling about her in a whirl of delicately beautiful confusion. She came down only after she was tired and out of breath. Imagining an audience applauding her performance, she executed a deeply extended bow toward the ocean.

"Bravo! Bravo!" a masculine voice called behind her, and the sound of real applause sent an ice spear through her stomach. She spun around, her first thought being flight, but she had nowhere to go. She could not run back across the rocks barefoot, and he was standing at the end of the pathway, between her and the place where she had carefully stashed her shoes. She took a good look at her audience. He was young and reasonably tall, with short, butter-tan hair, and wore summer-weight flannel slacks and a collarless white shirt, sleeves rolled up over sun-browned forearms.

"You frightened me half to death!" she snapped when she could manage to draw breath.

"I'm so sorry. I didn't mean to. I couldn't help but watch you dance. It was so beautiful. You're very graceful, you know." He picked up her hat, which lay in the sand at his feet, and came forward to return it to her.

"Thank you. I didn't realize I'd lost it." She made him wait until she had tied her hair back, then she took the hat, mostly to give her nervous hands something to do.

His face immediately assumed a wistful expression. "I wish you hadn't done that."

"Done what?"

"Tied your hair up again. It's so lovely down."

"It's also very hot. Now if you'll let me past, I really do need to go home."

"I must apologize again. I see that I've frightened you. I'm really very harmless. By the way, I'm Noah Canning. Who might you be?"

"Elizabeth Talbot. Now, please…" She looked up into eyes nearly the same shade as Paul's, her initial panic settling.

"Of course, Miss Talbot." He stepped away from the path with a bowing gesture. "But it's such a small island and such a big summer. I very much anticipate seeing you again." Trying to salvage her dignity, she packed up her art supplies and reclaimed her pumps, sitting on a rock with her back pointedly to Noah as she donned them. He still waited patiently at the side of the path when she rose and tucked the box under her arm.

"May I carry that for you, Miss Talbot?" he inquired with meticulous politeness. She took her first discerning look at him then, finding square shoulders, regular features, and an enchanting hint of dimples in his cheeks. The knot inside her unwound.

"Thank you, Mr. Canning," she responded, relinquishing the box. It was indeed rather heavy, but he took the weight without seeming to notice it.

"So, where do you live, then?" he asked.

"Not far. Just over the headland. Brookhaven Cottage."

"I've always been curious about how that place got

its name. The others all have nautical names like Tern, Gull, Driftwood...you know. Brookhaven seems somehow out of place."

"Brookhaven is the name of Father's family's ancestral plantation in Virginia. He inherited this cottage, but some of his family still live on and work the plantation. Somehow the place survived the Civil War with only minimal damage."

"I see. Now it makes sense to me."

"Are you on the island for the summer?" She was slightly puzzled. She knew almost all the Sand Island summer residents, and he was not one of the regulars.

He shook his head. "I'm a mainlander. It's a summer home, though. My family is from Boston."

"Then what are you doing here?"

"Just out for a day's sail. My catboat is docked around the other side." He gestured vaguely southwest, toward the end of the island most residents did indeed refer to as the "other side."

"Quite a walk, I'd say."

Noah shrugged. "I was just wandering, out of curiosity. I'm immensely glad I did." Elizabeth did not rise to the bait, nor would she have expected him to believe he could engage her that easily. She was, after all, a lady.

They walked in silence for some time, until they had crossed behind the brushy rise and were approaching the cove. From the shelter of the windswept brush, Elizabeth could see her mother and father sitting beneath a beach umbrella, watching Clara and two of her friends poking about the surf line. Her father had some sort of legal publication perched on his knees, while her mother worked on her tatting. Or at least she held her tatting, looking as though her hands were busy. Elizabeth never saw her add more than a knot or two at a time; the same piece had lasted her fully two years.

"Is that your family down there?" Noah asked, coming to a stop.

"Yes, all except my brother Robbie. Providence alone knows where he went."

"Well, then, this had better be as far as I go. It's a little early in the game to present me to your parents, especially since we haven't even been properly introduced." He set her box down.

"Thank you for your aid, Mr. Canning," she said almost tersely; politeness dictated she express some sort of gratitude, whether she felt it or not.

"It was my privilege and my pleasure, Miss Talbot. And I sincerely hope we meet again soon."

"As you said, it's a small island and a very big summer." She took up the box by its padded leather handle still warm from his grasp, and he bowed to her again. She had the feeling he would have kissed her hand had she offered it. Instead she started down the path to the beach, feeling his eyes on her. Then she realized she was still wearing the locket. Without breaking her stride she reached behind her neck and tripped the catch, feeling first the weight of the locket, then the heavy chain, slither down into her camisole, where it nestled warmly between her breasts.

As she crossed the beach, her mother looked up from the tatting lying idly in her lap.

"Back so soon, Elizabeth?" she asked.

"The lighthouse cove was occupied. I didn't want to crowd anyone."

"Someone we know?"

She shook her head. "No. Some day sailors from the mainland were having a picnic. I may go back again later when the sun is lower. Right now the shadows are quite sharp."

"Well, then, sit down with us." Rose gestured to one of the five weathered Adirondack chairs that spent each summer perched above the high-tide line. Elizabeth put down her burden and unobtrusively removed her shoes and hose for the second time that morning. Rose looked at her and cocked an eyebrow.

"My pumps are completely full of sand, and I don't want to snag my hose on the chair," she explained, thinking she had to justify herself yet again.

"Well, if you'd wear proper oxfords, that wouldn't happen." Elizabeth let the remark pass, but she pulled up her knees and sat sidesaddle on the chair so she could cover her bare feet with the bottom ruffle of her petticoat. But she soon grew restless.

"I think I'll go in for a while," she announced, scooping up shoes and her art supply box. Her nod toward the cottage yard hinted at a necessary visit to the backhouse beyond. Her mother nodded.

"Perhaps you'd consider changing your clothes while you're there."

"Perhaps. But as dated as it is, this outfit is comfortable in the heat." Her father looked up from his book in a way that precluded any revisit of the breakfast argument. Elizabeth twitched her hips almost insolently and did not see her mother shoot a sharp look at her before turning her attention back to the children at the tide line.

She entered the house through the kitchen, nodding

to the cook, who was paring potatoes at the sink. She made her way through the front parlor and up the stairs to the quiet of her room. Her great-grandmother's diary called to her across the years, a siren song she found irresistible. She settled herself comfortably on her bed, took the first volume out from beneath her pillow, located the page where she had left off, and started to read.

May 19, 1821

I had no opportunity to write until now, but there was precious little worth setting down anyway. Rob and Charles Junior fell out over who knows what, and it came to fisticuffs. Rob bloodied Junior's nose and received a black eye as repayment. Mother was so incensed that she gave them both over to Cicero, who is at present overseeing them while they labor in the flower beds. Yesterday they had to split and haul wood, then collect shells to resurface the path leading to the beach. I know that as soon as the plantings are in order Cicero will find some other heavy labor to set them to, as hard work and the resulting fatigue will blunt their adolescent tempers.

I think all the worry and strain of the fire is finally manifesting itself; Mother's placid temperament is showing a crack here and there. When she heard Rob complaining of being set to work like a field hand, she threatened to double their punishment. Moreover, when Mary laughed at them, Mother threatened her with the hairbrush. So I have retreated to the room Mary and I share, and I am keeping my nose down, hoping to go unnoticed. Even though I am nearly seventeen and much too old to punish, I know Mother has her limits and would have no compunction about taking that selfsame hairbrush to me.

~*~

May 20, 1821

Every summer when we come to Sand Island I experience a few days of melancholia; I always miss Brookhaven terribly. But then I find my old friends here, and I am once again sanguine. Sally Lawton, who lives in the next house down the beach but one, has been my bosom summer companion since her family started coming to Sand Island when we were only eight years old. But she is not here yet; as I previously wrote, we have come early. I did stroll down to their house on the off chance that they might be in residence early as we are, but it is closed as tightly as an oyster, windows shuttered and windblown sand everywhere. I will keep walking down there every day or two until I find her family's servants there making ready. It gives me something to do and serves as a good constitutional.

How I miss home! I wish I could be there and not exiled to Sand Island like a child! I know I could have been a good right hand to Father and Phillip, but when I expressed that opinion, Father told me Mother needed me more. I could help keep the twins in hand and watch out for Mary, who is only eleven and still needs minding. Of course we have Nanny Pearl for that, and it would snow in that famous hot place before the twins paid me any mind at all, but Father would brook no arguments. So here I am, without even Pansy for companionship. I did question Father as to what he was going to do without Cicero, but he opined that Titus would do just as well.

Titus is our overseer, Cicero and Penelope's eldest son. I know most plantations have white overseers, but

Titus is just as level-headed and dependable as his parents and enforces Father's rules with an even hand.

Father, like Grandfather, is good to his people. They have excellent food from their community kitchen, sound housing—including an infirmary where the ill can be nursed—and serviceable clothing. I have seen many other field hands going about in rags, but our people all have two or three sets of clothes, at least one of which is presentable enough that they can be seen when we entertain. He never allows them to be cursed at or struck, even with provocation. He even goes so far as to reprimand anyone who is discourteous to our house staff. Another unwritten law is that he does not break up families. Consequently his people know they are in a good situation and are fanatically loyal to their Marse Edward.

At our plantation, jumping the broom is cause for a good party. When Titus married just a week before the fire, Father even declared that Saturday a holiday and, except for necessary services, no work was done. But for all that, our people were busier than they would have been on a regular workday. Everyone was cooking, and those who were not were busy decorating a new cabin for Titus and Ophelia.

Ophelia is not from Brookhaven. Instead she came from Green Hills, a few miles south of us. It is owned by a family named Greenhill (how unoriginal), who have a reputation for mingling with their blacks—not that it is widely considered a bad thing, since they are, after all, chattel property—it is just something we Morgans do not do. Feli (which I later discovered is also short for felicidad, *which means "happiness" in Spanish) is what many people term a "child of the plantation." Ophelia*

Lael R. Neill

was sired by some unnamed white man and is bright of complexion, and also bright in manner. She smiles, laughs, and sings, and she is devastatingly pretty. I understand why Titus was smitten with her. Since our plantations are too far apart for them to have sneaked away for a tryst here and there, he had to ask for her. In the end, Father purchased Ophelia. I almost expected him to free her, since Titus was free by Grandfather's will. However, Ophelia remains his property, at least for the present. Titus has set himself to purchasing her freedom, but since Father paid a premium price for her, that will take time and diligent saving on Titus's part. I have no doubts, though, that he will be successful.

I do not think it matters to the happy couple. Since Titus is a freedman, their wedding ceremony was conducted by a preacher from the little church for blacks that Cicero's family attends every Sunday. Everyone from the entire plantation gathered in the garden beside Brookhaven. The bride wore a white lace dress that had been mine until I grew so tall that it no longer fit me. She was crowned with a garland of roses and ribbons and carried a matching bouquet (Mother's doing—she is talented with flowers), and Father proudly gave her away. At the end of the ceremony the oldest woman on our plantation placed a flower-decked broom on the ground and they jumped over it into wedded bliss. Everyone sang to the fiddle one of our house servants played, food was served in abundance, and there was music and dancing until well after sundown. After Mary and I went to bed we could still hear the blacks singing and drumming, but the character of the music had changed. It was now dark and African sounding, reminiscent of the music I hear when Nanny Pearl takes me to visit Mama Lou in her strange little village near the river.

Some people look down on us for what they term Father's "coddling" of his people, but it has made them more than loyal to him. Even though he is free, Titus would never think of leaving Brookhaven, any more than his parents would. He has vowed to work until he can buy Feli's freedom, but I fully expect them to stay with our family until we are all old and gray.

Chapter 4

When Elizabeth awoke the next morning she took the diary out from beneath her pillow and secreted it in the cubbyhole. Then, since she and some of her friends had planned to visit The Landing, the little town on the "other side," she donned a pale yellow serge walking skirt and sensible, high-laced shoes. After breakfast she set off with a packet of letters to post, including the obligatory notes to family her mother wrote with grim determination, a couple from her father to members of his firm, and, slipped in between them, her own daring letter to Paul.

She had not made it a quarter of a mile down the informal wagon road before she caught up with her friends.

"Hello, Elizabeth," Judith Tanner said with a wide smile. Elizabeth liked her. She was not inclined to gossiping and backbiting like some of the other rich girls in the Sand Island summer crowd.

"Good morning, everyone."

"So what will we do with the day, then? Aside from going to the general store, that is?"

"I need to visit the postmaster. I need to check our mail and post a few letters."

"Oh? To anyone interesting?" The source of the question was Luci Graham. Elizabeth found the question intrusive simply because it came from Luci, who had just come out last Christmas and still flaunted her status.

"No, in fact they're all from my parents," Elizabeth fibbed.

"To elderly family and stuffy clients, I suppose."

"To elderly family and on behalf of stuffy clients, actually," she said rather quickly, remembering Paul's address on one envelope. "Father's clients are bankers, after all."

"How boring, and how utterly beyond our feminine minds," Judith sighed.

Feminine minds, my foot! Elizabeth thought. *If you'd only been at Jenny's wedding.* Her thoughts drifted off to the reception, where she and Paul had danced the night away, until... Grace, Luci's fifteen-year-old sister, brought her back to the present. She still wore a childishly short skirt, and her strawberry hair had been in two fat pigtails to confine its wild curl.

"So what was the most exciting thing that happened to you this year, Elizabeth?" she asked, filling the gap in their conversation.

"It had to be in my cousin's wedding party. It was only two weeks ago."

"That's right. You were her maid of honor, weren't you?" Judith asked. "You simply have to tell us all about it. That wedding was New York's social event of the year."

"Oh, it was. Believe me, it was. It was simply beautiful, all white and gold." She launched into a long, rambling account over every aspect of the nuptials, except for Paul. That was a secret she would not share, even with her best friend. The three hung on her every word like the shallow beauties they were. The juicy topic carried them half way to The Landing.

"But why did Jenny wait so long?" Luci asked. "Wasn't she afraid of becoming an old maid?"

"Jenny is a doctor. She didn't think she'd marry at all until she met Inspector Adair."

"Why on earth should she want to become a doctor? I can't imagine it. All that blood, all those sick people..." Luci broke off with a shiver.

"She has always lived to help others. You forget Uncle John is a physician, too. Aunt Catherine died when Jenny was just a child, and of course she idolized her father. She's also the most brilliant woman I've ever known. It was natural for her to aspire to medical school."

"I'm ever so glad I'll never have to work for a living," Grace put in. "Of course I plan to marry, but if I shouldn't, I'll still be of independent means."

"And with all those brothers of yours, one of them is bound to need a maiden aunt," Judith said with a laugh. The others tittered, and Grace blushed.

Just then they came across a small rise, and The Landing hove into view, a loose collection of half a dozen weathered buildings scattered about a small cove housing the marina and the ferry dock. A few hardy year-round residents lived there, catered to tourists in the summer, and fished during the off season. Elizabeth and her companions headed for the general store. Several ice cream tables crowded its large farmer's porch. The occupants of one of the tables waved vigorously to the girls as they came down the little hill.

"Look. That's Mary and Silvie. Let's go join them. After that long walk I'd welcome a lemonade," Judith suggested.

"That would be lovely," Luci agreed.

"I'd like one too, but I need to visit the post office first. You three go ahead and sit down."

"We'll save you a place. Do you want lemonade too?" Grace asked.

"That would be wonderful. I'll pay you back once I've posted these letters. All I have is a half-dollar."

"No, it'll be my treat. All four of us," Luci offered. She was prone to magnanimous gestures, but Elizabeth knew she could turn nasty just as quickly as she could be generous. For a long time Elizabeth had suspected Luci cultivated her friendship just so she could have someone against whom she could play off her petite blonde beauty. And Lord help sweet, naïve Grace unless Luci was married by the time she came out. That harpy of an elder sister would eat her alive.

"Then it's my turn next time," Judith said.

With Luci giggling over something inconsequential, they arrived at the general store. The girls claimed the table next to Mary and Sylvia and sat down into what resembled a flock of chatty sparrows. Elizabeth went on inside, to the back counter, where the mail had been sorted into pigeonholes with the names of the houses on them. It had been that way forever, obviating the necessity of rearranging all the names when any of the summer cottages changed hands.

When she stopped at the counter, the wife of the store owner greeted her. "How can I help you, ma'am?" she asked politely. At first Elizabeth had had a hard time with people acknowledging her as an adult, but she had learned to accept it with equanimity.

"Mail for Brookhaven, please? And I'd like to post these letters." She drew the stack from her pocket and laid the letters and her fifty-cent piece on the glass countertop, opaque with scratches from decades of coins. The woman took the letters, stamped them, made change, and then turned to retrieve the mail from one of the top pigeonholes. Elizabeth thanked her mindlessly, then riffled through the stack of mail. At the third letter down, her heart stopped. It bore her name, and when she turned it over, the return on the back read "R.N.W.M.P., Elk Gap, Ontario, Canada." She resisted the impulse to tear into the envelope then and there. Instead she put it in her left pocket and everything else in the right. It would require her best efforts not to give away her excitement to her friends, but after a lifetime of living with her mother she had developed a good poker face. When she rejoined the girls outside at their adjacent tables, none could have had the faintest inkling her heart was racing and her stomach still fluttering over the delicious secret buried in her skirt pocket.

While the girls chatted, Elizabeth noticed a catboat douse its sail and glide up to the marina float. She had the odd flash telling her it could be the same one that had brought Noah Canning to the island the day she'd put on her impromptu dance performance, which still inwardly embarrassed her more than she wanted to admit. She squirmed uncomfortably as three young men stepped onto the float and took their time mooring their craft. One was indeed Noah. The jauntiness of his gait bordered on arrogant, and while he wore a straw boater this time, his sleeves were still rolled up over muscular, sun-browned forearms.

Just then she felt the wind tug at her hat and run flirtatious fingers around the hem of her yellow walking skirt. Midmorning was usually when the breeze started in from the ocean. She caught her hat and paused to reset a hatpin.

"Why don't you let it go?" Noah and his friends had covered the short distance to the store, and he spoke to her with a brilliant smile. "That way I'd have an excuse to chase it down and return it to you again."

"Good morning, Mr. Canning." Deliberately she kept her tone cool, an easy thing when she thought of him in the same mental sentence with Paul.

The obligatory introductions went around, and, without asking permission, Noah pulled up a chair from an adjacent table and wedged himself in between Elizabeth and Sylvia. For the present, Luci, who fancied herself a *femme fatale*, found she was being ignored by the alpha male of the group. Instead, he focused his attention on Elizabeth, who watched with no small amusement as her friend became more animated, smiled more brightly, talked a little louder, and tried to dominate the conversation, but did not succeed in capturing Noah's attention.

"So, Mr. Canning, are you new to Sand Island?" she asked. "I don't remember seeing you here the last few summers." Noah's eyes moved reluctantly to Luci, then back to Elizabeth's face before he answered.

"No, ma'am. I'm a mainlander. My family just purchased a summer place up on The Bluff." The area to which he referred, informally called The Bluff, contained a string of palatial vacation homes constructed within the last ten years or so.

"Then where are you from?" she asked, leaning her chin on her hand, flirtatiously childlike.

"Boston," he responded, not rising to the bait. Instead he shifted in his chair until his knee brushed

Elizabeth's skirt.

"Well, then, we hope to see more of you this summer. You know there are dances at the pavilion every Saturday evening?"

"No, I hadn't known that. What's the pavilion?" He directed the question to Elizabeth, but she let Luci jump in since she seemed determined to dominate the conversation. She sipped her lemonade and let the byplay pass over her.

"It's over the water on the south end of the bay. There's a long dock attached to it, so you could come in your boat."

"Oh. So that's the pavilion. I saw it yesterday when I sailed around the island. I'll keep it in mind, then. If you'll grant me the first dance, Miss Talbot." Elizabeth turned and looked at him, stifling her surprise with uplifted eyebrows. With Paul in the forefront of her mind, it would have been perfectly all right with her for Luci to steal Noah Canning out from under her nose. However, he had deftly established his territory and brushed Luci off at the same time. Luci's eyes narrowed, and she gave Elizabeth a sharp look. Then she ventured a glance at the gold pendant watch pinned below the yoke of her blouse.

"Goodness, I had no idea it had grown so late. Grace, we need to go home. As much as I've enjoyed everyone's charming company, I did promise my parents I'd have my sister home by lunchtime."

"But I haven't finished my lemonade," Grace protested.

"Well, hurry, then. You don't want Mother to be cross with you."

"I think I'd best be returning too," Elizabeth said.

She rose and shook out her skirt, feeling Paul's letter concealed in her pocket. It nearly shouted at her. Noah stood at the same time.

"Then, ladies, it's been a pleasure," he said, tipping his hat to them. "Miss Talbot, I shall plan on seeing you Saturday."

"I haven't really made up my mind whether I'll attend or not. I'll see."

"Then I'll cling to hope until the last final moment." Theatrically he covered his heart with his hand. Behind him, Judith rolled her eyes.

Farewells behind them, the group of girls climbed the hill behind The Landing, leaving Noah and his companions on the porch.

"I'm surprised at you, Noah," one of them said. "That little blonde is cake and ice cream and had her cap set for you, and you go for the giraffe who doesn't talk."

"And Luci would be as cold as ice cream when it comes down to it," he responded. "That's why I paid attention to Elizabeth. It's always the sad-eyed loners who'll give a man what he really wants."

"Her? Bullshit. She's as tight as an oyster," the other said, taking cigarette papers and tobacco from his trouser pocket and casually rolling himself a smoke.

"I'll make you gentlemen a bet. A hundred dollars says I'll have her by the end of summer."

"You're on!" the smoker scoffed, holding out his hand.

Chapter 5

Elizabeth walked between Judith and Sylvia, silent in the anticipation of the letter deep in her skirt pocket, and let Luci's chatter flow over her like the easy summer breeze from the ocean.

"Don't you think Mr. Canning is just the handsomest?" she said, her voice habitually breathy and quick, as though she had run a mile. "I mean, those lovely blue eyes? And he noticed me, too. I know he did."

"It seems to me he noticed Elizabeth," Judith said dryly. It was obvious she had hit her tolerance limit for Luci's fatuous gushing.

"He did mention something about returning your hat to you again. What was that about?" Sylvia inquired.

"Oh, nothing, really. I was walking on the beach yesterday morning, and my sun hat blew off. He retrieved it for me, that's all."

"That isn't nothing," Luci continued. "Circumstances like that are how young ladies meet their future husbands. Aren't you the least bit excited?"

"No, actually I'm not. Mr. Canning seems very sure of himself," she responded, then thought, *If you only knew about Paul you would know all about blue eyes. Deep, like the sky opposite the sun, and blond hair that sparkles when the light hits it. Tall, strong, a man, not a callow boy. And as for the dance Saturday night, I already spent almost a whole night dancing with Paul. Not to mention what happened when we parted. Nothing could ever again be as special, as poignant, as that marvelous evening.*

"I don't know about Mr. Canning being overly sure of himself. But maybe he has reason to be. He seems all of twenty-two to me. And I just know he'll notice me. He did talk about the dance Saturday night, after all." Luci rattled on, her words only so much rain on the roof as Elizabeth recalled the night of Jenny's wedding reception.

"Yes, he did speak about Saturday night. He asked her for the first dance." This time it was Sylvia who tried to put the damper on Luci, but the latter seemed oblivious.

"I have the most charming brand-new frock, with lace around the collar—Alice blue, of course. What else is anyone wearing this year? It's just the thing for the dance. I can scarcely wait. Everyone who matters is here at the Island now, after all. Tell us, Elizabeth, what do you plan to wear now that your first dance is spoken for?"

"I haven't given it a thought," Elizabeth replied airily.

"You're the best dancer among us," Judith put in. "He's bound to be impressed with that."

"I did study ballet when I was younger, but that doesn't translate to ballroom dancing."

"I'm certain it does. It teaches you to stand and move, and to pay attention to the music and to your partner."

"I never got far enough for a partner. I woke up

one morning and found I was too tall."

"But it made you elegant."

"If that's what you call it." She shrugged, drawing herself up and looking down her nose at Judith, who burst out laughing. Of all Elizabeth's friends, she had the sunniest temperament, and Elizabeth loved her for it.

Eventually the conversation drifted away from the opposite sex, the dance, and new frocks, and after what seemed an eternity, she found herself back at Brookhaven Cottage. The front door stood open to take advantage of the breeze. She opened the screen with its squeaky spring and out of habit held it until it closed quietly behind her.

"Bet!" Clara called, skipping into the living room to give her a hug. Then Elizabeth had to acknowledge a make-believe lick on the cheek from her little sister's stuffed dog. "You're just in time for lunch. Barkley and I have been walking on the beach. He doesn't like the tide pools too much. They taste funny. But he loves to chase the seagulls."

"You shouldn't let Barkley drink salt water. It'll make him sick to his stomach," Elizabeth said solemnly.

"Do you hear that, Barkley? No drinking seawater." Clara shook her finger at Barkley while she tagged Elizabeth into the kitchen, changed her mind, and exited the back door, letting the screen slam behind her. Mrs. Hall and the maid were busy at the stove, while her father sat at the table with a legal pad in front of him.

"Here's our mail, Father," she said, handing over the stack of letters from her skirt pocket. "One is for

Mother, from Aunt Eleanor. The others are all your clients. Where is Mother, by the way?" She took the liberty of sitting in her usual chair.

"Upstairs with a headache. Too much sun yesterday, I think. Did you have a nice walk down to The Landing, then?"

"Quite, thank you."

"By the way, what's the envelope I see sticking out of your pocket?"

She felt her cheeks redden. "Sergeant Weller wrote to me. And I'd appreciate it if you don't tell Mother. I know she wouldn't approve." Her father gave her a conspiratorial wink. It was not the first time they had shared a secret.

"I won't breathe a word, Queenie. I like him. He's a stellar young man. It's too bad he lives way up in Canada. Still, I suppose you could arrange to visit Jenny and Shane once their immediate honeymoon is over with." His teasing made her blush to her toenails, especially since Paul had suggested just that. "If your mother does find out, I'll tell her I gave you my permission to correspond with him."

"I appreciate that."

"And if you want to go read your letter, you're excused. I'll call you down for lunch." She jumped from her chair with a hasty "thank you" and planted a kiss on her father's burgeoning bald spot.

Pausing to remove her shoes at the bottom of the stairs, she tiptoed up to her room, avoiding all the squeaking boards. She breathed a sigh of relief when she made it without rousing her mother, who could hear an ant cough a mile away. She closed the door softly behind her and locked it, another action that would have brought her mother down on her. Then she sat at her vanity table and slit the flap of the envelope neatly with a nail file.

The two pages inside the envelope gave her such a rush of excitement she had to close her eyes and take three or four deep breaths before she could begin to read. Then she made herself take in the salutation. Paul's handwriting looked as she'd expected it to, large and bold, and though he wrote an obviously educated hand, still idiosyncratic and distinctive.

Dear Elizabeth,

Thank you so very much for allowing me to correspond with you. I will never forget the night of Jenny and Shane's wedding reception. The ball was quite an experience for a small-town boy like me, although you are such a dab hand at things like that, I doubt it so much as ruffled a hair on your head. It would be my fondest wish to repeat the whole night again and again if I could. I can still hear the music playing and feel you in my arms. You are such a lovely dancer that it made me feel that I could dance too.

I spent a night at my parents' home on the way back to Elk Gap. They are well, and my sister Lorena is in the throes of puppy love. She goes around sighing like a furnace, and I'll admit I did my share of sighing, too, every time I thought of our last dance.

When I arrived in Elk Gap, all was as we had left it. I did have to ride to North Village yesterday because three or four men got into a brawl after someone sold them illegal liquor. Of course, nobody there would tell me who they got it from. They won't even tell Shane, and he speaks their language, where I have to rely on French, which I speak only passably and they not at all when they don't want to. I suspect the Camerons are at it again. Someday we'll catch them red-handed, and then all this nonsense will stop.

I did have to bring one of the men to town with me. He suffered a clout over the head and Angus had to sew up his scalp. As you can guess, our esteemed Dr. MacBride was not overly thrilled with the idea of having a dirty, smelly drunk in his clinic and was something less than gentle. And when I took the man back home he was still so drunk that he went to sleep and fell off his horse twice on the way. I told him if he fell off a third time I'd tie him across his saddle. As much as I hate to say this, I believe Elk Gap will have to build a jail, even if it's only to give people like old Jimmy Whitehorse a place to sleep off the latest binge.

By the time you receive this I will already be on rounds. I expect that to be routine, since it's only June, and August is when strange things happen. I will try to write to you at least once and post it at Castlereigh. That's the far end of the territory. It takes two weeks to ride the whole thing if I don't encounter any time-consuming problems and if I don't tarry. Shane likes to visit the Indian villages, so he's usually gone longer, but since I can't talk to those people I only make certain everything is all right and go on my way. I am even packing my dictionary in my saddlebags so you won't reap the benefits of my poor spelling. It took me quite some time to write this letter, as I made myself look up any word over the length of five letters.

And the souvenir you placed in the left breast pocket of my dress uniform is now in the left breast pocket of my working uniform, where it will remain, close to my heart, a reminder of the loveliest evening I

*can remember, and also of the loveliest of ladies who
danced with me.*

*I hope by the time I return, a letter will be waiting
for me in the post office. Until then, I beg to remain*

Your servant.

Paul

She read the letter three times, then returned it to
the envelope. She resisted her first impulse to put it in
the box where she kept all her correspondence, because
she was not at all certain it would be safe from prying
eyes. Instead she opened the door to the cubbyhole, felt
around for her great-grandmother's diaries, and inserted
it behind the cover of the first volume. Then she went
back to her vanity table, took out her stationery box,
and began to pen a reply.

Later that night she lay awake, a slice of moonlight
slanting over her bed. Deciding it was light enough to
read by, she took the precious diary from its hiding
place and opened it.

May 25, 1821

*Junior and Rob have worked off their punishment
and are once again bosom friends. We are all trapped
inside by an unseasonable rainstorm, so they are
playing perhaps their twentieth chess game. Mary is
whiny and restless, bored with reading her little tome
on the proper behavior of young ladies and considering
herself too old to play with dolls. Mother has set her to
needlework while Penelope and Nanny Pearl are
preparing supper and Cicero lounges in the kitchen,
keeping them entertained while they labor. I have
divided my time between reading the Bible and poring
over my journal entries. It is an altogether dull day.*

One family did arrive last night, just as the storm

*set in. The Randolphs from New York are always
among the first-comers to Sand Island. He is a retired
banker; this year they have brought their son and
daughter-in-law, along with their first grandchild, a
frail little girl of some six months. They are convinced
that the more sanguine climate of Sand Island will be
good for the child's health. Nanny Pearl, however,
opines that a strong dose of Mama Lou's herbs would
put her right in a day or two. After all, Mother's five
children were raised on Mama Lou's concoctions and
we have all turned out strong and healthy. And in truth
it is rare for a woman to bear five children and lose
none; it is even more rare for twins like Junior and Rob
to flourish as they have, since they were born early and
small.*

*Everyone agrees, however, that Sand Island is a
healthful place. There is neither malaria nor cholera
here and there has never been an epidemic of any other
summer disease, including dread afflictions such as
scarlet fever, typhoid, smallpox, or infantile paralysis.
It may be because there are only about fifty families on
the island, most of whom are summer residents. The
dearth of social events leads to much walking upon the
beach, bathing in the surf, and generally taking the air,
which due to the breezes from the ocean is always clean
and fresh.*

*It is true that life at Sand Island is not as
convenient as life at Brookhaven. One cannot dig a well
close to salt water, so all our water is hauled from a
well at the center of the island. Each day an eccentric
old man drives a mule wagon laden with water tuns and
refreshes our rain barrels for a nickel. He labors from
dawn to dusk, since at the peak of the season there are*

at least thirty-five households to serve. He actually has two wagons; he leaves one to be filled while he makes his rounds with the other. An equally eccentric man delivers cords of alder quarters as needed. He saws them to stove length but they need further splitting, especially in the making of kindling; hence Junior and Rob's punishment.

~*~

June 9, 1821

At long last the rain has stopped and our neighbors have begun arriving! The Weatheralls, the Claridges, the Lawtons, and the Sandersons are now in residence. Amelia Sanderson has been a summer friend only two years less than Sally Lawton. We spent most of yesterday walking on the beach and trading the sagas of coming-out parties. Since Amelia is slightly older, she came out into society winter before last. She has a lively wit and is always the center of any party she attends. She kept us all in paroxysms of hilarity, even Mary, who had been allowed to tag along with the stern warning that children (most especially little sisters along on sufferance) should be seen and not heard.

We ended our day at the Lawtons' sharing cool mint tea and a promise to meet tomorrow morning for another long stroll on the beach. I confess now that my two bosom friends have arrived, I do not miss Brookhaven as much as I did. However, given the choice, I would still rather be there helping Father than here trying to ride herd on my siblings.

~*~

June 12, 1821

I have met the man I am going to marry! The first of the Saturday night dances was held tonight (or *yesterday—it is so close to midnight that I am unsure, but I am much too excited to sleep, hence I am writing). As I wrote earlier, we all have new wardrobes, and for me that included two fancy gowns. They are not quite the ball gowns I owned at Brookhaven, since these smaller affairs on Sand Island do not warrant fully formal attire, but they are lovely nonetheless. Last night I chose to wear a seafoam green tulle with a band of pink ribbon roses below the bust, and Nanny Pearl did my hair with pink and green ribbons. I went to the dance feeling very elegant indeed. I am glad I was up to the challenge. George was there.*

George. George Mayweather Bryant. Someday I will be Mrs. George Mayweather Bryant. It is too bad I am only seventeen (nearly). It will be a full year and a half before he can speak for my hand, but I know he will do so in the course of things. It would not do for us to become engaged before I come out into society; it might call my virtue into question.

George and his family are newcomers here. They purchased their place from the estate of the truly ancient and venerable Miss Maudie Adams, a very rich spinster who has been the unofficial grand duchess of Sand Island ever since I can remember. No social event ever had its true start before Miss Maudie showed up to give it her blessing and to preside over it with steely omniscience. I had not known that she passed away around Christmas, but it seems her two quarreling nephews were very eager to get their hands on every cent of Auntie's money as quickly as possible, and effected a prompt sale of Tidelands—which is, I might add, the grandest and largest of the island's summer cottages—to the Bryants. George's father is president of the bank with which Miss Maudie's family conducted its financial business time out of mind.

When we arrived at the dance, it seemed odd not to have Miss Maudie in her position of preeminence, banging her cane and demanding that this young man or that bring her a cup of punch. Instead there was practically a receiving line dedicated to introducing the Bryants to Sand Island society. I had not been paying much attention to them, my mind on a bit of gossip Amelia Sanderson had whispered in my ear, and when I looked up my heart all but stopped. There he was, George Bryant! The first thing I saw was sapphire eyes looking down at me from a height well over six feet, the sensitive face of an artist, and curling black hair. He bowed over my hand and asked me for the first dance in spite of having been presented already to both Amelia and Sally (and it is always pretty, blonde Amelia to whom young men gravitate).

From the first dance, George had eyes only for me. I found out that he is twenty-one as of March and is reading for the law so he can join his uncle's Boston law practice. Until then he is clerking for the firm and learning as much as he can. We danced almost every dance, only changing partners now and then to be polite. Even when he was dancing with Amelia, I saw his eyes seek me out.

He is so unbelievably handsome. He's fully half a head taller than I am, which I find enchanting. Some men with black hair have coarse complexions, but his skin is as fine and fair as milk. He's slim, with long, lovely hands. I could prattle on for pages and pages about the shape of his lips, or how his eyes seem half hidden in long, black lashes. Suffice it to say that he is a gentleman, with a soft voice that makes every word seem like a secret between us.

He said he will ask my parents for permission to call on me. I realize that should not happen until I have come out into society, but this is, after all, Sand Island. The rules are much looser here, and what happens here need not follow me back to Virginia. Meanwhile, there is church tomorrow and a large picnic afterward. He asked me if I would consider meeting him there. I tried not to say yes too fast. Sand Island or not, it would not do to seem too eager.

In the meantime, I must go to bed, though I am much too excited to rest. In just a few short hours Mother will wake us for church, and I do not want to look like a sleepless shipwreck.

~*~

June 13, 1821

George did not disappoint me. He and his family were entering the church just as we arrived. He looked so handsome in his summer suit with a white silk stock about his throat. My heart nearly stopped when he nodded at me from some distance away. We did have a brief opportunity to chat after the service, when his parents and mine greeted each other outside the church. Then came the picnic! The young people always have their own tables, and George asked if he might join me. I demurred properly and let him charm me into acquiescence. He is so good at that! I could feel the jealousy from at least half the girls present, most notably Amelia, who is accustomed to bringing young men to heel with a flick of her eyelashes, and Emily Wellborn. No one likes Emily, though we are all forced to deal with her. She is a self-important prig, terribly beautiful and terribly rich, spoiled, and self-centered. I could fairly hear them both wondering how plain, tall Eliza attracted such a charming, handsome beau while they are both going begging. I will not say that I gloated or stuck my nose in the air, but oh, I was sorely tempted!

Eventually the Saturday dance claimed Elizabeth's attention. With Luci's braggadocio still lingering in her ears, she passed over her own new Alice-blue frock and instead selected a dress of antique rose silk crepe. Its wide cape collar came halfway to her elbows, caught up in front with a large rosette of the same silk crepe. The rest of the dress fit closely at her waist, flaring softly over her hips to the hem of the skirt. Giving the nod to the formality of the occasion, she pinned a matching rosette into the back of her hair, thanking her Brisbane ancestors for its compliant curl. But nothing could make up for the fact that she missed Paul to the depths of her soul.

With a last glance in her cheval glass, she told herself she was being silly to feel so keenly about a man she had known only a week. Puppy love, he had called it in his letter. But she was twenty, a little old for a crush. Perhaps Nana had fallen head over heels in love here on Sand Island, but she had been just sixteen, a mere girl. Twenty, and out in society, equated to a lady.

The entire family, with Robbie complaining bitterly about the necessity of a suit and tie, walked the three-quarters of a mile to the pavilion. By the time they arrived, the music had already begun. An older man sat at an out-of-tune upright piano, banging out a waltz, while his wife scraped away on a violin. Their music, spirited and skillful, had entertained the summer populace of Sand Island time out of mind.

They arrived early enough no one was dancing yet. Instead, groups drifted here and there, mingling and catching up on the winter's news. Her father gravitated toward Benjamin Tanner, standing nearby with his wife and Sylvia, who greeted Elizabeth with a friendly wave and a smile. There were greetings all around, and the men shook hands.

"So where is Arthur, then?" her father asked, referring to Sylvia's older brother.

"He's wandering around here with some of his friends. The bachelor pack, you know," Ben responded, gesturing vaguely around the crowd. At that moment Elizabeth caught sight of Arthur, heading back toward them with three young men in tow. She realized his charges were Noah Canning and his two friends from The Landing. Elizabeth's stomach tightened when he introduced the three, afraid Sylvie might let something slip in front of Rose, who would have no compunctions about scolding Elizabeth in public for talking to strangers. Instead she pretended innocence and politely greeted her brother's new friends.

"So, Mr. Canning, yours isn't a common surname," Ben Tanner said. "Are you any relation to Archibald Canning?"

Noah's mild gaze met the older man's. "Yes, sir. I'm his son."

"Oh. You live up on The Bluff, then, don't you?"

"This is our first summer there. The house was just completed this spring. I have a sailboat, so I can come and go as I please without being limited to the packet boat. I've already met some very enchanting people on

Sand Island." He looked pointedly at Elizabeth, who saw her mother's eyes widen in momentary surprise, then narrow again with delight.

Elizabeth had wondered from the beginning if Noah could be related to the Cannings of railroad fame. Now the relationship was confirmed. Everyone in the country knew Archibald Canning, a baron in the business world, whose family had made millions during the westward expansion after the Civil War. His venture from railroads into banking had made him undisputedly one of the richest men in America.

At the pavilion the oldest married couple customarily started each Saturday dance. Only after the older generation had the floor would it be permissible for the young, unattached couples to dance. Finally Commodore Tobias Finch of Gull Cottage rounded up Millicent and proceeded to the center of the floor. The two musicians paused politely, then struck up the old favorite "Lorena." It was easy to see the former debutante in the white-haired Mrs. Finch. She held herself erect and gazed lovingly into the faded eyes of her husband of over fifty years, dancing as she had doubtless danced at their wedding. Elizabeth felt a warm rush at the obvious love the couple shared, then sadness washed over her. *Never for me*, she thought. *Never for me.*

As they waited the dance out, Luci, minus Grace, slid up to stand next to Elizabeth. She had piled her honey-colored hair high and wore the blue frock she had bragged about at The Landing. As always, she looked like a carefully dressed and coifed doll, all soft, sweet frills and wide blue eyes. She greeted them both, obviously having been introduced to Noah in the general course of things. However, beyond a polite acknowledgment, he ignored her. Then the piano player switched to a waltz, which his wife picked up after an introduction. Noah turned to Elizabeth.

"Miss Talbot? You promised me the first dance, remember?"

"I said I'd consider it."

"Well, then? Please?" He held out his hand to her, and she capitulated, letting him lead her onto the dance floor. The large pavilion did not crowd the dancers; nevertheless, Noah moved calmly with small steps and did not cover too much ground. Elizabeth remembered the way she'd fit in Paul's arms and drew an inevitable comparison in which Noah Canning, for all his family's money, came out far the loser.

After a polite interval to allow her to accustom herself to his rhythm, he spoke. "I say, Miss Talbot, you do look quite lovely tonight. That color suits you very well."

"Thank you."

"That pink is such a relief from all that dreary Alice Blue one sees everywhere these days. I like a woman who thinks for herself instead of blindly following the latest fad."

"I'll assure you, Mr. Canning, I do think for myself—truth be known, far more than is good for me."

He tossed off a quick laugh, flashing perfect teeth. "Good. That makes life all the more savory."

"Absolutely. A bland life simply won't do." She finally felt herself smiling, but it fell far short of the smile she had bestowed on Paul.

When the musicians took a break, he for a cup of punch and she to retune her violin, the young people drifted out to the promenade over the water. The moon, just short of full, had only recently made its appearance, gilding the fine wind chop stretching away over the Atlantic, deceptively calm at high tide. Elizabeth leaned her elbows on the railing and adjusted her great-grandmother's beautiful shawl, allowing the light offshore breeze to caress her cheeks. While she listened idly to Luci's mindless chatter, Noah came up to stand beside her.

"It's on the cool side tonight," he observed. "Are you warm enough out here?"

"I'm quite comfortable, thank you. We'd best enjoy the cool evenings while we can. Soon the weather won't be so pleasant."

"Quite so," he agreed, as though she had said something unbelievably profound. "Would you like some punch, then?"

"Thank you, but not right now. Perhaps later. I'm just enjoying the moonrise."

"Then if you don't mind, I'll just enjoy it with you." He propped his elbows on the rail in an unconscious imitation of her pose and leaned so close to her she could feel his warmth. She edged away, relieved when he did not crowd her again, and occupied herself in watching the moon begin its stately ascent into the cloudless sky, where it began to pull the ocean toward ebb tide. Not that she would have minded the touch of a sleeve, she thought, if only it had been the blazing scarlet of a certain red tunic.

Later, as they walked home, her thoughts were still full of Paul. When her mother broke into them, the intrusion was almost unwelcome.

"Well, Bet, you certainly caught the eye of at least

one young man tonight," she began.

"Oh? Do you mean Noah Canning?"

"Yes, I do. Why, his father is one of the richest men in the country."

"I know, Mother."

"And you're not impressed? You're not flattered that he's paying attention to you?"

"Not particularly."

"You're not still mooning over Inspector Adair's partner, are you?"

"No, Mother," she said with a sigh.

"Good. Because it wouldn't do to lose your heart to one of those small-town boys who'll never amount to anything. Mr. Canning, on the other hand, has a brilliant future ahead of him." Elizabeth decided not to answer, instead concentrating on her steps in the dark. "Well, don't you agree?" Rose demanded at length.

"I suppose so," Elizabeth replied, eventually having to say something.

"He does seem a fine young man," her father agreed. "At least he has his manners in place." In point of fact, Noah Canning made her uneasy, but she decided, as she usually did, to keep her opinions to herself. She had learned early that airing them only courted arguments. Over time he would probably shift his attentions to someone more attractive, like Luci, and she would be rid of the entire situation.

"Perhaps he'll be at tomorrow's picnic after church and accept an invitation to sit with us," Rose continued. "Will you invite him, Tal?"

"Of course, if it's so important to you." Her father's eyes over her mother's head let Elizabeth know the statement was really a question directed to her. In reply she shrugged her indifference.

"Naturally it is," Rose replied, oblivious. "Elizabeth needs to attract the proper kind of husband, you know."

Chapter 6

Dear Paul,

With luck, this should be waiting for you when you return from rounds. Hopefully it will prove a pleasant surprise.

The weather here has turned warm, and Sand Island society is picking up its pace for the summer—a pace, I might add, which is never very lively. The high point of the week is a dance at the Pavilion, a sort of dock on pilings over the water. Every year I expect a hurricane to blow it away, but every spring when we arrive it is still there, closed up as tight as an oyster, with its storm doors in place. Once it's opened up for the season, there are dances and once in a while even a concert there. Nearly every Sunday afternoon everyone brings food and makes a potluck picnic after church, and then a new week sets in and everyone settles down. I am glad I brought a goodly supply of needlework with me. It's about all there is to do. I walk about on the beach and try to sketch now and then, but I've never been a very good artist, and when I think of Shane's staggering talent I want to put my pencils in their box and throw it as far out to sea as I can. But with my luck it would probably drift back in and wash up at my feet, and there would be a little hermit crab in it, busily drawing much better than I can.

Last week Father and Robbie rowed Clara and me

over to Wreckers' Island to beachcomb before the winter's wrack is picked over. Of course Mother, being prone to seasickness, stayed behind. I've always loved beachcombing. I found some unusual shells and one piece of scarlet sea glass. Legend has it that a ship carrying red bottles of French wine broke up on the reef a hundred or so years ago, and people have been finding the red glass ever since. It's a custom to have a local artisan set it in silver costume jewelry and to wear it here during the summer. It marks one a true resident of Sand Island. I may have him make this piece into a pendant or perhaps a bracelet; it's of goodly size and a proper shape.

I did make one more surprising find. However, it was not on the beach. My great-grandmother Talbot was known for her journals. They have become a cherished family heirloom and have proven most interesting. However, they seemed to have begun with her marriage at age twenty-two. We always suspected there were a few more volumes somewhere. The day we arrived, this year, I found them hidden away in an old trunk in the storage cubby in my bedroom. I have not told anyone of my find. I've been savoring them, since she was close to my age when she wrote them. It makes me feel some special connection with her. She passed on shortly before I was born, so I never had the privilege of knowing her, but now that I read her words, she comes alive for me. Up until now I only knew her as the chronicler of the War Between the States, speaking of privation and strife and unsettled times. But in these earlier entries she is a charming, lively young woman, full of ideals and hope for the future, and very much in love with a beau she met here on the island. I see that, despite nearly a century between us, she and I have much in common. In fact, were I to meet her tomorrow I am certain we would instantly become bosom friends.

Were it not for your letters and my great-grandmother's diaries, I fear I would be languishing of boredom right now. Mother insists on dragging me to the Saturday night dances. They pale in comparison to the one night we spent dancing at the Waldorf ballroom. That is a memory I will cherish always. If I were the diarist my great-grandmother was, I should have filled pages and pages just on that one ball.

The night is growing dark, and my eyelids are growing heavy. If I am to post this in the morning, I will have to bid you good night. From my bedroom window I can see the moon. It's high, and just at half. I wonder if you could be looking at it now and thinking of me as I am thinking of you. Good night, then. I wish my last dance could have been with you. My first, too, for all that, and all the others between.

Your friend always,
Elizabeth

After breakfast the next morning she set out for The Landing. She wore her favorite yellow walking skirt and her great-grandmother's hat embellished with its yellow-and-blue silk scarf. Feeling aloof and dignified, she nevertheless managed to collect Judith and Mary on the way to the post office. There were no letters for Brookhaven; she posted her missive to Paul without letting the other girls see the address, then stood back while they collected their respective mail.

"Shall we have a lemonade?" Mary suggested. "My treat this time."

"I'd love it. It was a warm walk," Judith

responded.

"My treat next time, then," Elizabeth appended. The three sat down at one of the ice cream tables on the long farmer's porch of the general store.

"So you had a letter this time, Mary?" Judith asked. The reply was interrupted when the daughter of the store owner came out with lemonade for them.

"Goodness, Lenore, are you a mind reader, then?" Mary said, handing over a dime and declining her penny change.

The girl giggled. "You always order lemonade. It's all we have, after all."

"It's all you need. It's delicious," Elizabeth said, picking up her glass for a delicate sip around the welcome chunk of ice. Lenore curtsied in acknowledgment of the tip and disappeared back into the depths of the store.

Mary took up the thread of Judith's inquiry. "I did have a letter. It's from my sister Beatrice. She's expecting a child in September, and she's over the moon about it. All her letters are full of her coming baby. She thinks she invented motherhood."

"As I suppose we all shall feel when our turn comes." Judith sighed. Elizabeth looked down at the wet ring her glass left on the table. *Never for me,* she thought.

As they sat chatting, a catboat doused its mainsail and coasted up to the float. Elizabeth recognized it instantly; she did not have to watch as the three young men piled out.

As usual, Noah led his posse up the walkway to the store. He doffed his hat and bowed. "Good morning, ladies." His two yes-men made identical obeisances.

"Good morning, gentlemen," Judith responded. Mary nodded, and Elizabeth raised her eyes lest she seem totally rude.

"May we join you?" he asked.

"Certainly," Mary responded. Noah pulled a chair around from an adjacent table, wedging it in next to Elizabeth. He was not quite touching her, but he moved so unpleasantly close his leg prodded her skirt. She gathered it closer and moved a few inches away.

"It's a lovely day, isn't it?" he said to no one in particular.

"A trifle breezy, though," Judith allowed.

"Perfect sailing weather. I had thought perhaps the three of you would like to join us for a little jaunt over to Wrecker's. We can sail up the back way and catch the tide back here to Sand. I can even deliver you ladies to the cove afterward, so you won't have to walk all the way home."

"Why, what a lovely idea!" Mary gushed, her eyes on Noah.

"Providing we're back by lunchtime," Elizabeth added.

"Oh, you will be. The tide turns at eleven twenty. But that gives us at least two hours for a walk along the beach."

"But how are we going to go ashore? I mean, I don't see how you can bring your sailboat that close," Judith said with a worried frown.

Noah laughed, his eyes sparkling. "It has a centerboard, not a fixed keel. It started life as a skipjack. If you're through with your lemonade, ladies, I'll show you." Elizabeth drained her glass and, sucking on the remainder of her ice cube, rose after Judith and

123

Mary. She tagged behind as Noah led his gaggle down to the dock.

He had moored his sailboat to the float in seamanlike fashion, bow and stern lines fastened with neat clove hitches. He had reefed both sails neatly and lashed the tiller even though he had not intended to leave the boat long. Whatever else could be said about Noah Canning, he respected his boat, Elizabeth reflected. He stepped in, then held out his hand.

"Ladies? Welcome aboard *Pleasant Folly*." Mary smiled at him and gave him her hand, stepping delicately over the gunwale. "On such a calm day she'll hold six. There's plenty of freeboard. But still, you need to sit in the stern. The bow does take spray now and then." Judith banished her distrustful frown and gave him her hand. Then it was Elizabeth's turn. She gathered her skirt and reluctantly held her hand out to him. His palm felt warm and strong, if somewhat soft; Paul's had been hardened by years of cavalry gauntlets.

When Noah had arranged the girls in the stern and untied the reefs from the sails, he slid the loop off the tiller. A moment later Asa and Theo shoved off. The little sailboat nosed out into the glassy water, the boys raised the mainsail, and they tacked against the fickle breeze in the lee of the island, picking up speed as the sail bellied out.

After a short time they rounded the end of Sand Island. Noah countered the current that would have taken them seaward crossing the channel, and they glided up to the remnants of an ancient riprap groin that had held the dock when the lighthouse was in service. He raised the centerboard and lowered the sail at the same time, so they coasted up and *Folly* nosed gently against the rocks.

Elizabeth was glad of the low heels on her walking boots, because picking her way over the seaweed-slick rocks was fiddly business. This time she was even glad of Noah's aiding hand. An air of clandestine excitement always hung over the ruined lighthouse, a reminder, perhaps, of the island's less than savory past. Wrecker's Island even smelled different, a cold hint of dark, pelagic mysteries barely concealed by the deceptively calm surface of the water.

The six walked down the path around the ruined lighthouse, toward the seaward side of the island. A blow a week ago had turned up the beach, potentially leaving fresh treasures for the picking.

The only practical way to beachcomb was barefoot. The girls sat on a weathered log, Mary and Judith giggling about trying to take off their stockings without exposing their legs. Elizabeth set about the task in workmanlike fashion, working her garters down through the outside of her skirt rather than fishing under her hem. Then she wadded her stockings into her walking boots and started down toward the tide line. Noah, who had dispensed with his comfortably worn deck boots, promptly joined her.

She took up a stick to turn the sea wrack and made serious work of searching for shells. For a long time Noah walked beside her, hands in pockets. She wondered why she felt ill at ease with him and decided the reason had to be that her heart lay elsewhere. He had been pleasant, meticulously polite, and seemed genuinely interested in her. What more could she ask? But before her mind formed the question, her heart answered it. *He isn't Paul.*

She bent to pick up a slipper shell. Rather small but perfectly formed, it had the vivid coloration that often fades as shells grow. She put it in her pocket and wandered down through a spray of fragments to the water line. Noah followed along, stopping to roll up the legs of his summer flannel slacks before wading ankle-deep into the retreating water. However, a wave chased him back, making her laugh.

He stopped suddenly, a look of surprise coming slowly across his face. Then he leaned down and dug around in the sand at his feet, coming up with a muddy, dripping object.

"Hello! What's this?" He squatted down and rinsed the trinket he had picked up, then stood up again, brushing the sand off. She came over to inspect his find. He dropped it into her hand: a small heart-shaped blown glass perfume bottle of the type ladies carried in their reticules. Years in the relentless pounding of the water had given the surface a delicate frost like an acid etch, but she could still see threads of red, blue, and gold running through the glass.

"I think it's a scent bottle," she said. When she took hold of the stopper it twisted out easily, and around the minimal amount of sea water inside, she smelled the residual fragrance of the perfume it had once held. She made as if to return it to him, but he took her hand in both his and folded her fingers around it.

"Sweets to the sweet, they say. You keep it."

Despite herself she felt her cheeks flush. "Thank you, Mr. Canning."

"Noah. If I may call you Elizabeth." He still held her hand. Self-consciously she withdrew it from his grasp.

"Yes, you may. We've known each other an acceptable length of time, I believe."

"Especially since this is Sand Island, not Boston or New York."

"Or even Arlington," she finished for him. She raised her eyes to his, and he gazed at her, his face soft, somewhere between admiration and longing. She watched as the breeze toyed with a stray lock of his butter-blond hair and suddenly longed to smooth it back into place.

"Elizabeth, I..." Whatever he was going to say was cut off by a shriek of feminine distress. They both looked back to see Mary dancing around with a small but very determined crab dangling from her foot. Amid general laughter, Asa chivalrously removed the offending crustacean and hurled it back into the surf.

"Are you all right, Mary?" Elizabeth asked, trotting over to her friend.

"I know better than to put my feet where I can't see them. There's a deeper place where the surf washed out the sand around a rock, and I stuck my toes where they didn't belong."

"Yes, you do know better. And now you know why."

Theo and Judith arrived on the scene a little late. "Mary?" Judith asked.

"You missed the show," she said. "A crab pinched my toe and frightened me half out of my wits."

The spell broken, the six young people straggled down the beach a respectable distance, then turned back. The restless tide was close to high slack.

Noah looked at the water and consulted his pocket

watch. "I think it's time to head back," he announced. "If we hit the tide just right, when it's completely slack, we can tack across the channel and deliver you ladies to the Pavilion. It's only a short walk home from there."

Once again Elizabeth sat with Mary and Judith on the abraded old deadhead, dusted the sand from her feet, and pulled on her hose and walking boots. When she looked at Noah, it was not exactly with new eyes, but with the gift of the perfume bottle and permission to use her given name, something had definitely changed between them. She dared not hope it would be anything more than an exchange of pleasantries and a summer friendship. She knew, as sure as God made little green apples, a grand romance like Cousin Jenny's lay completely beyond the pale for her. And besides, another had ensconced himself deep within her heart.

When she arrived at Brookhaven Cottage, lunch was just being brought from the kitchen. She hung her hat on the hall tree and hurried to take her place at the table.

"Sorry I'm nearly late. Mary, Judith, and I went over to Wrecker's."

"With Noah Canning and his sidekicks?" her father asked. She nodded, waiting for Robbie, whose duty it was to seat her. Practicing his most formal manners, he pulled out her chair, helped her slide it in, and asked if she were comfortable. She thanked him, taking her napkin from its ivory ring and draping it over her lap. In Arlington the napkin rings were sterling, but this was Sand Island, and her mother gave a grudging nod to a slightly less formal table.

"When can I go to Wrecker's Island with you?" Clara asked.

"When Mother says you can," she responded.

"We'll see about it the next time Robbie and I row over," her father replied.

"But I want to go in the sailboat," she protested.

"No. You're not a good enough swimmer yet, and that sailboat belongs to someone else. He'd have to invite you. It would be rude to invite yourself. How was the beach, then?" He turned away from Clara, who looked down at her plate but knew better than to pout.

"The storm turned things over nicely. I found some good shells. Oh, and there was this. It looks to have been in the surf for years. Perhaps it's even from the wrecker days." She dug the scent bottle out of her pocket and handed it around.

"Oh, it's lovely! How did you find it?" Clara inquired.

"Actually Mr. Canning found it and gave it to me."

"How nice," her mother said as she passed a plate of last night's pot roast, warmed over and resurrected for lunch. "I approve of that young man, Elizabeth. I think you need to encourage his attentions."

"Yes, Mother," she said, with the proper mixture of submission and boredom.

"What's the matter? He's not good enough for you?"

Her father gave his wife a sharp look. "She doesn't have to make her mind up tomorrow. After all, she's barely twenty."

"When I was her age, twenty was practically an old maid."

"Well, times are different now. We're going into war. That should give anyone cause for caution. Besides, Mr. Canning told me he is planning to enter

West Point as soon as his congressional appointment comes through. West Point cadets can't marry," Tal said, carefully dishing up some potatoes and carrots. Hopefully his comment would put an end to her Mother's train of thought. But that hope proved futile.

"Nevertheless, he's a stellar young man. It would be a shame to waste that kind of an opportunity. Of course you must agree, Elizabeth?"

"Yes, Mother." The same passive tone drew a knowing look from her father, saying he would intervene if Rose went much farther. It would not be the first time he had taken her side against his assertive wife.

Elizabeth turned her attention to her food, nibbling at a limp carrot and letting her mind wander. It was time she spent an afternoon in her room, reading Paul's correspondence and her great-grandmother's diaries. She had decided long ago to spin the volumes out as long as she could rather than yielding to temptation and reading them all in one thrilling gulp. Consequently she was only halfway through the second one.

Dear Elizabeth,

Shane and Jenny have returned from their extended honeymoon. That's about all I can say. Shane is here physically, but he's as absentminded as a crazy old sheepherder. I've never seen him like this. As Mother says, he'd lose his head if it wasn't fastened on tight. I sincerely hope this is temporary and he'll eventually pull around.

They bought the Widow Timmons' place, or rather, Jenny's father and Richard gave it to them as a wedding present. It's on the southwestern outskirts of Elk Gap. The house itself is large and quite nice and included furnishings, though I imagine Jenny will want her own things eventually. It's slightly smaller than Richard's farm, with thirty-six acres, mostly in pasture. A few cows and one harness horse came with the place, so Shane hired a couple to take care of the stock and the land and keep house, and a day girl comes in except on weekends. After all, Jenny can't run a house and a medical practice at the same time.

You wouldn't believe it, but three days ago they returned from North Village with a puppy. It's one of those white wolf-looking things that are all over the village. I gather they descended from a dog Shane's grandfather had when he was small. They even call it Loup-Garou, which is French for Werewolf, or Lupi for short. So far all it has done is nearly get kicked for barking at Brandy, wet on the floor, and offend the barn cats, but it has at least learned to leave the rooster alone. I saw that happen, and I laughed for hours, every time I remembered the look of stark terror on that pup's face as it came yelping around the porch with that old red rooster flapping and squawking along in hot pursuit. Obviously its short little life was flashing before its eyes. It'll be a long time before he takes it into his head to chase another chicken.

I may have to get another horse. Brandy had a bad colic last week and is still lethargic and unfit to ride, although she's eating again and all seems well there. I've heard that once a horse is colicky it will be colicky forever. I hope that's not true, because she's a good hill horse. I borrowed Fleur from Jenny for the duration, which irritated Josh Barnes to no end. He thought he was going to sell me one of his broken-down nags. I asked him whether he thought I was outright dumb or just plain stupid. Shane and I did ride up to Thomas Wise Hand's place, and he has a bay gelding I like. It's by his old codger of a thoroughbred stud, and it's a nice, sound young animal, tall enough that my legs don't drag the ground. I think I'll go ahead and buy him. If nothing else, we can use a second pack horse on rounds. Since Shane is keeping Midnight at their place now, there's a vacant stall in Josh's stable, so I'll have somewhere to keep him.

And speaking of rounds, August is coming up. This time it's Shane's turn, so he's taking Jenny with him. I hope feminine presence is enough to break our August Curse. We've already had one forest fire up near Castlereigh, and the weather is getting hotter and drier every day.

I hope your summer is going as smoothly as mine, and I also hope you can see your way clear to visit Jenny sometime soon. I'd love to take you riding with me while the weather is still nice.

Yours always,
Paul

~*~

Dear Paul,
It's hard to believe, isn't it, that summer is nearly over? We always return to Arlington during the first week in September. By then the worst of the hot weather is generally past. Then we shall be coming up hard against the holiday season with all its parties and social events. Though somehow I suspect this year's season will be somewhat subdued. Even in a remote place like Sand Island, all anyone hears are reports of the war in Europe. It is especially chilling to me that Britain has declared war on Germany, but Britain had

no real choice, since if Germany takes France, it is only a short hop across the Channel to British soil. Now that Britain is involved, I know Canada will be too. It makes me glad to know that you will be safe from all that even if there is conscription (God forbid). That's all my friends speak of right now, even though President Wilson has vowed to keep the United States neutral and out of all conflict. Father says he can foresee circumstances under which the United States would have no choice but to go to war. It reminds me of the ancient Chinese curse which is supposed to go something like "may you live in interesting times."

With the summer winding down, all my friends are busy planning farewell parties, outings, picnics, et cetera. Some of us will be sailing to Wreckers' Island in the next few days for one last session of beachcombing and probably one last picnic at the old lighthouse. I wish you could be with me, though, for all that, I've wished you could be with me for every one of the picnics, parties, and dances I've been to this summer. But on second thought, they probably would have bored you to distraction since you are accustomed to a job in which a surprise may lurk around every corner.

Elizabeth sighed, capped her fountain pen, and rubbed her eyes. She would finish the letter tomorrow. Right now sleep called. She rose from her desk, folded her shawl, and hung it over the back of her chair. After a stretch, she blew out her table lamp and made her way to bed. The soft glow of her bedside lamp gave her plenty of light to see by. Perhaps she would allow herself just a few pages of her great-grandmother's diary before she went to sleep.

She tucked her feet down into the softness of her

bed, pulled the light cover up over her shoulders, and dug the diary out of her pillowcase. Much to her relief, no one had discovered the volumes since she was meticulous about making her bed, and changed the linens herself. She found the bookmark and opened the diary.

July 28, 1821

Today I did something daring. George has a small rowboat, a dink such as people tow behind a larger sailing craft. He was paddling about the cove while I was walking upon the beach, and he asked me if I would like to join him.

Directly to the north of Sand Island is another island. I know it by no other name than Wreckers' Island, for at one time, legend has it, people would extinguish the lighthouse that sat upon the long spit and deliberately lure ships onto the sand bars for their cargo. Then a huge storm brought down the lighthouse and a better one was built here on the rocky promontory on the north end of Sand Island. Since it could be guarded more easily, the ruined lighthouse was abandoned, and Wreckers' Island has remained uninhabited ever since. I love the long, flat beach there. It harbors a wealth of shells and curious flotsam not picked over from day to day that makes beachcombing a grand adventure. The reason the island is not visited often is that a treacherous channel runs between the north end of Sand Island and the long spit where the ruined lighthouse sits. It is actually a better site for a lighthouse because it is farther out to sea, but the flat, sandy terrain is more susceptible to the sometimes violent hurricanes that strike the region. And while the passage between the islands is narrow and shallow, the tide runs strong there. Passage is best accomplished at low slack water during a neap tide, and one must be careful to return promptly or be forced to wait for the more dangerous high slack water.

Before I realized where we were going, he headed around Lighthouse Point and directly into the channel. Fortunately the tide was right, for I discovered then that George is no sailor. I, however, have been acquainted with the water all my life. So, among all my friends here, we will contrive to teach George about the sea over the summer.

We made it easily to Wreckers' Island, although the exertion of rowing brought on a soft cough that George attributes to the damp sea air. So we beached the dink well up on the shingle, tied it off to a log that had been washed up during the winter storms, and sat for a while on the warm sand.

At length we strolled down the seaward beach. Since the day was cloudy, I risked my complexion and used my big straw sun hat as a basket to gather some of the prettier shells that hid among the dried seaweed at the high tide line. At first George was picking up anything that was whole and unscarred, and laughingly I explained to him the difference among clams, oysters, limpets, and snails.

We nearly overstayed ourselves, to the point that the incoming tide almost took us around the leeward side of Sand Island, and we had to row back hugging the beach. All the way back I looked at George, his fine face flushed with the effort of rowing and his dark hair tossed by the breeze. He is so handsome. Like Amelia and Emily, I wonder what he sees in plain, tall Eliza Morgan. But when he took my hand to help me from the dink, he held it for much longer than necessary, and I confess I felt a lovely thrill clear down to my toes.

Elizabeth's eyes grew too heavy to read any longer. She set the volume aside and half rose to blow across the lamp chimney and extinguish the light.

Just like I wonder what Noah sees in me, she thought. But she felt an uneasiness she did not share with her great-grandmother, whose delight in George seemed complete and all-consuming. The touch of Noah's hand brought more anxiety than lovely thrills.

Chapter 7

The August sun beat down as if no one had yet told it summer had nearly run its course. Elizabeth stood on the float below the pavilion, inexplicably nervous at the prospect of a farewell picnic. Taking lunch and sailing over to Wrecker's had become customary, yet today she felt herself full of some ill-defined foreboding.

She had not waited long before she saw *Pleasant Folly* rounding the point where the channel cut between the two islands. To her surprise only Noah sat in her cockpit. A good ways out he lowered the sail, letting *Folly* glide up to the float. He threw her the bow line, and she dallied it around an iron cleat as he hopped over the short distance between the float and the gunwale with the stern line in his hand.

"Where's everyone else?" she asked without preamble.

He favored her with a bright smile. "Don't I even rate a hello?" he asked.

"Oh, sorry, Noah. Hello. It's nice to see you."

"You too, Elizabeth. And in answer to your question, the sea's a bit too rough for anyone else to sail with us in *Folly*. They'd be in for a soaking, although we'll be fine in the cockpit. So the rest are rowing over from the other side." He held out his hand as if to help her board, but she hesitated.

"I...I don't know..."

"Oh, don't worry. After this long you can trust me, can't you?"

"It's the others I don't trust," she replied tentatively.

"Come on, Elizabeth. They'll be there. Don't worry." He beckoned to her, and she gave in, letting him steady her as she stepped into the gently rocking boat. He cast off the bow line, then boarded, reached over to unwind the stern line from its cleat, and gave *Folly* a shove away from the float. A moment later he raised the sail, and with a combination of sail and tiller they tacked toward the northern end of the island. She had to admit to herself he was right about the spray. *Folly's* bow thumped against the waves, and even sheltered in the stern she felt tiny fingers of salt water cool against her face.

As he had done a hundred times, he lowered the sail, raised the center board, and coasted into the shelter behind the remains of the old dock. One truncated piling still stood near the shore, a convenient mooring. He wrapped a quick clove hitch around it, took up a picnic basket, and gave her his hand to negotiate the slippery rocks. By now she was used to the path; she dropped his hand as soon as she had her footing.

On their way to the stretch of beach, he paused to stash the picnic basket in the ruined lighthouse. "I thought we could have lunch there before we sail back," he said by way of explanation.

"Are the others bringing lunch too?" she inquired.

"I think so. Let's go down the beach. When they get here they'll find us." He led off northward along the tideline, and she tagged a short distance behind him. After a few minutes he dropped back to walk beside her, and eventually his hand caught hers. While a month ago she would have snatched her hand back from his touch, she let it rest in his. After all, this would be their last weekend at Sand Island. What harm could there be in a little flirting?

They walked down the beach hand in hand, pausing to examine interesting shells and sea glass. By the time they walked down the strand and back, both sets of pockets were bulging with their acquisitions. As they approached the ruins of the lighthouse, Elizabeth's anxiety ratcheted up a notch.

"Where are they?" she asked. Obviously she meant Theo, Asa, and their respective girlfriends.

Noah shrugged. "I don't know. They said they'd meet us at the lighthouse. Could be they didn't want to row over in this rough water."

"But…"

"I know, Elizabeth. It doesn't look good that we're here alone. So why don't we eat lunch and then go back? I don't think we need to wait for the tide today. There's a good breeze I can tack against."

"Well…all right. Lunch first, and then we leave. Promise?"

"Promise." His smooth, open smile missed its mark; she still felt uneasy. "I have quite a nice lunch for us," he continued. "My parents had a party yesterday, and we get the leftovers. As you'll see, it was quite a do." They sat in the shadow of a ruined wall. He unloaded the picnic basket, which showed the expert touch of a professional. She had the idea one of his family's cooks had packed it for him. He laid out a variety of delicate finger sandwiches, some tiny tarts, a selection of fruit and cheese, and lastly brought out two mismatched soda bottles that appeared to have been refilled with some sort of fruit punch. Noah uncapped his bottle and held it out toward her.

"Here's a toast to the end of a beautiful summer." She slipped the porcelain-topped cork out of her own bottle and touched the lip to the neck of his.

"To the end of a beautiful summer." She took a discreet sip. It was fruity and sweet, with a strange bite to it, leaving a dark, nearly bitter aftertaste in her mouth. She took up a small chicken-and-cucumber sandwich to banish the strange flavor.

"It's been a beautiful summer for me, Elizabeth," he said. When she looked up at him he still held his punch bottle, and his eyes regarded her intently. "It's been the summer when I courted a lovely young woman I'll never forget."

She felt her face grow warm. "I'll never forget this summer either." Mentally she crossed her fingers. Noah had not made the summer unforgettable. Rather, its singular memorability lay in the collection of letters secreted in her steamer trunk in the cubby under the eaves of her bedroom.

Finally he turned his attention from her and took up a sandwich, vanquishing it in one bite. Then he scooted down to recline on his left elbow. The sun caught his tousled hair, turning it to liquid honey. Perhaps in some ways he could be considered better looking than Paul, she considered, but nothing could approach the tall Mountie in his spectacular uniform. Not even the son of a man with more money than he could possibly know what to do with in one lifetime. She selected another sandwich, more to have something to do with her hands than to assuage her hunger. The ham tasted salty, and she washed it down with a liberal draft of punch. This time the aftertaste did not seem so foreign. It went to the depths of her stomach and flared into gentle warmth. She toyed with a cube of cheese, put it in her mouth, and sucked at it until it dissolved, following it up with more punch. Soon the level of liquid in her bottle had diminished significantly, and she found herself almost sleepy. The warmth of the sun became even more languid and the breeze softer as it toyed with Noah's hair and caressed her cheeks. She lifted the punch bottle to her lips only to find that less than a spoonful remained. She drained it and set the bottle aside, then folded her hands in her lap. The sun was so bright. Perhaps if she closed her eyes only for a moment...

"Are you sleepy, Elizabeth? We did take quite a walk and it's a warm afternoon, after all." She heard his words as though from a distance.

"That must be it. The sun's so warm. But we have to get back..."

"Not quite yet. We have a few minutes. You can nap if you'd like." She struggled to keep her eyes open. "No, sweetheart. Don't try to stay awake. I'll just watch you. You're so beautiful like that." She felt him scoot closer to her, stroke her hair, and then take her hand, but sleep opened in a great whirlpool and sucked her down, and with a sigh she was lost. She only half felt him touching her here and there, where she never had allowed anyone to touch her. Even a great pain deep within her could not rouse her to protest beyond a feeble whimper.

Later she could not really remember coming back to Brookhaven Cottage. She had been violently sick in the rough water, and had barely made it upstairs to her bedroom. Fortunately no one had been home, and later that afternoon when her mother discovered her upstairs in her bed, she made a vague excuse about an impromptu picnic and bad food, then slept through until the next morning.

Chapter 8

August 22, 1821

Hurricane season is now upon us. It appears to be coming earlier than usual this year. Last week I had the fright of my life—worse, even, than the fire—but paradoxically it was also the most beautiful experience I could ever imagine. George, who is becoming quite proud of his seamanship, was insistent upon rowing us to Wrecker's Island. I demurred, saying we should not be doing this alone. Not only was it unseemly, but it was also dangerous. George dismissed my concerns and rowed across the little channel while the water was still moving toward low tide. Since the moon was exactly at half, this would be one of the gentler neap tides and we would not have to watch our timing as closely. But water being water, one must always respect it. Deep in my heart I wondered if George could be the slightest bit overconfident of his new-found abilities.

I had noticed the clouds building up to the northeast, but other than that it was a lovely day. We spent our time beachcombing and poking through the ruin of the old lighthouse. George found a piece of red sea glass and gave it to me as a keepsake. With my back modestly turned I tucked it into my camisole and promptly forgot about it, as a minor storm the week before had cast up some lovely shells that claimed our attention.

Lael R. Neill

We walked side by side, enjoying each others' company and making satisfying small talk, not realizing we had nearly covered the length of the seaward beach. Nor had we watched the gathering storm. Finally the slanting afternoon light revealed a solid black wall of churning cloud making its way toward the island, driven by a freshening breeze out of the northeast. In alarm I called George's attention to the approaching squall. He agreed that we should hurry back to the boat, but it was well over a mile and the storm was moving much faster than we could. When the wind stripped away my hat and sent it flying, I knew we were in genuine trouble. This was going to be quite a blow, and Wrecker's Island was bare save for sea grass and the ruin of the old, tumbled-down lighthouse.

We made it to the lighthouse just as the storm broke. We were instantly in a maelstrom of lightning, thunder, and icy, pouring rain. I knew it would be suicide to try to make it back to Sand Island with the wind so high, driving the current before it. We had no choice. We were stranded, marooned, with a miserable night looming ahead of us. George kept trying to reassure me as the sun went down and the wind beat against our makeshift shelter.

The only place we could find, and a dubious one at that, was beneath the bottom of the staircase in the base of the lighthouse. We stuffed ourselves into a corner and draped my shawl over our heads. Nevertheless, with the wind howling and the rain pounding around us, we were both instantly soaked to the skin. We wrapped our arms about each other for mutual warmth and long before I began to take the cold seriously I felt George shivering against me. Then I realized there was

144

nothing more I could do. Mother and Father would be deathly worried over us, not to mention George's family. The colder and wetter we became, the more helpless I felt. Eventually I broke down with quiet tears, and George tried his best to comfort me—too well, I later discovered.

As a child on the plantation I had seen cows served and mares covered, and all along I had thought that humans must do something similar. I was not wrong. And so we consoled each other with the greatest joy I have ever known.

The storm tore our dink from its moorings and cast it up on the landward shore west of Sand Island. It was found, and almost immediately a rescue party came for us. I had survived the night and the wetting with nothing worse than a ruined coiffure, but George was feverish and shivering, and his cough, never completely cured, returned. He spent the next two weeks in and out of bed and was still unwell when we said a very sad farewell and returned to our winter lives.

Nanny Pearl knew something had gone on when George and I were stranded on Wrecker's Island. I felt it in those blue-ringed black eyes that met my gaze with an unspoken question. Normally all she had to do was stare at me in that pointed fashion and I would confess every detail of my latest childhood peccadillo without prompting. But now I was no longer a child. I had become a woman. I would wait her out.

We had not been home a fortnight when I received my first—and my last—letter from George. It was elegant, eloquent, and ineluctably sad. His cough had not been the result of the damp salt air of Sand Island. When he and his family arrived home, his physician

*diagnosed him with the consumption and told him he
would be dead before Christmas. So, he said, this letter
was farewell. He pledged me all his love throughout
eternity, wished me a long and happy life, and told me I
was so desirable that I would easily find another who
would love me as deeply as he did. With this letter he
sent me a beautiful gold locket with a miniature portrait
of himself on one side and a lock of his hair on the
other. I love the portrait; I always will. He looks like a
romantic poet, his curling hair flowing and an
introspective half-smile on his face.*

*A few days after George's letter, Nanny Pearl
caught me alone coming back from the necessary
house. She remarked that my flux had not made its
appearance since we returned.*

*"Has you had doin's wid a man, den?" she asked,
her variable accent coming out, for the moment, pure
slave. I wanted to toss my head and give her the lie, but
I felt the bright spots come to my cheeks. None of us
could lie to Nanny Pearl. Ever. "I done t'ought so," she
grumbled. "Well, den, dere ain't but one t'ing to do.
Tomorrow we's goin' down to see Mama Lou. She
know what to do 'bout girls as don't need to be in da
fambly way." I regained my poise and started to turn
away from her, but her thin, incredibly strong fingers
gripped my arm painfully. "You lissen to me, now,
Missy Liza, and you lissen good." She always elided my
name so that instead of "Miss Eliza, it came out "Missy
Liza." "Yore ol' Nanny Pearl gonna make dis right.
You ain't gonna tell yo' mama you gots a baby. It be fit
ta break her poor sweet, lovin' heart plumb in two. And
dat Mister George, no matter how much a ge'mans he
be, he ain't gonna be able to come down here and do*

right by you. So tomorrow you come wid me down by da river to Mama Lou. Bring yo'sef a handful a nickels an' dimes an' sich, like you goin' to buy her herbs, and nobody eber gots to know what you and your Mister George done got up to de night ob de storm."

Nanny Pearl was not to be denied. She took me to see old Mama Lou in her strange little shack in the middle of the settlement where many free blacks live. When we were children, an outing there was a rare treat, like a trip to a decidedly foreign country. The rapid patter of Gullah sounded like rain on the rooftops after our parents' cultured but drawly English, and when it first fell upon my ears, I knew that I was no longer home. But this time was far from a lark. My skin crawled and my arms prickled as Nanny Pearl drove the mule cart down the open space that passed for a street in the settlement. Dark faces peered around half-closed doors and peeked from windows at the sight of a white lady in their midst. But Nanny Pearl ignored them, looking neither left nor right, until she pulled the beast to a halt in front of her mother's leaning shack. The moment she stopped, a ragged little boy of perhaps eight years old appeared from nowhere to take charge of the animal.

"Here we is, Missy Liza," she announced, gathering her skirt and stepping down. I followed a moment later.

The door to Mama Lou's shack stood open to catch any breeze that might relieve the heat of the late-summer day. I had been in her home before. A baffling array of dried things, some plant and some animal, hung from the rafters and from nails in the walls. Gourds incised with weird designs held mysterious components for Mama Lou's African medicines. Of course there were hushed rumors of Voodoo spells and dark rituals. I had never really believed them, but they made delicious fodder for scary stories to be told after dark on rainy nights. Now I feared I was about to become much more intimately acquainted with Mama Lou's black magic than I had ever dreamed.

Finally Mama Lou herself made her grand entrance through the back door. She was dressed much like Nanny Pearl, and it was easy to see where the family lines lay. They were alike in their slim, wiry bodies, very dark skin, and black eyes that saw beyond the depths of one's soul.

"Wha'choo doin' here, gal?" she asked, addressing Nanny Pearl with an abruptness none of us would have dared. In deference to me she did not speak Gullah. I would have understood it anyway, but it served to keep a well-defined distance between us.

"Dis'n heah, she gots a baby started."

"So you done come to Mama Lou to keep yo' secrets where dey b'longs?" Her eyes looked at me as though I were a bird and she a cobra. I swallowed against my dry throat and nodded.

"He'd marry me, but he's ill with the consumption, and he…"

"Nobody don' care none about dat, Missy," she interrupted, dismissing me with a wave. "Sometimes beginnins jus' gots to be ended." Yes, this beginning has to be ended, I agreed within myself, though I wanted George's baby more than anything before or since.

"Yes, Mama Lou," I replied, albeit reluctantly. "It's the last thing I want, but this beginning does need

to end."

"Well, den, Missy, you just lay yourself down on dat dere bed and let Mama Lou do what she gots ta do."

I did as I was bidden.

In my fevered imagination I thought she was going to give me some foul concoction made from bat ears, toad livers, and mushrooms picked from graveyards at the dark of the moon. Instead she took up a long, slender wand carved of dense, very smooth wood, stained with many uses. After thoroughly washing it and me, she worked it up into the center of my body, and that which had begun in such joy ended abruptly in an equally scathing agony. Tears ran down my face and back into my hair, but I willed myself not to cry out. I only managed that by forcing my throat open so that my screams came out as hoarse whispers. Afterward she did give me some sort of potion to ease my pain. As I was sinking toward sleep, through the open front door I heard Nanny Pearl, doubtless speaking to the little boy who had come to care for our mule.

"Here, Isaac. Dis here nickel, it be fo' you. Go back to da Big House an' find dat yeller gal Pansy. Nobody but Pansy, heah? She be Missy Liza's house girl. You tell her Missy Liza done fell off de roof, an' we gonna stay heah wid Mama Lou for two or t'ree days until she can ride home. Now git, and don' choo tarry none nowhere, heah?"

Two days later we rode home from Mama Lou's cabin. No mention was made of our errand to the village by the river, and life at Brookhaven went on. I felt an ineffable sense of loss, and I took to my bed with what I told my mother were exceptionally bad monthly pains. If she suspected anything else she turned a blind eye.

It was terribly difficult for me to drag myself through the dull and lackluster days, knowing that I had lost not only a precious part of George but George himself. Then, just around Thanksgiving, when the nights were cool and quiet, I received a note from George's mother. It was bordered in black, only a few gracious and proper sentences, informing me that George had passed in his sleep, peaceful and without pain at the end, and he had asked her to send me his love. I mourned then, my grief all the sharper because of the necessity that it go unacknowledged, hence uncomforted. After all, in everyone else's eyes, George's death was of course unfortunate but our relationship was only a summer flirtation, doomed to oblivion with the autumn leaves. Only Nanny Pearl seemed to understand the depth of my heartache, beginning with the loss of my first deep love and compounded by what was left behind in Mama Lou's shack. She spoke of it to me only once, when she told me there would be more. Whether she meant beaux or babies I did not know, nor did I care.

Elizabeth sighed and set the diary down on the bed next to her left hand, aching for her great-grandmother and for George, their romance gone so terribly, so tragically awry. Earlier she had awakened, ill yet again. Ever since the day at Wreckers' Island she had been nauseated in the mornings. But then she considered what had passed between herself and Noah during their own last trip to Wreckers' Island and wondered. Could the same thing have happened to her? Could she be in what Nanny Pearl had termed the "family way"? She shifted against her pillows and started to pick up the diary again, but her mother's footsteps in the corridor outside her room made her tuck the slim, secret volume beneath the covers and under her hip for good measure.

Without announcing herself, Rose walked into the room. She crossed around the foot of the bed, drew up the chair from the vanity table, and ensconced herself next to her daughter.

"You're ill again, Elizabeth?" she asked without preamble.

"Yes, Mother. I've never really recovered from whatever I caught at Sand Island."

"I think perhaps you won't recover very soon, either. Not for nine months, anyway," she sniffed.

"What do you mean?"

"Your monthly infirmity?"

"Not yet. Why?"

"When you were at Sand Island, were you…alone with a man? Did you have any physical contact? Of an…of an intimate nature, I mean." The words came out strangled and unsure. Her mother had never spoken of that sort of thing; now, when she had to, she choked on her own propriety.

"What? Do you mean…did a man do anything to me?"

"Is there any chance you could be…could be with child?"

Elizabeth felt the puzzled frown that drew her brows toward each other. She did not immediately grasp whatever Rose was aiming at. Then she remembered the last day she had seen Noah, and her stomach twisted. This time it was not the nausea she had come to expect in the morning. It was sheer terror.

"Mother!" she exclaimed, the word ripped from the depths of her soul.

"Well? There was the day you went to Wrecker's Island alone with Mr. Canning."

"The day I came home sick from the picnic food?"

"Yes. That day. I think it was more than bad food that made you ill. Did you by any chance drink wine?"

"I don't think so. He gave me punch he said was from a party his parents had given the night before. I did get sleepy, but I think it was just the sun and the fresh air. And I admit I don't exactly remember everything that happened afterward."

"Did the two of you have carnal knowledge of each other?"

"I don't really know what you mean, but he did touch me. I was too confused and too sleepy to know exactly what he was doing, but he did…he did hurt me. Down there."

"Oh, Elizabeth! No! Don't tell me you let him have you! Get you *pregnant!*" Rose's voice swept upward into a wail.

"I didn't let him do anything, Mother. I couldn't. I was…"

"There were spirits in that punch, as sure as God made little green apples. He got you drunk, and now you're… Oh, the scandal! And now I shall have to tell your father!"

"You mean I'm going to have a baby?" The realization nearly made her vomit again. A thousand horror stories flooded her mind, blotting out all rational thought. Like all girls of her age and station, she knew what became of "bad girls" who brought shame on their families and ruined their own lives by having bastards.

A bastard. That was the right term for a child who had no father, borne by a woman who had no husband. And now that stigma, that opprobrium, had come to rest squarely on her shoulders. Shock immersed her so completely she could not think.

By this time Rose was in tears. She drew a handkerchief out of her pocket and sobbed into it. "I never thought I'd see the day when a daughter of mine did such a terrible thing! You've ruined the family name forever! That is, unless we can persuade Mr. Canning to do the right thing, face up to his responsibilities, marry you to give your child a name."

"Oh, Mother, I don't want to marry Noah! I couldn't! I don't love him. I don't even *like* him!" Elizabeth felt the tears come too, and blotted her face on the sheet.

"Nevertheless, you will do what must be done. I will have your father contact his family and demand that he marry you, quickly and quietly. Of course everyone will know what's happened, and tongues will wag, but that's the best that can be made of the situation."

Elizabeth had never wanted to be held and comforted as much as she did at that moment, but she knew better than to turn to her mother, who at the moment was totally absorbed in her own histrionics. Elizabeth's whole life came apart in an instant, and uppermost—Paul was lost to her now. For that reason, more than anything else, she turned over and buried her face in her pillow, whispering his name and letting the tears come. When she sobbed herself out, she was alone. Her mother had left the room without another word.

Much later that evening, with Robbie and Clara banished upstairs with their governess, she and her mother and father sat in the family parlor. Her father claimed his favorite overstuffed leather chair, while she sat primly on an ottoman and her mother took one end of the sofa.

"So, Rose?" Tal asked, holding a match above his pipe and drawing on it until the tobacco caught. Taking in careful little puffs to make sure the pipe stayed lit, he waved the match to cool it before depositing it in the silent butler at his elbow. "What is so important you needed to talk with us in private?"

"It's a matter of the utmost importance. We could all be embroiled in scandal unless this is handled discreetly."

Tal raised his eyebrows. "Oh?" he prompted.

"Yes. It concerns Elizabeth."

"I gathered it concerns her or else she'd not be here. So what have we?" He looked directly at Rose.

"Elizabeth has...allowed an unwonted familiarity. It appears she is with child."

Tal's eyebrows went up. "Elizabeth?" he asked.

"I didn't allow it. He...gave me something to drink. It made me so sleepy I had no idea what he was doing."

"Then you are sure, Rose?"

Her mother nodded. "Yes. Her courses have stopped, and she is sick in the morning. You must contact Noah's family and demand that he marry her." Her father drew gently on his pipe, a thing he did often when he did not know what else to do and wanted to cover indecision by appearing thoughtful.

"The Canning family is quite well placed," he said,

allowing his doubt to show.

Rose drew herself up tall. "Our families are not without influence," she sniffed. "The Governor, after all, is my uncle, and I need not reiterate the Talbot family lineage."

Tal shook his head slowly, as with great regret. "I had no idea young Noah would turn out to be a rakehell. He was always such a polite young man," he said to no one in particular.

"The Bible says the Devil can quote scripture and assume a pleasing appearance," Rose replied, her voice dripping sarcasm.

"Certainly I'll write to Mr. Canning." It seemed as if that decisive action was his own idea. "They'll simply have to marry."

"I don't want to marry Noah Canning," Elizabeth stated flatly.

"You'll just have to swallow your pride, young lady. You're a fine one to puff up now," Rose snapped.

"But aren't there...things that can be done?"

"What are you talking about?"

"To make you...you know...not pregnant anymore?"

Rose rounded on her. "Elizabeth! Wherever did you get that idea? Of course there simply aren't!" Elizabeth opened her mouth, then closed it again, realizing she would have to reveal more than she was willing to at the moment.

"Well, there are, but they're barbaric and dangerous, not to mention against the law, and people like us simply don't do that," Tal put in, trying to defuse his wife's growing ire.

"But I can't marry Noah! I simply can't! It would

mean the ruin of my whole life!"

"It's ruined now, along with your reputation and, I need not add, ours. What's this all about, anyway? That police officer you've been secretly corresponding with all summer?" That hit her below the belt. So her mother had been spying on her. What else had she learned?

"Yes, I've been writing to Sergeant Weller. He's a gentleman. Not like Noah Canning, who, remember, you virtually ordered me to encourage. You were all for it." Long ago she had learned the best defense was a swift offense.

"I didn't mean lie down and play the whore for him," Rose snarled. Her voice dropped an octave out of sheer fury, and she advanced on her daughter. Elizabeth rose, using her height to her advantage.

"If I'm a whore, what does that make you? Mr. Canning was your idea, not mine. I never liked or trusted him, but you practically threw me at him."

Elizabeth never saw it coming. Her mother took a full swing and slapped the side of her face so hard a sheet of white light flashed across her vision, and she staggered back against the couch. But she caught herself and was back in an instant, fists clenched with rage.

"Don't you ever touch me again! Ever!" she spat.

"I'm your mother. I'll do as I..." Elizabeth moved toward her mother, but her father came between them.

"Rose! Enough!" Tal barked. "Elizabeth, I think you should go to your room while your mother and I talk things through."

"Gladly," she shot back, finally taking control of the anger that raged hot in her chest. She ran for the stairs, taking them two at a time with her skirts hiked up like a tomboy. The resounding slam of her bedroom door fairly shook the house. Still in a fury, she locked the door, then threw herself on her bed. Her mind raged and roiled; she was too upset and too angry even for tears. Pregnant! Her mother had actually used that word! Then she had used a worse one. Anger toward her mother had simmered just under the surface for a very long time. Now it boiled over into red-hot hatred. She would never look at her mother the same way again, even if they both lived to be a hundred. She had been betrayed and vilified by the very person she was supposed to be able to trust most. Then her thoughts turned, as they did several times every waking hour, to her cousin's wedding and the tall Mountie in the iconic red uniform.

"Oh, Paul, I always hoped I'd see you again. But now I can't. I could never face you, after what's happened," she whispered into her pillow. And when the tears came, they rivaled Noah's flood.

She had almost cried herself out when she heard a tap at her door. "Go away," she said irritably, blowing her nose on her petticoat like a little girl.

"It's Robbie."

"Go away, Robbie."

"Please let me in. I know what a bother Mother can be. What did she do to you?"

"Were you listening? If you were, I'll kill you."

"No, honest. Please let me in, Bet." Finally she gave in, got up, and unlocked the door, ushering him in and locking it again behind him. She sat down on her mussed bed, and he took the chair from her vanity table and drew it up beside her.

"What on earth happened to your face?" he asked.

She raised her hand to her cheek, and he reached back to the vanity table for her hand mirror and gave it to her. She touched the pronounced swelling over her cheekbone and explored the coming bruise.

"Mother struck me," she said truthfully, not coming up with a convincing excuse in time.

"Mother struck you?" he echoed. "But then, she's slapped me before."

"Yes. Well, I guarantee she'll never strike me again. If she does, she'll wish to high heaven she hadn't." She handed the mirror back to him, and he returned it to the table.

"Believe me, I wasn't listening to what went on between you and Father and Mother. But I did hear that voices were raised."

"Yes. I'm in no position to tell you why. That'll be up to them."

"I'm not here out of curiosity, Bet. Truly. I don't want to dig any dirt on anyone. I just…I'm concerned. You're my big sister. And if I can help you, I will. You know that." She felt a rare rush of affection for her younger brother; it had not been so long ago they were sworn enemies.

"Thank you. It's true. I'm in some difficulty. I imagine I shall have to go away soon." She had no idea where that prophetic statement originated.

"If this is more of Mother's tiresome picking on you, I'll take your side. Whatever happens, you can count on me. If I can do anything to help, you I will." His open, innocent face pronounced his sincerity; Robbie had turned out to be part and parcel of his father.

"I know. I appreciate your concern, and I thank you

for it. But I think I may be beyond your aid. Time will tell. Now you'd better get back to your own room before you get into trouble along with me." She stood to usher him out, and with the manners that had been ingrained in him he rose with her. When she had closed the door behind her brother, she returned to her bed, feeling even more lost, alone, and naked against a hostile world.

The next few days she holed up in her room, illness only partially feigned. She spent most of her time sleeping, ate little, and spoke to no one. Even the precious secret diaries went untouched, and Clara's sweet offer of a fall nosegay brought only a brief, sad smile.

It seemed as if her entire world held its breath. When she absolutely had to leave her room, she tiptoed out, first scanning the hallway to make sure her mother was not in sight, accomplished whatever she needed to, and immediately scurried back to her haven. And for Rose's part, she completely ignored her oldest daughter. The only people Elizabeth saw were Robbie, Clara, and the maid who brought her meals and tended to her room. Her father put in one appearance to inform her he had indeed written to the Cannings and would let her know the response as soon as he received it. He seemed ill at ease, as though wanting to reach out to her but not exactly knowing how to go about it. For her part, she resisted the temptation to throw herself down and rest her head in his lap as though she were Clara's age again and wanted an all-powerful Daddy to keep the nasty world at bay.

So a fortnight passed, and she received a summons to come down for dinner, as though she had been subpoenaed to appear before the Supreme Court. She picked her way through her meal, leaving almost all of her food on her plate. Robbie and Clara, sensing the tension in the dining room, stayed uncharacteristically silent, eating with meticulous politeness and minding their own business. The meal dragged on, only Tal seeming to enjoy himself, but, Elizabeth considered, it took something truly cataclysmic to put her father off his feed.

Finally the tense meal dragged to its conclusion, and Robbie and Clara were duly dispatched to the upper reaches of the house, while Elizabeth and her parents withdrew to the small front parlor. Elizabeth had long ago learned to hate that room, for it was there all the children went for criticism, lectures, and punishment. She took up the ottoman again, while her parents sat in their accustomed places. This time her father did not light his pipe but instead sat stiffly in his favorite chair.

"Tal?" Rose prompted.

Her father drew a breath, and Elizabeth watched him withdraw behind his lawyer façade.

"I have corresponded with Mr. Canning," he began. "The results were not satisfactory at all. Without going into detail, he denied any wrongdoing on the part of his son, and questioned your virtue. Your mother and I have decided that the only course of action is for you to leave until circumstances are again suitable for you to return home." He looked at his wife, subliminally handing her the baton.

"I have written to Jenny. You will go to Elk Gap until your child is delivered. She can help you arrange a suitable adoption. After that, you may return here if you wish. As far as anyone here in Arlington is concerned, you have gone to visit my cousin Grace in San Francisco, and to attend finishing school there in lieu of doing the continent. After all, one does not travel to Europe when there is a war on."

"So I'm banished."

"It's the only course of action. There will be gossip, of course, but can you imagine the scandal that would ensue if you remained in Arlington? Why, it would make a forest fire look like a candle flame. You'll leave tomorrow. The train ticket has been purchased, and all arrangements made."

"And then I can come back?"

"Only if you wish. And then I would suggest you do not re-enter society. You are the first child, after all, and it's your duty to stay here with us against your father's and my old age."

She had heard that one before, too, but It had never been laid before her so boldly. She looked down at her hands; the silence in the room wrapped around her like a shroud. She could almost imagine the screws in her coffin lid being tightened for the final time.

She dared a glance at her father, since he had been her refuge against her mother's rigidity. However, his expression was blank. There would be no solace from his direction this time.

"It seems that is the right course of action for you, Elizabeth," he said at length. Rarely did he use her full first name. She heard the final turn of the last screw. What a future: a life sentence as a drab and colorless maiden aunt in a luxurious prison fenced with the iron bars of propriety and gentility.

Suddenly her stomach turned over.

Knowing she could never make it to the water

closet in time, she ran for the front door and out across the porch, to be violently sick behind a lilac bush.

Chapter 9

The train slowed at the outskirts of Elk Gap. Elizabeth, gazing out the rain-streaked window into the cold, bleak October day, felt deep relief. The long journey had finally come to an end. It did not matter if the small town looked like the meanest backwater she could ever imagine. It would provide a refuge when she needed it most.

She could see the train station for perhaps a mile before the engineer blew for the stop. It appeared deserted, as did the main street itself. Her heart hit the soles of her shoes as it became evident her mother had not made any arrangements for her. Instead, she had been dumped on her cousin's door, a foundling left on the church steps, discarded like an incriminating piece of garbage.

When the train finally stopped, she let the conductor give her a hand down the steps, then waited for the porters to unload her camel-backed steamer trunk. She came around the end of the building, looking about her at the scene her cousin Jenny had described, the same scene that had launched her on the path to her medical career, and the love of her life. Hard on the heels of the thought came the one she lived with every waking moment: there would be no love of her life, for Paul had become an impossibility. To boot, he was probably so close to her he could appear at any moment. What would she do if she saw him?

As she looked across the street toward a three-story white board-and-batten building sporting a sign reading "Mrs. Hammill's Boarding House," a tall figure in a distinctive Northwest Mounted Police uniform stepped out onto the porch and glanced across at the train station. Her heart gave a huge hitch in her chest, and for a moment her breath failed and her vision faded. She took hold of a convenient post in case she fainted, or her lurching stomach rebelled even further. But then she recognized the insignia on the sleeve of Shane's tunic. Though relieved, she felt she was not yet ready to face her cousin by marriage. She bowed her head, hiding her face.

She watched as Shane looked down the street, then waved at someone. Following his line of sight, she saw another tall figure in a Red Serge posting toward her on a big chestnut horse. The shock of recognizing the sergeant's stripes on Paul's sleeves translated itself into a sheet of lightning before her eyes and a sudden constricting pain flashing through her chest. She clutched at her post with gloved fingers growing rapidly strengthless. Then her vision grayed out around the edges, and as the scene spiraled into a small dot before her eyes, she sank to the board sidewalk, an unconscious bundle of fur coat and widow's weeds.

The next thing of which she became aware was a voice persistently calling her name. A hand firmly patting her cheek had some connection with the voice that now encouraged her to wake up. As she came to, her stomach turned over, but she was spared the indignity of retching by the fact that between the motion of the train and her condition, she had not eaten anything for almost forty-eight hours. Eventually she gathered her courage and opened her eyes, looking up to see Paul on his knees beside her. A moment later Shane arrived and added another concerned face to the scene above her.

"What's going on here?" Shane asked.

"She fainted," Paul replied. "Come on, Elizabeth. Wake up and tell me what happened." As her eyes swept up the sleeve of the Red Serge, she realized the warm palm under her cheek belonged to Paul.

"I'm...I'm all right," she said, hearing her own voice weak and far away.

"Obviously you're not," Shane observed dryly.

"No. I'm just... It's been a long trip. I think I'm just too tired..."

"Too tired to think. Let's get you across the street to the clinic. Jenny's there. She'll take care of you. Just hang on. Let me carry you." With those words Paul slipped an arm around her shoulders and another behind her knees. She was about to protest she was too heavy to carry when he took an easy step back off the boardwalk and scooped her into his arms. She tried to aid him as much as she could, but her uncoordinated arm around the back of his neck felt doubtful at best. Still lightheaded and confused, she retreated into a welter of emotions she could not readily identify. Humiliation and despair played equally large roles, and never in her life had she so wished the ground would simply open up and swallow her. Then the tears, long bottled up, broke loose, and she buried her face in Paul's shoulder and simply let them come.

"Elizabeth, don't cry," he murmured, and she felt his cheek momentarily against her hair. "Whatever's wrong, it's not worth tears. You'll be all right. You're here with us now."

She barely noticed when Shane opened the clinic door and let Paul into the waiting room. Then she heard Shane calling to Jenny.

"I'll be right there," her cousin's voice responded from the depths of a hallway.

The world slowly came back into focus, and Elizabeth raised her head from Paul's shoulder as Jenny came into the little waiting room.

"Elizabeth!" Jenny exclaimed, obviously shocked to her core.

"Mother didn't tell you," she replied dully.

"No, I haven't heard from her. What happened to you?"

"I'm all right. I just… I fainted."

"Paul, bring her in here." Jenny opened the door to the nearest treatment room. Paul carried her in and helped her lie down on the examination table. When she protested and tried to sit up, Jenny's hands came down gently around her shoulders. "No, Bet. Lie back. I don't want you fainting again. Don't worry about anything. Whatever's wrong, we're going to fix it, understand?"

"There's a snowball's chance in hell of that," Elizabeth whispered, feeling tears straggling back into her hair. She withdrew into some far part of her mind where misery was the only reality, and only half heard Jenny shooing the two men out of the room. She closed the door behind her and came back to Elizabeth.

"Honestly, Jen, I'm all right. I just haven't eaten in two days, and I've been riding that awful train with the coal exhaust and cinders, and I think I'm just exhausted."

"You haven't eaten in two days?" Jenny echoed.

"No. I was motion sick all the way. That and…and…. Oh, Jen, I'm in trouble. It's just awful, and now Mother just packed me off without even the courtesy of asking you…" She turned away, burying her face in her hands, trying to sob silently. Wordlessly Jenny handed her a towel, then drew up a chair beside her.

"Bet, believe me, you'll be all right. Whatever you need, you can stay with Shane and me. You're safe now. Nothing bad is going to happen to you here." She felt Jenny stroking her shoulder, and after a few moments she got hold of herself, dried her face, and blew her nose. Jenny repossessed the towel and dumped it into a bin. "I think you can sit up now. Hold onto me and let me help you, and if you're the least bit dizzy, let me know, all right?" Elizabeth nodded in agreement and let her cousin help her sit up. Then Jenny raised the head of the examination table so she could lean against it. Elizabeth accepted the glass of water her cousin held out to her. Surprisingly, her head stayed put. She was desperately thirsty, but she had sense enough to heed Jenny's warning to drink slowly.

"What if I throw up?" she asked between sips, then noticed Jenny was holding an enamel basin.

"It wouldn't be the first time for either of us. Just take it easy. I think dehydration was probably half your problem. Drink that, and I'll give you more in a few minutes. Now let's get your coat off, and you can tell me what's gone on." Jenny unbuttoned Elizabeth's coat, and she had a flash of *déjà vu* that led her back to childhood, when her older cousin had helped her in and out of winter wraps. Elizabeth managed her gloves and reached up to unpin the fur toque that matched her coat.

"Mother said she'd write to you."

"I haven't heard from her. That doesn't mean she didn't write. This far out, mail doesn't always make it timely." But Elizabeth knew the truth of it. Her mother had simply foisted her off on Jenny without explanation or permission. She felt the blush of shame staining her cheeks, and she looked away from her cousin's keen gaze.

"You're just being kind. This is such an embarrassment. I should have known to write to you myself instead of believing Mother did it," she sighed, then felt Jenny's gentle, warm hand on her wrist.

"And what would you have had to tell me?"

"That I'm…with child. Mother concocted a story, and told me to pass myself off as a widow. She told me to come here, introduce myself to everyone as Mrs. Morgan, and let it be known my husband had been killed in an Army training accident and I left Arlington for a change of scene. But you can figure out the real reason. There'd be scandal for the whole family from now until doomsday if the truth were to be bandied about."

"Oh, Bet…" Jenny reached for her cousin's hands. "Don't worry. As I said earlier, you're safe here, and of course you can stay with Shane and me. You'll be all right."

"Mother also told me you could arrange an appropriate adoption."

"I could, it's true, but let's just wait and see what happens. We've plenty of time. How far along are you?"

"It…it happened on the fourth of September. I

didn't let him, Jenny. He gave me something to drink that made me very sleepy, and he…he took advantage of me when I couldn't resist him."

"Probably laudanum. That's criminal, Bet. He could be charged with rape."

"But you know how difficult that is to prove. I'd be blamed, and my name would be dragged through the mud for all the world to scoff at. Not to mention that his family is one of the richest in the United States, and they could buy all the judges they wanted to. No, Jen. This is the only way."

"I know your family. They would have tried to make him marry you."

"That didn't work either. You see, he's supposed to be entering West Point next fall, and those cadets have to be bachelors. So his parents sent him off to the Army, where he's firmly out of reach. He'll undergo basic training, and probably be put in some safe little corner of the United States, doing paper work until his enlistment is up. Then he'll go to West Point and become an officer, and I'll be totally forgotten. No, it's much easier for Mother to ship me off to an obscure place like Elk Gap and tell everyone I'm visiting family in San Francisco in lieu of doing the continent. After all, one can't do the Grand Tour while there's a war on. Then after this all blows over, she has assured me I can come back to Arlington and pick up my life again."

Jenny's dark eyes fixed attentively on her, making Elizabeth wonder just what her quick-minded cousin was thinking. "If that's what you want to do, yes. The choice is yours, not hers. As I said, you have a long time to make up your mind. Your baby won't be due until early June. That's quite a while to consider your options."

"Options?"

"Yes. You may think there's only one course of action open to you right now, and that is to hide until your baby is born, give it up quickly, and go back home. But a lot can happen between now and then. Don't hold too tightly to any one idea."

"What else could I do?"

"For one thing, you might find you like it here, away from the restrictive life you've led. When your baby is born, you may not want to give it up. But we won't talk about that right now. Like I said, you have a lot of time. For now, come home with me, get settled in, and see what comes along. But there is one more thing."

"Yes?"

"You're going to have to see Angus MacBride, and let him treat you. You're family, and physicians don't treat their own families. However, I'll be available to keep an eye on you, and to answer any questions you may consider too intimate to discuss with a gentleman. And knowing Aunt Rose, I imagine she filled your head full of every old wives' tale there is."

"Well, she did give me some...advice," Elizabeth admitted.

"Like what? Eating for two?"

"That's part of it. But I haven't been able to eat much. I'm still ill."

"Morning sickness is miserable, but it does go away eventually. If it's too bad, there are some medications we can try, but I don't like to prescribe medications during pregnancy, because whatever you take does get to your baby. And eating for two will just make you fat. It's probably how Aunt Rose became so stylishly stout. Eat as you always have. One thing I don't recommend, though, is wearing a corset. If you don't like how you look, wear a loose afternoon dress or put on a long scarf or an apron. You'd be surprised how much you can cover up with a nice apron."

"That's well and good for you to say, Jenny. You've always been so slim you've never even worn a corset. Mother says I need one."

"You evidently haven't looked at yourself lately. How much weight have you lost? Do you even know? You're as small around as I am."

"I'm not certain."

"Well, we'll try to keep your weight gain to around twenty pounds from where you are right now. That's enough to be healthy, and the extra will be easy to lose. Now, anything else?"

"I've always heard you couldn't…that it wouldn't happen the first time."

Jenny slowly shook her head. "No. Theoretically, any time you have physical relations you can conceive. In point of fact, it seems women are fertile during only a part of their menstrual cycles, but more research needs to be done on that."

"Physical relations? I've heard the term, but I don't understand."

Jenny's eyes widened, and she took a deep breath. "Oh, Aunt Rose! I could just wring her neck. She didn't tell you anything, did she? I mean, not even enough so you could protect yourself."

"No. She didn't tell me anything, even afterward. All she did was wring her hands, and tell me how it was all my fault. And I don't even really know what happened."

"What happened is you were raped, and that was not your fault. You were in the wrong place at the wrong time. You didn't do anything blameworthy. If you think you did, get that idea out of your head right now. I'll tell you what. I'll give you a book to read when we get home. It's dry, and kind of deep, because it's one of my medical texts. You read it, and then we'll have the discussion you and Aunt Rose should have had years ago, and I'll explain what you can do to take care of yourself. But back to the topic at hand. Do you remember when your last period started?"

"It was about two weeks before. I have it written down somewhere."

"Good. Be prepared to tell Angus when you see him. Do you want to do that now, or do you want to wait until you've rested up from the trip? I know a long train ride isn't fun. And I think you're right. The reason you fainted is that you're overtired and you haven't eaten in way too long. There's nothing really wrong with you."

"If I can just go home with you... I'm absolutely exhausted."

Jenny patted Elizabeth's hands reassuringly. "Certainly. I'm ready to leave for the day anyway. I'll go pick up my buggy, and we'll go home. You'll have your own room, and all the privacy you want. Fair enough?"

"It sounds like heaven, after what I've been through. And the last thing Mother told me was to stay away from Paul. I certainly managed that, didn't I?" She felt the small, wry smile that twisted her lips.

"Fainting at his feet might have been a

little…ah…dramatic, Bet."

"I suppose Shane will have to know about me. And I don't think he'd keep secrets from his partner."

"Shane doesn't carry tales out of school. He'll tell Paul what you want him to know, and no more."

"Maybe, for now, telling people I'm a widow will work."

"It will for the bulk of Elk Gap. And if Aunt Rose told you to sequester yourself in the house, I'm going to say phooey on that right now. You'll need to get out and get fresh air. This isn't Arlington or, heaven forbid, New York. Here, ladies have quite a bit more freedom. You can attend church and the Presbyterian Ladies' Handwork Society and whatever else you may want to without stigma. Oh, they'll all be as curious as cats at first, but you're an old hand at social situations. You'll handle it all very gracefully, and I'll be there to back you up. Now get your coat and wait for me in the anteroom. I'll bring my buggy around."

Fighting the worst fatigue of her lifetime, Elizabeth did as Jenny directed, and sat on one of the mismated straight chairs in the anteroom until she heard a buggy stop out front. She carefully picked her way down the three steps to the board sidewalk, then stepped in to sit next to Jenny.

"My trunk is still at the station," she said.

"It'll be safe there. When we get home, I'll send our hired man for it," Jenny reassured her. She shook the reins, and the gelding started up in a gentle trot.

"Jen, do you think I could ride? Mother says no, but…"

"Of course you can. Just don't jump. We even have an extra saddle horse now. Why don't we plan on going out Sunday and seeing some of the countryside after church, if it isn't raining?"

"I'd love that." Jenny smiled at her, and she could not help returning it. For the first time in a month, a glimmer of hope slipped in.

Chapter 10

After stopping for the mail, Jenny drove an easy three miles, heading south from town, and eventually turned into the driveway of a big house. Richly ornate, it boasted an elaborately irregular footprint and fairly dripped gingerbread millwork and stained glass. A graceful tower surmounted the left-hand corner of the second floor. Though the grounds had gone dormant, Elizabeth could see how the multitude of rose bushes would grace the front yard in the summer. As Jenny pulled around the house to the barn, they passed a large vegetable garden whose orderly hay-mulched rows still contained some winter truck. In the pasture adjoining the barn, two horses and two milk cows grazed.

"So this is the place Uncle John and Uncle Richard bought for you. It's a beautiful house, Jenny," she remarked.

"Thank you. And it does have indoor plumbing and a telephone. We'll have electric lights, too, as soon as electricity makes it out this far. Until then, kerosene isn't that bad."

As soon as they pulled up, the hired man opened the barn doors, but Jenny did not drive in. Instead she stopped in the yard, where there was adequate room to turn around. The man came out to meet them and took the hack's reins.

"Thanks, Clancy. And by the way, Elizabeth, this

is Clancy Jacobson. Clancy, my cousin, Mrs. Morgan." Clancy took off his knitted watch cap and made an old-fashioned bow.

"Mrs. Morgan."

"Hello, Clancy," she replied, a little nonplussed. Jenny evidently maintained a more informal household than the Talbots did; Rose would never have introduced anyone to a servant.

"Please don't unhitch Jasper yet," Jenny continued. "Mrs. Morgan's trunk is still at the train station. If you would go for it, I'd be grateful."

"Right away, ma'am," Clancy responded, pausing to give both women a hand down before he climbed into the driver's seat and clucked to the gelding.

"I left a bag with my trunk," Elizabeth said as he came past. He nodded in acknowledgment.

"I'll get 'em both, ma'am."

Jenny started toward the house, but Elizabeth stopped, gazing across at the pasture. "So that has to be your famous Fleur," she said, pointing to the gold mare next to the fence.

"That is. And the sorrel gelding is Feather. He's another of Thomas Wise Hand's horses. Shane and Paul have kept him as a spare ever since Paul's horse had colic. You can ride him if you'd like to. He's as well broke and dependable as Fleur is." Evidently one or both horses heard its name, because they trotted up to the fence. Elizabeth saw where Feather had acquired his name. He had a stripe that looked for all the world like someone had dipped a huge feather in white paint and pressed it to his face. He reached out toward them, soft-rimmed nostrils quivering with friendly curiosity.

"He looks young," she said as she patted his neck

and let him sniff her.

"He is. He's only five. He's still coltish in a lot of ways, aren't you, silly boy?" Jenny tickled him under the chin, and by then Fleur had had enough. She nudged him out of the way to claim the attention for herself. "Somebody's jealous." Jenny giggled, rubbing Fleur beneath the jaw. "Both Feather and Fleur have the same sire. He's a Kentucky thoroughbred."

"You can tell it. They have similar lines."

"Well, then, Bet, let's go in. It won't do for you to get tired. You can play with the horses later."

The back door was closest. Jenny led Elizabeth past the wide screened porch to the large, airy kitchen, just the first of many times she would come in that way to be greeted by warmth and the fragrance of cooking. Half a dozen crusty loaves of bread lay cooling on the big table in the center of the room, while at the stove the cook, a sturdy fiftyish woman with silver hair in a severe bun, stood dropping dumpling batter into a steaming pot that smelled temptingly of chicken stewed with vegetables.

She looked up briefly. "'Afternoon, Doctor Jenny," she said.

"Hello, Lydia. This is my cousin, Mrs. Morgan. She'll be staying with us for the present."

"Hello, Mrs. Morgan. If there's anything you need from me, don't hesitate to ask And I hope you like it here." Lydia paused a polite interval before returning to her dumplings.

"Thank you. I'm certain I will. And dinner smells wonderful."

"It'll taste as good as it smells," Jenny said. "Lydia is a great cook. We're lucky to have her. If I had to cook, we'd all starve."

"I'm on your side. I don't know how either," Elizabeth agreed.

"I'll take you up to your room. You can lie down for a while before supper if you'd like, and Clancy will be here with your trunk before you know it."

"I think I do need to lie down. This afternoon has been…somewhat demanding, if you will." Elizabeth tagged her cousin through an elegant formal dining room and into the capacious front parlor. It did not escape her notice that no dust rested on any of the shiny surfaces, not a speck disfigured the carpets, and not an item was out of place in the whole house. A quiet fire rippled on the parlor hearth, illuminating the richly carved walnut case of an enormous square grand piano.

"I didn't know you'd started playing again," she observed.

Jenny's response was a light, rippling laugh. "Not me. We bought this place furnished. That big old Beckstein was part of it. It's actually in tune, and there's a bunch of music in the music chest. You can play any time you'd like to. Me, I swore off the piano as soon as Aunt Eleanor would have it."

"I think I just may take it up again," Elizabeth responded, wondering where the idea had come from. She, like all accomplished ladies, had endured years of piano lessons. She had actually come to be a competent pianist without ever really enjoying it. However, she reflected, she had a reasonable amount of talent, and now there was no dour old Professor Barnstable smacking his insufferable pointer against the score, she just might find she liked playing.

Jenny led up the stairway to the second floor. "Our

master bedroom is down the hall this way, toward the tower. That's the sitting room. I really love it. It has a beautiful view down over the lane," she said, gesturing to the right down the hallway. "Your room's over here. It's one of the front ones, so the view's almost as good. We keep the bed freshly made up, so it's ready for you to move in." She showed Elizabeth into a large, comfortably furnished room with green velvet drapes flanking two large windows that looked out over the wintery yard. It had its own fireplace set off by a sculptured tile surround, a large four-poster bed and two matching armoires, a highboy, and a capacious vanity table that would serve double duty as a writing desk. An upholstered rocking chair with a needlepoint footstool had been placed strategically close to the hearth and draped with a dizzyingly bright crocheted afghan. The room, only a hair smaller than her bedroom at Arlington, welcomed her. She took off her coat and hat and hung them in one of the armoires, and instantly felt at home.

"Thank you so much for opening your home to me when I just showed up on your doorstep like an orphan of the storm."

"You're as welcome as the flowers in May, Bet. So why don't you just make yourself at home now, and as soon as Clancy comes back with your bags I'll have him bring them up. I need to go back downstairs now and see to supper. Shane will be home in a few minutes. But I know you're tired. Shall I have a tray sent up for you?"

"That would be very welcome. It's not that I don't want your company, but I'm absolutely exhausted."

"I'll do that, then. And if you care to freshen up,

the bathroom is right across the hallway. Believe it or not, we're part of the civilized world. We have both hot and cold running water here."

"Jen, you've been so good to me," she said, feeling an involuntary quiver seize her chin.

Jenny turned to her and enveloped her in a typically Brisbane hug. "Nonsense. You're family. I love you, Bet. You're the little sister I never had." With a quick squeeze and a grin, Jenny took her leave, letting Elizabeth accustom herself to her accommodations.

With great effort she bit back tears. She had been crying entirely too much lately. She remembered her Grandmother Brisbane telling her that in heaven the angels had a lovely crystal pool of tears, with a beautiful jewel-handled golden dipper to ladle them out to humans when they needed them most. However, one had to be very careful not to use more than one's share. She had certainly exceeded her allotment over the last month. It was going to require a great deal of restraint over a very long time to make up the deficit.

The next afternoon she sat tucked up on the long sofa in the front parlor, her feet comfortably covered and a contraband penny dreadful hidden behind a volume of Tennyson selected randomly from the bookcases flanking the fireplace. Absorbed in the printed word, she had wandered far away from her turbulent world, into another time and another place where knighthood was in flower and *amor* did indeed *vincit omnia*, when someone rang the front doorbell.

"Maddie, please get that," she heard the cook call from the depths of the house.

"Coming," the maid responded. A moment later she bustled down the hallway toward the foyer. The bell rang a second time before Maddie made it to the front door. Even though the door between the parlor and the hallway was open, Elizabeth could not see Maddie. However, she heard the girl greet their visitor, and then her heart turned to ice.

"Good afternoon, Sergeant Weller. Come in."

"Hello, Maddie." The familiar, resonant voice, somewhere in the upper baritone range, made Elizabeth's spine tingle. Given the choice between fight or flight, she would have chosen flight, but she had nowhere to go. She closed her penny dreadful and tucked it down behind the sofa cushion as though she were at home in Arlington; it had not yet dawned on her no one in Jenny's household would care what she read. The volume of Tennyson went face down across her lap. "Is Miss Talbot at home, then?" Paul continued.

"Miss Talbot? Oh, you must mean Mrs. Morgan. Yes. She's in the parlor." Maddie ushered him in, and Elizabeth felt the heat flooding her face. This time she could not faint or throw up. She had to face the music.

Paul came into the room, carrying a basket of oranges. "Good afternoon, Mrs. Morgan," he said, his normally bright, open face clouded.

"Good afternoon, Sergeant Weller."

"I brought you something in lieu of flowers, since they're not available here in Elk Gap this time of year. I trust you're feeling better, then?" He set the basket down on the low table in front of the sofa.

"Thank you so much. It was very thoughtful of you. Won't you sit down?"

"Thank you, no. I really don't think I ought to." He towered over her, his hands behind his back as though at parade rest. The level intensity of his gaze made her want to babble out the whole sordid story. No wonder he made such an efficient police officer.

"It's true. I was married. It was very brief. It was a…a whirlwind summer courtship, since he was going into the Army in mid-September. We barely had time for a honeymoon. He hadn't been gone three weeks when I received word he had been killed in a training accident. I…I came here for a change of scene. I couldn't stand Arlington anymore."

"My condolences." His flat voice had a glacier behind it.

"Thank you." She could not meet his eyes. It felt like trying to lie to her mother. She never got away with that, either. When she looked back up at him, he was regarding her with an expression she could not read.

"And yet you kept writing to me."

The blush stained her face a second time. She said the first thing that came to mind. "I didn't want to hurt you."

"So you deceived me instead. Well, then, I know you're in good hands here with Jenny and Shane. I hope you find the peace you seek. Good day, then. I'm sorry for the intrusion." He unbuttoned the left pocket flap of his Red Serge, fished around, laid a small object on the table, and turned to go. When she looked down, she recognized the ornate silver button hook she had given him a six-month eternity ago, when they were both full of ideals and exploring the concept of falling in love. He crossed the room, quiet for a large man in heavy boots, and stopped at the hall tree for his hat and gauntlets.

She considered her course of action for all of three seconds, then went for broke. She followed him, stocking-footed, into the hallway, the button hook in her hand. "Paul?" she said tentatively. He froze as though struck, then turned slowly to face her. "Paul, if you can find it in your heart to forgive me, I would like very much for us to remain friends." She heard her voice husky and unsteady. "Please bear in mind that many situations are much more complex than they may appear at first glance." Her words did not relieve the serious lines around his eyes.

"I daresay that's often true," he said, his voice level. But when she reached for his pocket flap to return the button hook, he interposed his hand. "No, keep it. It was much too forward of me to accept a token of your favor in the first place. Good day, then, Mrs. Morgan." With a nod to her, he took his leave. She closed the door behind him, her mind and heart once more in upheaval. She had all but laid her shame bare before him, and he had not even seemed to heed the revelation. Yes, she had gone for broke, and gone broke. But it was no more than she expected. Paul had been an impossibility from the start. *It's enough that Jenny and Shane have graciously accepted me into their home. I can't have Paul too. That would be way too much to ask.* Then, as her heart resumed its heavy burden, she returned to the couch, wrapped the afghan around her legs, and took up her dime novel again, not bothering with Alfred, Lord Tennyson. However, she found it impossible to read through her tears.

Outside, Paul moved as one in a dream—or, in his case, a very bad nightmare. He untied Brandy's reins from the cast iron hitching post and mounted, demanding a canter the moment he cleared the front yard.

He had lost his first love to his profession; Louisa Chase Carter's pretentious parents had rejected his suit because they did not want their daughter marrying anyone as common as a police officer. Had he gone into his father's business, it might have been different, but he knew he had to be true to himself and to his calling or he could not be true to anyone else. Then in the fullness of his pride he had dared raise his eyes to a girl even more aristocratic than Louisa—and had been firmly set in his place.

Well, it's no more than I deserve. Stupid, stupid, stupid. Shane with his university education and polished manners could get away with it, but I was an idiot to think I could aspire to a lady like Elizabeth. I got only what was coming to me.

All those letters. I sat with a dictionary for hours, until I knew I had every word spelled right, and I went over punctuation rules for every comma and period. I must have made three or four drafts of every single one. I worked way harder on those than I've ever worked on a report, and what good did it do me? Absolutely none whatsoever. The minute she's out of sight she lets some worthless rakehell sweep her off her feet, and then he gets himself killed.

His mare's ground-eating stride carried him back toward town, the last place he wanted to go. He needed a long ride to clear his head. At the intersection of the North Village road, he turned west and let Brandy have her head. Her sometimes hot temperament made her a real runner. Today he let her indulge herself until the cool breeze leached the heat of humiliation from his face, and with the ebbing of his initial anger, sanity set in.

While his partner operated on gut hunches and almost never erred, Paul approached life's more complex situations like geometry proofs. That basic difference was part and parcel of the reason they worked so well together. And somewhere in this chain of logic, a vital link had gone missing. He slowed Brandy and turned his mind loose on the problem.

Well, there are two sides to this coin. Either she told me the complete truth or she didn't. If she did, it's very strange that her family allowed her to marry so suddenly. Even if there were no reason, it would call her virtue into question. That's just not the way people of the Talbots' social station do things. They would have held out for a long engagement until he returned from the war, if nothing else, just to avoid the possibility that she could become a young widow with virtually no future. And if there really had been a whirlwind courtship like she told me, why did she keep writing to me? That makes absolutely no sense. Elizabeth isn't the kind of girl to dissemble, to lead me down a garden path. She would have been straightforward and honest about it. If she were double-dealing that way and Jenny knew about it, she would have found a way to warn me. She wouldn't have let me get blindsided like this. No, there are too many holes in this story. Something is far wrong.

That leaves only one other possibility. She was caught in a compromising position, and she had to be sent away. If her rake had his way with her and then abandoned her, that makes more sense. Her family conveniently tucked her away here in Elk Gap for the duration and made up some tale about where she went. She wouldn't be the first wayward girl foisted off on a distant relative with a grandmother's wedding ring and a story with more holes in it than a pistol target. Whoever that hell-hound was, his family has to be way more influential than the Talbots. That would take some real doing. But then, they went to that fashionable summer residence that positively reeks of rich people. She must have met him there, and he courted her like a princess, took advantage of her, and then denied everything. That entire scenario is not out of the question. In fact, it makes much more sense than the story she told me. And how I wish I could get my hands around his throat!

So where does that leave me? She said she wanted us to remain friends. She left that door open. I just don't know what I want to do about it yet. I haven't enough information to draw a firm conclusion. In that situation it's always best to wait, investigate, and only slap the cuffs on that criminal when I have the evidence. Of course there's already gossip and speculation that she's here only until her indiscretion can be swept under the rug with a quick, quiet adoption. I'll just have to wait it out. If she's indeed with child, it'll become obvious soon enough. And if I still have aspirations, the time to make them known will be afterward. Yes, she dealt my pride a blow, but she did say something that gave me food for thought. She said the situation is more complex than it appears on the surface. Someday she might be ready to explain that to me. My best course of action is to stand back, not involve myself with her, and see what happens.

As he passed the trailhead for North Village, to his chagrin he saw Shane picking his way down the last few hundred yards of the rocky defile. His partner raised his hand in a wave, and Paul halted Brandy.

"So you've been up to the Village?" he asked rhetorically. "Is everything quiet, then?"

"Not totally. I really thought hard about taking Billy Wise Hand and Moses Richardson down to River Bend for a few nights in jail. Instead I took them before the Tribal Council. They got drunk last night and beat the living daylights out of each other. Now they're hung over, sore, and sorry. I wish I could make them sorrier. I also wish I could get my hands on whoever is making the illegal liquor around here."

"We've been fighting that battle for years."

"I know. But I feel we're close. Nobody cares about what goes on in North Village, but they've started selling to the town kids, and some of the parents are getting their hackles up about it. They'll go too far pretty soon. I just have a feeling about it."

"I know about your hunches. You think it's the Camerons again?"

"I know it is. We just have to find their still, and them with it. Destroying a still doesn't help. They'll just build another one. We have to catch them in the act."

"Hopefully somebody'll come up with a tip."

"Hopefully," Shane echoed. "But what are you doing way out here? I left you riding patrol east of town."

"I finished. Brandy needed a run, and I hadn't been out here in a while."

"Well let's have a run, then!" Shane whooped and pounded on Midnight's sides, and Brandy leaped into action. She could be quicker off the line than the larger gelding, but in a distance race he had a slight edge.

Neither horse was consistently faster than the other, so when they raced, it usually boiled down to which one had a head start. This time Paul did not press Brandy, so when they pulled up, Shane was ahead a length or two. Hopefully his superior's victory would take his mind off what Paul had been doing way out of his patrol area.

Chapter 11

By Sunday, Elizabeth had made up for the lack of sleep on the train, and with Jenny's advice had staved off her morning sickness by eating dry toast before she got up. Jenny bounced into her room, her morning face bright. Surprisingly, she sported one of the white shirtwaists and black serge skirts she normally wore to work. Elizabeth's first thought was she had been called to someone's house.

"So you're not going to church today, then?" she asked.

"No. I'm going. So are you. Remember we planned to go riding afterward?" By way of explanation Jenny pulled on the sides of her skirt, revealing it to be not a skirt, but divided culottes. "I only have one sidesaddle, and it fits Fleur, so you ride her and I'll take Feather. People at Calvary are used to seeing me show up in work clothes. No one will think a thing about it. Now get up and get dressed. It'd be a shame to waste such a beautiful day."

Elizabeth complied, pulling on her underclothes and the hated long black skirt and waist. As she combed her hair out, she looked sadly at the narrow gold band on her left hand, its engraving of flowers all but worn smooth by the years. It had belonged to her great-grandmother Morgan. She felt an even deeper connection with her every time she read a diary entry or looked at the ring. *It just worked out better for you, Miss Eliza. There was no Mama Lou to make things right for me.* But from somewhere in the depths of her heart a small voice spoke. *You haven't given time a chance. You don't know what may lie just around the corner. Patience, Elizabeth. Patience.*

Somewhat reassured, she piled her hair up and pinned it, set her black toque at just the right angle, and thrust a long, jet-trimmed hatpin through the back to hold it. Her mother would have had her wear an old-fashioned crepe veil, but she drew the line at something so melodramatic. Hers was of very open net, nearly chic, coming only to the tip of her nose. When she was satisfied she looked properly mysterious, with just the right touch of understated glamor, she took up her jacket and gloves and went downstairs.

Shane stood in the side yard with an immaculately groomed Midnight patiently beside him. Jenny waited astride the sorrel gelding, while Clancy held Fleur's reins, anticipating Elizabeth. She stepped up on the mounting block and took the reins with a meticulous thank-you.

"Ready, Elizabeth?" Shane asked, taking a long-legged, easy step up onto his tall warmblood.

She flashed him a smile. "I'm as ready as can be. It's been so long since I've ridden."

"Fresh air will do wonders for you," Jenny said, falling in beside her as they started down the long lane.

"I know I look as pale as a prisoner. I haven't really been outside since we came back from Sand Island. I didn't feel like it, and Mother would have had apoplexy if anyone had seen me. You'd think I had the Scarlet Letter tattooed on my forehead."

"You can put Arlington behind you now, Bet. Just enjoy the beautiful day. This Indian summer won't last. Winter will be with us soon, and we won't be doing this sort of thing." Jenny gestured around her. Though the trees had gone bare and the grass brown, the sun shone warmly through a sky so blue it looked like paint. Elizabeth was certain it would smear if she could touch it.

Jenny reined back, letting Shane lead them through the front gate. The early morning light played across his freshly pressed Red Serge and glimmered off Midnight's glossy, groomed coat, all but burning into Elizabeth's eyes. Her mind drifted back to the day they had ridden in Central Park, and how elegant Paul had looked on Aunt Eleanor's big Saddlebred. Unconsciously she straightened in the saddle, as though she were back in New York riding Polly and the world lay before her, just beginning to unfold its limitless possibilities.

The three miles to town passed quickly with small talk while she gazed around like an unabashed tourist. They rode past the post office and continued for a block north, to where the church stood upslope of the old log pond. Spring fed, it held the source of the small creek that meandered around the north side of town.

"What a handy swimming hole," she observed.

"And a hockey rink as soon as the ice is thick enough," Shane responded.

"As I remember, you said you played hockey in college."

He smiled with the memories. "Yes, I did. Six years. I was the captain of my team for the last two. Our last season went undefeated."

"Quite an accomplishment."

"It was my ticket into polite society. Before hockey I was just an ignorant country bumpkin and the butt of a lot of bad jokes." He halted Midnight in front of the church, then took Fleur's reins and led her to a mounting block where Elizabeth could step down. Jenny, however, kicked her right foot out of the stirrup, and bounced from the saddle. She shook her skirt out while Elizabeth smoothed her clothes. Shane took all three horses, tethered them at a long hitching rail, then offered Elizabeth and Jenny an arm apiece.

"Ladies?" he said with a grin. Jenny accepted his arm, but Elizabeth fell in beside him, feeling butterflies in her stomach.

"What's wrong, Bet?" Jenny asked. "You look worried."

"I don't want to be an embarrassment in front of your friends."

"You won't. Don't worry. People here are a lot more open and accepting than you're used to."

"But if they guess the truth?"

"They'll keep their mouths shut. Or at least they'd better."

"Jen, I've never known you to be a social lion."

"Big fish, small pond," she shrugged, acknowledging the greeting wave of a middle-aged couple shepherding three teen-aged boys. The woman held a little girl by the hand. "Will and Millie Tillman from the general store," she continued. "And the older lady right behind them is Mrs. Hammill, who owns the boarding house across Main Street from the train station. Shane lived there before we were married; Paul still does. Oh, and look! Uncle Richard!"

The farmer's wagon Richard had driven since moving to Elk Gap rattled up. His hired man stopped the old, mismatched mares and stepped down, then gave Richard's housekeeper a hand. Richard himself followed suit and trotted over to them.

"Elizabeth! Jenny telephoned me and said you'd come to stay with her for a while."

She gave him a hug and pressed her cheek against his. Even though he was properly Jenny's uncle and not hers, all the children on both the Brisbane and Weston sides claimed him. "Uncle Richard. So good to see you again. So you...know?" Her voice dropped to something like a whisper on the last sentence.

He nodded privately. "I had to know. Nobody else needs to." He released her, and she thrust her hand through his arm as they walked up the path to the church. Richard took up Jenny's running commentary regarding the who's who of Elk Gap as they filed into the sanctuary. They arranged themselves in a pew, with Shane on the end and Elizabeth comfortably between Richard and Jenny. Then, as the organist, an older man who reminded her of her hated piano professor, began his prelude, Paul slid in next to Shane. They exchanged brief greetings that did not include Elizabeth, who sat too far away for a politely discreet whisper. Soon the strains of *Jesu, Joy of Man's Desiring* died a merciful death, and the pump organ wheezed out an introduction to the first hymn. Everyone rose, with a shuffling of feet, coats, and hymnal pages. Paul sang with spirited confidence while Shane, tactfully sparing the others his dodgy pitch and worse voice, stood respectfully silent, and the service began.

When they sat down, Elizabeth felt the eyes of the

congregation boring into her back, while the occupants of the two pews in front of her cast curious glances over their shoulders from time to time. She sat ignoring them, as upright as though she had an iron rod through her spine, a book on her head, and her mother critiquing her every move.

After the service she met most of the town. They treated her gently after Jenny explained her widowed cousin had come to visit. Since Paul had not even bade her good morning, she pretended to ignore his presence, even though her heart was shouting at her and trying to pound its way out of her chest.

In her turn she was greeted by Reverend Aubrey, with whom she traded a few polite words about his message, and received an introduction to his recent bride, who cordially welcomed her into the congregation and extended an invitation to the Ladies' Handwork Society.

Afterward, Elizabeth and Jenny walked down the lawn toward the hitching rail where the patient horses waited, with Shane and Paul ahead, ostensibly talking shop.

"So you're going to ride patrol, then," she heard Shane say. "I thought we'd wander out east to the White Fork. It's an easy ride for Elizabeth, since she hasn't ridden for a while."

"I'm going on short patrol, unless you tell me I need to go to North Village," Paul responded.

"No. Everything was quiet up there yesterday. I doubt anything strange could have happened between then and now." Shane unhitched Fleur and handed Paul the mare's reins. He interlocked his gauntlet-clad hands and held them down for her.

"Allow me," he said politely.

"Thank you, Shane." It took a major effort to keep her tone detached as she looked at Paul, but she had a great deal of practice behind her. She took hold of the saddle, set her left foot against his interlaced fingers, and let him lift her up onto Fleur's back. She hooked her right leg over the top pommel and felt Shane set her toe into the stirrup. Paul handed her the reins, and she smiled thanks at him. She took a long and careful look at the left breast pocket of his Red Serge, where it lay against his chest, flat and obviously empty.

Paul turned as someone caught Shane's attention. She looked over the men's heads as Paul joined his partner, who was now speaking earnestly with a man who looked like most of the rest of the farmers in their Sunday best. He wore a heavy woolen jacket over freshly pressed overalls, and had slicked his thinning hair down on both sides of a center part. He held a much-worn fedora in both gnarled hands, sparing one to gesture northward toward the woods as he spoke.

In the interim, Jenny mounted and directed Feather around next to the mare. "I wonder what those three are talking about," she speculated idly. They did not have long to wait, as Shane broke away from the other two, climbed up on Midnight, and came over to Jenny, his expression serious.

"Well, Jenny, it looks like you two are on your own to go riding this afternoon," he began.

"Oh? How so?"

"I think we may have our moonshiners. Clyde Short told me he found evidence someone has been cutting across his wood lot and going up the hills to the north of his place. They tried to hide their trail but didn't do a very good job, and yesterday when he followed the tracks up into the hills to see what was up, he found their still. He lit out like his shirttail was on fire and doesn't think they realized he was there. Looks like Paul and I have our work cut out for us tonight."

"You're leaving now?" she asked.

"We have to. The moon will be full, ideal weather for firing up a still. We have to locate it and be in place before they get there."

"Do you need anything from home?"

"No. I can borrow Paul's extra parka. Other than that, all the gear we're apt to need is back at Mrs. Hammill's."

"Well, then…be careful."

"We will. If that still belongs to the ones I think it does, they're trigger happy and they're awfully good shots. But don't worry if you don't hear from me for a while. If we round them up, we'll have to take them to River Bend. The best way to do that would be to ride straight through and come back tomorrow. If that's what we finish with, I'll call you in the morning after Millie has her switchboard up."

"All right. I won't worry about you. Much, anyway." He leaned over, gave her a quick kiss, nudged the gelding with his heel, and was off. Paul followed a moment later, kicking Brandy into a canter to catch up. He did manage a quick glance at them over his shoulder.

Elizabeth's heart twisted at the yearning, loving look on Jenny's face as she watched her husband ride away. "They'll be all right, won't they?" she asked.

"Probably. They know what they're about. But, as Shane said, those guys are dangerous. He's been after them as long as he's been here. They make illegal liquor and sell it to the Indians in North Village. It's been a real problem around here for years. Maybe this time they'll catch them and put an end to it."

"Aren't you worried?"

"No more than usual. Being married to a police officer certainly has its moments. But it's part and parcel of who Shane is, and I wouldn't change him by a hair or he'd no longer be the Shane I know and love." Elizabeth nodded as she watched the two Mounties ride back toward their constabulary in the boarding house. Jenny was right, as usual, she concluded.

Paul resisted the impulse to look over his shoulder again as Jenny and Elizabeth rode down the street behind them. However, he did watch them pass the boarding house as he and Shane gathered up their gear. A flush of anger ran through him, and he irately jammed rifle cartridges into his ammunition pouch, almost pounding them in to make them fit. Shane looked at his partner with a raised eyebrow but said nothing as he calmly refilled his own, adding .45 rounds for his pistol.

"I'll go up and get the furs," Paul volunteered. It came out more gruff than he had intended.

"Just the parka for me. You can wear leggings if you want to, but it's not cold enough out there for me to need them."

"Big tough warrior," Paul growled, not needing the reminder Shane's heavier and more muscular build gave him much higher tolerance to the sometimes bitter Ontario cold. He stomped up the stairs three at a time and shoved the door of his room open so hard it rebounded against the stop with a shuddering bang. He made a quick circuit of the room, picking up a few odds and ends and taking two bear-fur parkas from his armoire. He started back down the stairs the same reckless way he had ascended, but thought better of it when he saw his landlady coming up from the first floor.

"Sergeant Weller? Is everything all right? I thought I heard a loud noise upstairs," she said.

"What? Oh, yes. Nothing's wrong. My door stuck, and I pushed it a little too hard. I'm sorry if I alarmed anyone."

She flashed him a plump-cheeked smile. "Probably just the cold setting in that made the door sticky. Well, then, there we have it."

"Yes. And if you'll excuse me, Inspector Adair and I have been called out." He single-footed past her, and went into the room they used as their constabulary. He tossed Shane his spare parka and jerked the other one over his head, shoving his arms through the sleeves.

"Are we ready, then?" Shane asked as his head emerged through the neck of the parka.

"I am. It's not like we're going on rounds, after all."

"But we'll get hungry, or at least I know I will. I took the liberty of asking Mrs. Hammill to put up sandwiches and tea for us. Well, let's get going. We have bad guys to catch." Shane took up his Winchester, ushered Paul through the door of the constabulary, and closed it behind him.

Midnight stood at the hitching rail, a hind hoof rested, his head down, and his eyes closed. Brandy, by contrast, pranced nervously, and tossed her head to the limit of her martingale as they approached. She sidled as Paul mounted and received a vicious correction and a blunt spur to her ribs for her pains. Paul cursed under his breath. "I don't know what's gotten into this bitch," he said.

"I do," Shane responded, turning Midnight out along Main Street. "It's whatever's gotten into you. She senses it. We can trade mounts if the two of you can't get along."

"She'll settle down. Or else." His words came out through clenched teeth.

"Not until you do. What's bothering you goes right down the reins and into her head. Want to tell me, or do I need to guess?"

"Guess. I know you'll be right. Elizabeth deceived me. She married someone, and kept writing to me anyway."

Shane shook his head, a gesture that could have been denial or sympathy. "Do you remember a year ago summer when I thought Jenny was engaged to that Phillip whatever his name was? I couldn't have been more wrong."

"Are you saying... But you'd know, wouldn't you?"

"I know, but I can't talk about it. You have to understand."

"Yes. Family secrets and all. Mustn't air dirty laundry in public."

Shane reined Midnight in abruptly, forcing Brandy to stop too. He felt the steely eyes transfixing his very soul. "Paul, you and I have never even come close to a disagreement in six years. However, you're treading a very fine line right now. I'll give you one warning, and one only. Elizabeth doesn't deserve your anger. She's done nothing wrong. Back off. Back way off."

Paul's heart froze in his chest. His partner had never spoken harshly to him since their relationship had begun. But he had just bumped up against the Scorpio in Shane that would be pushed only so far. He had effectively drawn the line, and Paul, even though his temper ran hotter than Shane's, knew he dared not cross it.

His mind replayed the scene in the living room when Elizabeth had told him many situations were more complex than they seemed on the surface. Then the police officer in him, the part that lived to solve puzzles and unravel mysteries, kicked in.

That's how it is. And as his emotions settled down, so did Brandy. "I think I understand now," he said after they had gone perhaps a mile.

"I daresay you do," Shane responded, his tone still cold. "Whatever you do, don't blame her. Nothing has been her fault. If you still think you love her, be patient. Don't give up. The right time will present itself. Believe me, a Brisbane woman is worth waiting for." Shane's wry smile said everything.

Elizabeth and Jenny had made a loop down Main Street and around behind the railroad station, and from their secret vantage point they watched the two men ride out.

"So are we still going riding?" Elizabeth asked after a moment's pause.

"Do you want to?"

"Of course. It's a lovely day, the country's beautiful, and the company is good. What more could anyone ask for?"

Jenny turned to her with a smile. "I have a better

idea than the East Road where Shane was going to take us. I want to ride along the river to Denham's Crossing, then cut back and pay a call on Uncle Richard. Of course Mavis will serve us tea, so if we don't get home until supper we won't starve."

"It's all new to me. Lead on, *ma cousine*." Jenny returned her grin, touched Feather's flanks, and started down the rutted dirt length of Maple Street. Where it crossed Main, Jenny stopped, and Elizabeth reined Fleur in.

"You didn't get the grand tour of Elk Gap quite the way I did," Jenny began.

"No. In fact I didn't see much of anything before I fainted, as you put it, at Paul's feet."

"Well, here it is. Post office on our right, then down at the end of the block is the clinic."

"I remember that too."

"I imagine you do. The railroad station is across Elm on the left. On the other side of Main is the livery stable and smithy, then opposite the railroad station: barber shop, bank, Mrs. Hammill's boarding house, and the Tillmans' General Store." Jenny indicated each one with a gloved hand. "The last thing on the way out of our huge, bustling downtown is the schoolhouse across that little side street from the store. Thank heaven for Tillmans'. He stocks almost anything you could possibly need, and if he doesn't have it he'll get it for you."

"That's good to know."

"Otherwise we'd be forever taking the train to River Bend. Because of the timetable that trip requires an overnight stay. The only other option is a long, boring ride. Although the one time I rode to River Bend

I went with Shane, so it was anything but boring."

"Oh?"

"Yes. A year ago July. I know I wrote to you about it. Shane took me to that reception for the Governor. It was a full-fledged formal ball. After that I knew just how Cinderella felt."

Elizabeth felt the darkness well up inside her yet again. "That's all over for me."

"Oh, maybe not. Yes, you do have a little detour in your life right now, but after it all works out you can go back to Arlington and pick up where you left off. If you want to, that is."

"Why would I not want to?"

"Just wait and see. A lot can happen between now and June. And you may not want to go back home to Aunt Rose after you've been away a while."

"I know Mother can be difficult, but..." She let her sentence die. Jenny waited out a buggy coming down Main Street, then directed Feather across the intersection. They turned left down Main toward the river and were well past Tillmans' and the schoolhouse when Jenny spoke again.

"I telephoned Aunt Rose after you went to bed, day before yesterday. I let her know what I thought of her simply dumping you as she did."

"And what did she say?"

"She gave me some mealy-mouthed excuse and said that she'd written but her letter simply hadn't had a chance to get here yet. She also told me you had to leave as soon as you could because of your influence on Robbie and Clara. As if they would know the truth of the matter if it rose up and bit them. Doubtless they're as ignorant as you were."

"I read your book, Jen. It did explain things, but I still have questions."

"Go ahead. We're in private."

"Well, you know that Father's grandmother wrote all those journals?"

"Yes. I've read them. Fascinating, especially about the Civil War."

"The family always suspected she started journaling well before her marriage. We were certain there were lost diaries. Well, I found them this summer. Three volumes. They were in a trunk in a cubby at Brookhaven Cottage. She was fifteen when she began them. She…she found herself in my predicament, and her…lover was dying of consumption, so marriage was out of the question. Her mammy took her to an old African woman who, well, remedied the situation."

"You mean aborted her pregnancy?"

"Yes, if that's what you call it."

"And how did she do that?"

"Supposedly with some kind of special carved wooden rod."

Jenny winced. "That's as dangerous as all hell!" she exclaimed "She's lucky she didn't die or become permanently sterile. The medical term is dilation and curettage. You literally scrape the inside of the uterus, and a pregnant uterus is like curetting a cloud. You can perforate it with a breath, and then you have a patient dead either of hemorrhage or infection. It's also very illegal, and carries both a hefty fine and a long prison term."

"Oh, dear. I had no idea."

"There's really no good way to stop a pregnancy once it's started. Dilation and curettage is the only sure way; oral abortifacients are largely a myth. There are, however, precautions you can take to keep yourself from getting pregnant in the first place. Mostly they're illegal too, but the ban on artificial birth control is a law honored more in the breach than in the keeping, and violations are largely winked at as long as one is not a blatant crusader."

"So you and Shane…"

"We enjoy our marriage as we wish, but we won't have a child until we decide we want one. When you need the knowledge, I'll discuss the subject with you."

"I see."

Jenny shouldered Feather closer to Fleur, and reached out to pat Elizabeth's leg. "It'll be all right, Bet. Everything will work out the way it's meant to. Now let's relax and enjoy our ride."

They headed down to the bend in the river where Elk Gap nestled like a baby in the crook of an elbow. The soft roadbed cushioned the horses' footfalls, until the only sounds Elizabeth could hear were the occasional call of a bird, the wind in the autumn-bare trees, and the susurration of the river purling against its banks. The waning sun still fell warm on her shoulders, and the rhythmic gait of the big gold mare lulled her into a semblance of peace despite the situation that had brought her here in the first place. For the first time in two months she found she could consider her situation objectively. Jenny was right, as usual. More avenues lay open to her than she had been led to believe. She did not have to hide under a rock until she delivered, then turn her baby over to strangers and leave town under cover of night like a scalded hound.

They had covered perhaps a mile at a relaxed walk

when she turned to her cousin. "Jen, I know why you went into medicine. It was because of Uncle John. But I think what you do is so admirable. I love the idea of helping people when they really need it most."

"It's the only thing I ever really wanted," Jenny responded.

"Do you remember the conversation we had in the privet maze at Parkfield? I asked you about nursing?"

"Yes."

"Well, do you think… Could I possibly become a nurse?" She heard her voice small and timorous.

"Oh, heavens, yes, Bet! You're level-headed and intelligent. You're also sympathetic, and you connect with people. If you wanted to go into nursing you could make a success of it."

"What would it take?"

"Well, right now there are two ways. You could go to a school of nursing, which takes about a year—and incidentally, there is a school in River Bend—or you could work with a doctor and have him or her certify you. At least that's the way it was in New York. I don't know about here, but it wouldn't be difficult to find out."

"So maybe if I worked with you?"

"You could become my assistant. Right now, I'd recommend you put in a day or two a week at the clinic and see how you like it. At first it would just be seeing our supplies are in order and the patient records are straight. Of course, I'd have to ask Angus, but he's forever grumbling that he can't find what he needs because we haven't enough help."

"Would you really let me work with you?" A little thrill of hope ran through her.

"As soon as you're over the morning sickness."

"I'll get over it if I have to tie a belt around my neck and choke myself."

Jenny's soprano laugh fluted through the quiet air between them. "I really don't recommend that, Bet. It's a trifle draconian. But you're coming into your third month. It should let up soon."

"I didn't throw up this morning. That's progress."

They wended their way out of town, through the mixed conifer and hardwood forest, until they came to a strange collection of buildings next to a shallow run of river. An old man sitting in a porch rocker waved to them, and Jenny returned the salutation.

"That's old Mr. Denham. He admits to eighty-nine, but I have no idea if he even knows when he was born. He can't read or write, or count, for that matter. I see him every time I'm down here. Usually he's working in his garden."

"So he's the Denham of Denham's Crossing?"

"He's the patriarch. There's a whole batch of younger ones. They still maintain the ford, and they'll take your wagon across for a nickel."

"To go where?"

"Just generally south. I've never been much farther than a few miles over the crossing, because that's the end of Shane's territory. However, it goes way north and west. The country is beautiful farther north."

"It's not so bad here, either, spoken as one who thinks Central Park is woods."

"I was like that once too. Our Mounties will educate you."

"I wouldn't speak that way of Paul any longer," Elizabeth said darkly. "We had words. Maddie referred to me as Mrs. Morgan, and Paul asked me why I had kept writing to him over the summer when I was obviously involved with someone else. He accused me of deceiving him, and he walked off."

"Oh, dear. You truly were between Scylla and Charybdis, weren't you?"

"Yes. Admit to being…what my mother called me, or continue the ruse. And I had to continue the ruse lest it become common knowledge that I'm unmarried."

"I'll not ask what Aunt Rose called you. If you told me, I'd probably get angry enough to telephone her again and give her another piece of my mind. But I'd not worry overly about Paul. He'll get over it in time."

"I'll get over being pregnant in time, too." The dark mood closed down even harder.

"And it'll go fast. Seven months isn't that long."

Uncomfortable, Elizabeth changed the subject. "I'd like to start work at the clinic this week, if I can."

"When you go three days without throwing up. Otherwise you run the risk of letting yourself get so tired and run down that you'll be wide open to any infection that wanders by. The season for colds and influenza is coming, you know."

"I'm not too worried. I don't tend to catch things. So how do you and Doctor MacBride handle your hours?" she asked after a little pause.

"I take almost all house calls, and I'm in the clinic on Monday and Tuesday so he can have two days off in succession. I'm off Saturday and Sunday unless someone has an emergency, and if I wind up getting called out too much on a weekend, we sometimes rearrange things. However, since Angus actually has an apartment at the clinic, he's almost always around."

"So you'll be going to work tomorrow?"

"Bright and early at nine o'clock."

"Maybe…maybe could I come with you? If I'm a good girl?"

Jenny laughed again. "My, you're the eager one, aren't you? All right. If you're feeling well tomorrow you can come with me and see what the clinic is like. I'll take you home at noon."

Elizabeth felt a huge surge of excitement, and suddenly the day seemed much brighter. "Thank you, Jen. You don't know how much I'm looking forward to this. I need something to do."

The road had led them away from the river, northward between manicured farms where fat cattle grazed. The cool breeze had become damp, caressing Elizabeth's face with wintery fingers. With the deepening of autumn at this latitude the sun set noticeably earlier each day; dusk had a good start by the time they returned home. Jenny opened the barn door and let Elizabeth lead the horses in.

"Oh, look. Midnight's in his stall. It looks like the guys missed their moonshiners." Jenny gestured to Shane's gelding stretching his head curiously over the stall door.

"Will Shane be in a bad mood?"

"Probably not. He doesn't take setbacks too seriously. Well, let's get the horses put up, and then we'll go in and see what's what."

After a simple dinner, since their help had the day off, they opted for a few hands of cards and an early bedtime.

That night Elizabeth had trouble sleeping for her excitement. She had not yet gone to sleep when she heard the grandfather clock downstairs strike twelve, just before the storm moved in. At first the wind kicked up, and then she heard sleet tapping against the windows. She had no idea when she finally fell asleep. Nevertheless, the next morning she rose and dressed in the clothes she had laid out the night before: black serge skirt, white shirtwaist, and a crisply ironed apron. She braided her hair loosely, then wound it into a chignon, pulling out a little fullness around her face. Then, deciding she looked professional enough for any setting, she came downstairs.

The kitchen smelled of bacon and pancakes, immediately unsettling her stomach. She lunged for a piece of dry toast, broke off a crust, and chewed valiantly.

"Are you all right, Bet?" Jenny asked, looking up from her seat at the table.

"So far, so good," she said, sitting down next to her cousin. Wordlessly Lydia poured her a cup of tea. She took a sip to wash down the toast. Her stomach instantly knotted. Knowing Jenny watched her every move, she forced herself to relax and breathe through it. To her relief the tension eased. She ventured another sip of tea.

"So, Shane, you said you couldn't find your moonshiners?" she asked, trying to deflect her cousin's attention.

"They were gone when we got there, still and all. They must have figured out they'd been seen. We'll get them someday." He took a bite of pancake running with butter and syrup. Elizabeth had to look the other way and try to ignore the food odors wafting around her.

"So what are you going to do today, then?" Jenny

asked.

He shrugged. "Ride patrol, although with this storm I doubt anything will be happening. If it's not too icy, I may go to North Village and ask the men to keep a lookout for our moonshiners—not that they'd cooperate. I think the Camerons pay them off in product to keep their mouths shut. This time I may solicit Grandmère's cooperation. I don't often ask her for anything, but this situation is getting out of control."

"I think you're right. The storm will keep people indoors. If it's icy, though, we may get some slip-and-fall injuries. You may be in for a busy day, Bet."

"I'm ready." Her voice came out a little brighter than she actually felt. Her first priority remained controlling her rebellious stomach. But she had to admit Jenny might be right. A fortnight ago she would have already thrown up three or four times. With a boldness she did not feel, she broke off another piece of the dry toast.

An hour later Jenny introduced her to the clinic. After leaving Jasper in the tiny barn across the alley, they came in through the kitchen door. The sleet fell heavier now; she noticed ice coating the entire back stairs and felt relieved when she made it into the kitchen without slipping. Jenny led her off to the left, into the rather large office she shared with Angus MacBride, who presided from his capacious desk. He hauled his blocky body upright.

"So, I see we have company today," he observed rhetorically. "Good morning, Mrs. Morgan."

"Good morning, Doctor MacBride."

"Elizabeth is interested in helping out. She's thinking of becoming a nurse," Jenny explained.

"Well, lass, that's lovely. We can certainly use a little help around here."

"Is there anything you'd like her to start on?"

"How about alphabetizing the patient records? I'll admit I've been sloppy about that." He indicated a polished wood filing cabinet in a corner.

"All right," Elizabeth said. "I think that's something I could do."

"Well, then, you can start on the records, but first I'd like to finish showing you the clinic. You can leave your coat on the hall tree over there." Jenny led her toward the doorway. She divested herself of her sable coat, while Elizabeth added hers to the hooks on the elaborate hall tree. Then they went out into the waiting room, with its polished pine floor and six white-painted straight chairs. She immediately smelled lye soap and Lysol.

"We have two examination rooms in here. I use the front one, and Angus uses the one in the back. It's bigger and it's more private. And between them is a water closest and our supply cupboard. Actually it's more like a big pantry. You need to become familiar with everything in it and keep track of how much of what we have in there. Eventually you can do our ordering." Jenny opened the supply cupboard, and Elizabeth surveyed its contents, recognizing less than half.

"I don't even know what most of this is," she admitted.

Jenny laughed softly. "You will. I'll help. We do have quiet times now and then."

She surveyed the shelves a moment more, then turned to her cousin. "Do you really think I can do this?" she asked, her tone dropping to a whisper.

"I know you can, Bet. I have ultimate faith in you or I wouldn't let you within a mile."

Elizabeth sighed deeply. "Well, then, I'll begin with the records, if that's what you want. It's something I feel reasonably confident about."

"Great. When you're done, I'll go over the supply room with you." Elizabeth went back into the office, opened the top file cabinet drawer, and went to work, ignored by Doctor MacBride, who eventually gave her a nod when he went out to greet his first patient. Soon she fell into the rhythm of her work and began humming under her breath. When the last file fell into place, it surprised her that two whole hours had passed.

She left the office and walked down the short hallway past the stairs. As she came into the waiting room, a woman's scream outside the front door made her jerk it open.

"Help! It's Alice! She's choking! She's not breathing!" Nora Redfield, whom Elizabeth recognized from church, burst into the waiting room, the limp, cyanotic form of her daughter Alice cradled against her shoulder.

"What happened?" Elizabeth asked.

"She choked on a button off her coat! Please, somebody do something!" Without thinking, Elizabeth grabbed Alice from her mother's arms. She sat down and draped the child over her lap, her knee just above Alice's waist. Then she gave her a smart blow to the back with the heel of her hand. The offending button flew out of her mouth and clattered on the floor. Alice gasped, drew three or four breaths, and started to cry. Nora gathered her up as Jenny came out of the front examination room. She walked over and picked up the button, then fixed Elizabeth with a critical look.

"How did you know to do that?"

"It's what Nanny did when Clara choked on a quarter."

"Well, it was absolutely the right course of action. And in cases like this, seconds count. It could have been far worse if you'd had to wait for Doctor MacBride or me. Well done, Bet." Elizabeth felt her face flush at the unaccustomed praise. But more than that, a rush of excited satisfaction consumed her. She had reached beyond herself to help another. She realized it was only a vague glimpse of what her cousin must feel, holding human life in her hands every day.

After a cursory check Jenny pronounced Alice unharmed and sent them on their way. Then she turned to Elizabeth, who in the aftermath of the adrenaline rush, had lowered herself shakily to one of the chairs. "Saving a life is the greatest feeling there is, isn't it?"

"I don't know that I saved a life..."

"Of course you did. Nora was too panicked to have the faintest idea what to do. You were there, what you did was right, and a patient at risk of death walked away whole. To me that's the definition of saving a life."

"You're right, Jen. It's the greatest feeling I've ever known."

"So what do you think?"

"About what?"

"Becoming a nurse."

"It's almost too much to hope for. Just let me see how we get along for the next month or so."

"Fair enough. You can see a lot in that length of

time. Let's just take it day by day." Jenny patted Elizabeth's knee. "Now come on and let me show you the supplies."

By the next morning, the ice storm was in full cry. Madame DuBois had scattered ashes over the back steps and the boardwalk in front of the clinic to keep them passable. Nevertheless, Elizabeth held onto the stair railing for dear life. When they made it into the kitchen, the older lady had tea ready for them. She gestured to the chairs pulled up to the kitchen table.

"Sit down. It was a cold ride, *non*?"

"It was, Madame. Thank you." Jenny divested herself of her wraps and sat. Elizabeth accepted a cup of tea, relishing the warmth.

"I presume it's going to get much colder before it gets better," she said, blowing steam from her cup before she took a sip.

"The winters are harsher here, it's true. Wait until a blizzard comes roaring down from the north. You've never seen anything like it. Last winter we had to string a rope from the back porch to the barn so Clancy wouldn't get lost."

"Really?"

"Absolutely. One storm stranded Shane in the house for an entire week. I almost went crazy right along with him."

"So do you think it'll be a busy day today?"

"That's hard to say. It could be the ice storm will keep everybody indoors, but we're bound to get more slip-and-fall injuries like yesterday's. Well, then, I think it's time to get to work. Thank you for the tea, Madame." The taciturn older lady nodded in acknowledgment and continued to work on her sink of dishes.

As they started back to the office, the sound of footsteps outside stopped them both. "Well, Bet, here it comes," Jenny murmured as the waiting room door opened. At first all Elizabeth saw was a red sleeve. It resolved into Paul, holding a blood-stained towel around his left hand, followed by Shane.

"So, what happened here?" Jenny asked, her voice a study in calm even as Elizabeth felt her heart rate triple.

"I went outside with a cup in my hand and fell on the ice," Paul grated through closed teeth.

"Not exactly the smartest thing you've ever done," Shane put in. "I'll leave you in these ladies' good hands. I'll be back in a couple hours." He left Paul standing in the waiting room and closed the door behind him.

"Well, Paul, let's get you into the treatment room. Elizabeth, you come in too. I'm going to need your help." Elizabeth's stomach twitched, and involuntarily her hand went to her midsection. She sternly told herself she dared not throw up now or Jenny would send her home and never bring her back. Tagging them in, she stood as far away as she could manage. His eyes caught hers with an expression she could not read, but she was certain he would rather be on the other side of the world instead of on the opposite side of one rather small room. "Now let me have a look?" Jenny asked. He let go of the towel, and she unwrapped it gently. Elizabeth caught sight of the long laceration across the heel of his hand, and her stomach lurched again.

"Am I going to live?" he asked wryly.

"I think so. This doesn't look that bad, but you're

definitely going to need stitches. You're also going to need to take your jacket off."

"Oh, wonderful. Getting out of all this stuff is about as complicated as unharnessing a horse." Elizabeth had noticed before Paul enjoyed making Jenny laugh.

"Don't worry. We'll help you."

"Seriously, I should have taken off my sidearm before I came over here. I'm sorry, but it didn't cross my mind. Be careful. It's loaded, and there's a round in the chamber." Mindful of his warning, Jenny removed his crossover belt and carefully hung it over the back of one of the chairs.

"I'm going to try to get your tunic off without getting blood on it, but if I don't manage, it'll come out with salt water," Jenny said, preoccupied with the tunic buttons. She eased his Red Serge off, right arm first. Then she had Paul slip his injured hand backward through the left sleeve. A small, indrawn breath accompanied the tight look on his face, and Elizabeth's heart twisted.

"Sorry. I know that hurt, and I'll be frank with you. It's going to hurt worse before I'm done; fortunately, that part of the hand isn't too sensitive. Ever had stitches before?"

"Yes. I know it isn't fun."

"It isn't, but in this case it's probably going to save the functionality of your hand."

"It's that bad?" he asked, picking up his towel again.

"I haven't examined you that closely, but it looks like it could be. Now sit down, and put your hand right here." She flipped out a clean towel and laid it on the examination table before taking a graniteware basin from a shelf and setting it down next to his hand. "All right. Elizabeth, if you'd come with me, please? I have an errand for you." Elizabeth followed her cousin out of the room, trying not to look at Paul. Jenny pulled the door closed behind them and went back to the supply closet.

"I need you to go to the kitchen and get the iron teakettle from the stove. Madame always keeps hot water in it for us. Then I need you to watch in case our patient faints. It's always the big guys who pass out. Women and smaller men never do. But it'll mean being in there with him. Can you do that?" Elizabeth felt the cold knot returning to her stomach, but she nodded staunchly.

"I'll be all right."

"If you even have a hint you're going to be sick, get out. Understand?"

"I'll be fine, I promise," she reiterated.

"You go get the hot water, then. I need alcohol, gauze, and suture material. For now, just watch what I'm doing and keep an eye on Paul in case he reacts badly. Oh, and while you're in the office, pull the folder with his records in it, please." She took three bottles from a shelf and went back to the treatment room. Elizabeth scooted into the kitchen and took the teakettle from the stove, using a bright, quilted potholder. When she came back to the treatment room, Jenny had poured what looked like water and iodine, plus something else Elizabeth could not recognize, into the basin.

"Thank you, Elizabeth. Go ahead and fill it the rest of the way," Jenny instructed. Elizabeth complied, then set the kettle out of the way on the granite counter behind Jenny. Jenny tested the temperature of the water by touching the basin with the backs of her fingers. "All right, Paul. Put your hand in there. It's the easiest way to clean that wound." Gingerly he dipped his hand in. Elizabeth watched him bite his lip and force himself not to wince. Trying not to look at the blood in the basin, she moved around to stand behind him, longing to touch him, comfort him. Then she told herself she was being silly. He did not need, nor would he welcome, her touch. He had told her as much not long ago.

Before she proceeded further, Jenny washed her hands and rinsed them with alcohol, and had Elizabeth do the same. Then she took her time cleaning the wound.

"You can move everything?" she asked. In response, he flexed his fingers and his thumb. "Good. And you can feel all the way to your fingertips?" She squeezed each of his fingers, and he nodded. "All right, Paul. Here we go. I'd advise you not to watch what I'm doing. And if it gets to be too much for you or you start to feel sick or dizzy, let me know, and I'll stop and give you a rest." It crossed Elizabeth's mind that she should take Jenny's advice and not watch, but she was mesmerized by what her cousin was doing.

When Jenny placed the first suture in the center of the cut, Paul flinched and his right hand fisted into an ivory-knuckled knot. Elizabeth's resolution not to touch him flew out the window. She laid her hand on his right shoulder, and he glanced around at her with a small, tight smile. She felt him forcing himself to relax under her hand.

It seemed an eon passed before Jenny clipped the last suture and blotted the cut with a piece of sterile gauze, then applied a dressing and immaculately bandaged it down.

"There. All done," she announced. "Eleven stitches is no small thing, and you held up very well. I'm turning you loose. If it's painful, lie down and elevate your hand above your heart. Those stitches have to stay in for ten days. Come back every morning, and I'll change the dressing. After a couple of days you can go ahead and use it, within reason, because that will keep the scar from contracting. But I'm advising you not to ride your crabby mare. Take Feather, or trade with Shane for Midnight, but I don't want Brandy yanking you around. Also, don't get the bandage wet. If you do, come to me right away, and I'll change it." Paul nodded his acquiescence. Any questions for me?" Jenny concluded.

"No. Not right now, anyway."

"Well, if you do, you know where to find me."

"I do. Thank you for helping me."

Belatedly Elizabeth removed her hand from his shoulder; she had forgotten it was there. He looked around at her.

"I'll help you with your coat," she offered. While Jenny made a notation on his record, Elizabeth took his Red Serge from the chair where her cousin had hung it and held it up for him, carefully maneuvering it onto his left arm first. Then she pushed his hand away and buttoned it for him. She had more trouble with the heavy, stiff duty belt but finally buckled it around his waist and threaded the crossover through the shoulder tab. He looked down at her with a quirky smile.

"You forgot the lanyard," he prompted. She slipped it over his head and made it seem she had to reach up a long way to fasten his shoulder tabs over it.

"Better?" she asked.

The crystal blue eyes that had melted their way into her heart the first moment they met locked onto hers. "Much better. Thank you." It felt to her he had made a first, tentative attempt to bridge the gap between them.

"You're very welcome," she replied softly. "Watch out for the ice. It wouldn't do for you to fall again."

He smiled down at her. "I'm a big boy. I'll be careful." He picked up his hat and left the treatment room. Elizabeth followed him into the waiting room. He paused with his hand on the doorknob.

"Until tomorrow, then?" he said.

"Tomorrow."

Elizabeth spent the rest of her half-day refiling patient records and cleaning up, but she coasted along on such a lofty cloud she would not have minded shoveling manure. When Jenny drove her home at lunchtime, she had not yet come down from her cloud.

"So, Bet, what do you think so far?" Jenny asked as Jasper settled into his smooth trot.

"I think what you do is the most wonderful thing in the world. Being even a small part of it is more than I could have imagined. I can't wait until you let me spend all day in the clinic."

Jenny's soft laugh felt as warm as a hug. "You're the willing horse, aren't you? But you have to remember that you're going to get tired faster than you used to. We'll leave you on half days for a couple weeks. Walk before you run, after all."

"At least I haven't thrown up."

"No, but you're not eating well, either, and pregnant women tend to tire easily. That's another reason I don't want you working too much."

Elizabeth felt the world's weight descend on her again and sighed. "I'd almost forgotten about...about that. At least for a couple hours."

"I know, Bet. But it won't last that much longer, and it doesn't need to sideline you forever."

"I keep telling myself that at least a hundred times a day, and sometimes I still don't believe it."

"Just keep on telling yourself. It'll sink in eventually. Until then, remember you're coming back to work with me tomorrow morning. I'm going to give you a lesson on dressings and bandages." Elizabeth's stomach tightened. Jenny knew her entirely too well.

By the next morning the ice storm had turned to snow. Jasper high-stepped through a foot of new fluff while more fell sparingly from a sulky gray sky. Elizabeth huddled in her coat and muff and tried to shield herself from the snow, while Jenny seemed invigorated by it. She whistled the gelding up into a high trot as they turned down Main Street past the livery stable and the next door blacksmith shop. As they approached the clinic, Elizabeth saw Paul come out of the front door of the boarding house.

"We'll have to open up promptly this morning," Jenny said as she turned into the alley behind the clinic. "I see our first patient is on his way."

"You'll want his record again?"

"Yes. I think there are enough materials in the treatment room, but I may need you to go to the supply room for me."

"I'm ready," she replied, trying to sound as game as she could. Inside she still quailed at the thought of helping treat Paul.

"Jenny, how do you treat friends without letting it

upset you?"

"It's called professional detachment. Sometimes it's not easy, especially if the person you know is seriously ill. But something minor like Paul's hand is different. It may inconvenience him for a while, but he's fine. All we need to do is keep it clean and watch for infection."

"I see. Well, I'm certainly learning fast."

"You're doing very well, and you know I don't say things just because I think it's what someone else wants to hear. I'm still amazed about your first day, with Alice and the button."

"I didn't think. I just reacted."

"And you reacted correctly. That's what amazed me. You're cut from the right cloth, Bet. Now, let's put this horse up and go practice medicine, shall we?"

Angus MacBride sat at the kitchen table, finishing his breakfast, when Jenny and Elizabeth came in. He seemed in great good spirits.

"Good morning, ladies!" he crowed, raising his mustache cup as if in toast to them.

"Good morning, Angus," Jenny responded, divesting herself of her wraps and hanging them on the hall tree next to the kitchen door. Elizabeth did the same, a beat later.

"Won't you sit down for tea, then?" Angus asked.

"I have to open the clinic. Paul's on his way across the street, if he isn't at the front door already," Jenny replied.

"So what happened to his hand?"

"He fell down on the ice while he was holding a cup. He sustained a big, shallow flap laceration across the heel of his hand. It took me eleven stitches to close it, but I expect it to heal unremarkably."

"Those chaps do find the mischief to get into, don't they?" Angus sighed, sipping his tea again.

"Well, we need to get to work," Jenny said. "If there's time later we'll join you for tea." Jenny led Elizabeth out through the office, to find Paul in the waiting room. He rose respectfully as they came in. This time Elizabeth noted he had left his sidearm in the constabulary.

"Good morning, Jenny, Elizabeth." He greeted them with punctilious politeness, but when she looked at him, his pale face and the dark circles under his eyes evinced a sleepless night.

"Go on into the same treatment room, Paul. I'll be right with you," Jenny instructed.

"I'll get his records. I forgot the folder on the way in," Elizabeth said, deliberately looking away from him.

By the time she returned with the records, Jenny had already removed the bandage and was busy dabbing at the stitches with an alcohol-soaked twist of cotton on a stick.

"See what I'm doing, Bet? I'm just cleaning up the sutures and getting all the dried blood off. This is going to make it a lot less itchy, and believe me, it doesn't hurt."

"No, it doesn't. That surprised me," Paul agreed.

"I want you to watch closely because tomorrow it's your turn," Jenny announced. Elizabeth's first impulse was to run, but this did not square with her new idea of herself. She had just discovered the competence in her inner core, and she did not want to let go of it before she had fully explored herself. But just why under all holy heaven did this exploration have to include Paul?

Jenny kept up a running commentary while she worked. "This wound looks very clean and healthy. See? No inflammation, no discharge, no swelling. We want to keep it that way. But hands are tricky to bandage. It can't be too tight or it'll cause discomfort and swelling of the fingers. Too loose and it comes off. The thing is that hands are used almost constantly, so we have to achieve a balance." She held his hand up, placed a clean dressing over the cut, and slowly wrapped it down so Elizabeth could see what she was doing. Then she split the end of the gauze and tied it around his wrist, neatly tucking in the tails. It was clear Jenny considered bandages a fine art.

"All right, Paul. You'll keep until tomorrow. We'll see you first thing after breakfast, then? Or rather, our nurse will see you." Elizabeth felt Paul's gaze before he turned to look at her.

"I'll be here promptly, barring something unforeseen." As he rose, she could not be sure, but she thought she saw the barest hint of a smile around the corners of his mouth. But when he stepped around her to leave the room, she suddenly felt the burden in her belly. It lay within her like a boulder, and when his knee brushed her apron, that boulder became an insurmountable mountain range between them. She looked away from his gaze, and he was gone, his Red Serge blurring in the tears she fought to control. When the cowbell on the front door clanked with his exit, she finally dared take out a handkerchief and blow her nose. Of course Jenny studied her intently.

"I don't know why my feelings are running away with me. I'll be all right in a minute," she murmured.

"It's not your feelings. It's your hormones, that's

all. That's going to happen from time to time until after the baby is born."

"Then I won't take them seriously," she responded, resolutely returning her handkerchief to her pocket while Jenny uncapped her fountain pen and made a notation in Paul's record. She blew on the ink to dry it, then handed over the folder.

"You can put this back, if you would, please." Glad for something totally mindless to do, Elizabeth took the folder back to the office.

She had been proud of herself. No morning sickness for three whole days. She broke her winning streak the next morning but managed to conceal it from Jenny, who had already gone downstairs by the time Elizabeth found she had to renew her friendship with the commode. She swirled baking soda around in her mouth to banish the sour taste and disgusting smell, wincing at the flat, metallic salt flavor that nearly made her wretch again. She accepted a cup of tea but declined toast before they left for the clinic.

When they entered through the kitchen, Paul was already in the waiting area. Elizabeth hung up her coat, stopped in the office to pull his folder from the file drawer, and went to greet him. This was the big test. She needed to act as professionally as Jenny had, in order to prove her worth; she wanted nothing more at that moment. And of course it had to be Paul.

"Good morning," she said. Since she did not want to call him by his first name but using his title would seem stilted, she skipped any form of address.

He rose politely. "Good morning. I'm here like Jenny told me."

"She wants me to see you this morning, since it's

only your bandage." With cool detachment she led him into the treatment room. He sat down on the accustomed chair, pulled up his shirt cuff and the sleeve of his Red Serge, and laid his hand down on the towel she provided. This was the Moment of Truth. She took out everything she would need, washed her hands, and rinsed them with alcohol as Jenny always did. Then she sat on the stool across from him, very intentionally not making eye contact. Taking up bandage scissors, she clipped the knot, then carefully deconstructed Jenny's bandage, memorizing which way the wraps went so she could reproduce it. She hoped he did not notice how her hands were shaking at first; however, as she fell into the rhythm of her work, she calmed down and the chunk of ice in her midsection went away. Paul cooperated with her, flattening his hand so she could clean the stitches. She swabbed gently at them, removing the last of the gritty dried blood before laying a clean dressing over the cut and bandaging it down exactly as Jenny had done.

"How has it been? Painful?" she asked.

"Not especially, anymore. And before you ask, no, I haven't been riding Brandy. She's only difficult during her heat periods, and that's not the case right now, but I've traded with Shane for the present."

"Midnight is such a big pet."

"He does set a lot of store by that horse," Paul agreed.

"Well, we'll see you tomorrow, then?" she asked, dismissing him before her stomach tightened any further.

He rose when she did. "Thank you, Elizabeth," he said quietly.

"You're welcome." She wanted to answer him in kind but could not. She had her pride, and, after all, she was now acting as a nurse.

He left the clinic, the cowbell on the door announcing his departure. Elizabeth began to order her supplies, but before she was through, Jenny came in.

"So how did his hand look?" she asked without preamble.

"Healthy. As you said yesterday, no redness, discharge, or swelling, and he says it's not painful now. He'll be back tomorrow."

"Good. You did well with your first patient. Now you need to make an entry on his record. I'll countersign it for you."

"Oh, dear! What do I write?"

"Note that you cleaned the wound and changed the dressing, and your observation that it looked healthy."

"Are you sure you don't want to do it?"

Jenny made a wry face. "Your handwriting is lovely. Mine looks like Father's. Sometimes even I have trouble reading what I've written. Just take a deep breath and settle down, Bet. You're doing fine. You're going to make an exemplary nurse someday." Elizabeth felt herself grow two inches with pride, a feeling almost foreign to her. *I'm going to be a nurse! I can't believe it!*

Chapter 12

In the chill, cloudy morning, Shane and Paul parted ways in front of the boarding house, Shane to start out on rounds and Paul to make the usual check on North Village. It had taken all of six years for the people to trust him enough to open up. But at least now when they saw him ride up alone, no one ran and hid.

Habitually he slowed Brandy as he rode past the clinic. Two days ago he had caught a glimpse of Elizabeth in the window of the waiting room. It had been all he could do not to jump off his horse and run inside. But he knew he would subside into tongue-tied confusion as he usually did when he tried to converse with her on any topic more complex than the weather.

A burst of feminine laughter behind him made him turn around just in time to see Garver Finley, the son of the bank president, offer Elizabeth his arm to escort her across the street. He watched her smiling at Fin, who returned it with goofy rapture on his face. Feeling his cheeks flare, Paul looked away and dusted Brandy's rump with the reins. She went from a walk to a canter in less than a yard, and he did not look back until he was well around the curve between Main Street and the North Village road.

As he turned off the road and onto the trail up to North Village, his roiled emotions settled a little. Partly to take his mind off Elizabeth's proximity, he had offered to take Shane's rounds, but his partner demurred. Paul knew Shane liked to stop at the Iroquois settlements because he moved naturally among the native people and spoke their language, where he himself had to rely on his sometimes shaky French and always battled the divide between law enforcement and everyone else.

He gave Brandy her head up the trail. She got along better when she was not overly controlled, something he regularly had problems with. He watched his breath fog in the crisp air and fell into the rhythm of the mare's gait as she walked gamely up the trail. He stopped to let her drink at the usual watering place, then resumed the long pull up to the village.

Shane had taught him long ago the polite way to announce oneself was simply to linger in an obvious place and wait to be recognized. He stopped in front of Madame LaPorte's substantial cabin and schooled himself to calmness. Presently the door opened, giving a glimpse of a shy, middle-aged feminine face before it closed again. After an indeterminate few minutes in which Brandy fidgeted and earned a quick correction, Madame LaPorte, wrapped in her usual bearskin sleeping robe, came out to meet him. He stepped down, leading Brandy toward her.

"Madame," he acknowledged.

"Monsieur Paul." Her odd form of address had long since ceased to bother him.

"Everything is well, then?" he asked her.

"Yes, except for the outsiders bringing their liquor to our men. Last night three of them fought. One beat his wife, and her brother, who was just as drunk as the rest of them, beat them both."

"Who were they, Madame? They need to be brought to justice."

"The Tribal Council has meted out justice. Now it is for you to find the outsiders who brought the liquor."

"We know who they are. Has the Council any idea where they are?"

"The Council deliberated, and we decided to break our silence. Some of the men were hunting, and found their still where they moved it after you and my grandson came after them last full moon. They are at the place where the creeks from the lake come together. You will find them there if you go tonight."

"That's quite a ways from here."

"Yes, it is. Thomas Wise Hand's boys found them. It is not far from where they live."

"Do you know if they realized they'd been found?"

She gave him a quirky smile. "His boys can sneak up on a deer. Those white devils are not deer."

"Thank you, Madame. If I get on the trail, I can be there before nightfall." He touched the brim of his hat respectfully and turned Brandy toward the west trail out of the village.

"Que Le Bon Dieu vous aide," she called softly after him.

On his way out of the village, he stopped to check his Navy Colt, making sure he had racked a round into the chamber and then topped off the magazine. His rifle then received similar attention, while he kept Brandy moving with his knees.

He kept to the established trail until perhaps a mile from his destination. Then he broke off and started through the woods. He would have ridden in the creek, save the flow ran toward his target and any mud he kicked up would have been tantamount to approaching game upwind. Even though he would never be Shane's measure, he was still too good a woodsman for that.

Eventually he tethered Brandy to a tree and crept up on foot. Madame LaPorte's informants had been right. The still was there, and what was more, so were Ned and Charlie Cameron. He felt a small twist of disappointment. He had always suspected old man Cyrus, a mean drunk who would have spelled genuine trouble if he had been smarter, provided the driving force behind his sons, but he had no proof. It could just be the boys had taken off on their own.

Silently he advanced on them a tree at a time, until he knew he could not get much closer without announcing his presence. As quietly as a cat he undid the flap of his holster, but he did not draw the pistol. Instead he shouldered his deadly accurate Enfield. If he could only get a little closer, he would have the drop on them. However, he had not counted on the dog.

They had brought a scruffy mutt with them. Suddenly it jumped out from behind their woodpile and started barking furiously. It rushed Paul, stopping a few feet away. He had no choice but to go for broke. He stepped out from behind his tree.

"Stop where you are! Hands up! You're under arrest!" he ordered, bringing the Enfield to bear.

"Oh, shit!" Charlie exclaimed, swinging his axe toward the chopping block. In the instant Paul's attention was on him, Ned stepped behind a tree, whipping his pistol from his belt. He loosed a shot in Paul's direction while Charlie dived behind the woodpile. Paul felt a burn as the bullet grazed along the left side of his jaw. He returned fire, trying to keep Ned pinned behind his tree, but he could not cover them both at once. They were too far apart, and if they flanked him, he would be in genuine trouble. Damn that dog!

When things don't quite go your way, bluff.

"Shane, I've got 'em. You circle around," he called. "Ned, Charlie, come out with your hands up! Surrender now, before somebody gets hurt."

"Don't take me for a fool. Shane's not here. He left days ago. You're the one who's going to get hurt," Charlie responded, and Paul ducked out long enough to snap off a shot in his direction. It did little more than raise a shower of splinters from the woodpile.

"You're talking about a capital crime, Charlie."

"Not if they don't find you. And it's a goddamn big woods." Paul anticipated Charlie's quick move and ducked behind his tree as another shot dug out bark next to his head. Out of the corner of his eye, he saw Ned fade back toward their tethered horses. At this point he would be satisfied if he could run them off. There was enough evidence here for an arrest down the line.

He pretended not to see what Ned was doing and instead concentrated on Charlie. They traded two more shots, keeping each other pinned while Ned untethered the horses. A moment later, Ned screamed back through their makeshift camp at a dead gallop and handed off one of the horses to Charlie. Keeping the animal between himself and Paul, Charlie swung into the saddle and started after his brother, who raced through the trees as if pole bending. Paul stepped out from behind his tree, lowered his sights onto Charlie's retreating back, and fired. For an instant Charlie wove in the saddle, then righted himself and galloped off after Ned, the brown mutt in hot pursuit.

Paul followed them a short distance, looking for blood sign and finding nothing. He debated about trying to track them, but the sun had begun to drop toward the hills, and he knew he would not have much time. Better to go home, and go after Ned and Charlie in the morning. Giving up for the present, he spent a moment reflecting on a situation that could have gone wrong in a very bad way. He explored his cheek where the bullet had burned a long streak, found no real injury, and dismissed it. Then he went back, took his hatchet from his saddlebags, and methodically smashed the still. He spent enough time to make a good job of it, then he collected Brandy and started back down the trail as new snow started to fall.

Chapter 13

As morning rolled around, Elizabeth prepared herself for another day at the clinic. Her strength had all but returned, as had her enthusiasm and love for Jenny's medical practice. Every time she tied her hair in a modest chignon and donned her black skirt, white shirtwaist, and enveloping apron, she felt a surge of satisfaction and pride. She and Jenny ate a quick breakfast, then Jenny took up her medical bag, which she always carried with her since a call could come at any time, and went outside to collect Jasper and the buggy. A couple inches of new snow had sifted down overnight, and more filtered slowly from the gray sky. Elizabeth could tell Jenny did not love the idea of her husband on winter rounds alone, but she said little. After all, he had been doing this for years.

As Jenny directed Jasper down the alleyway behind the clinic, an unkempt man crossed in front of them and grabbed a rein. He rode a big bay gelding and had a rough-looking sorrel tied behind him, but the thing that chilled Elizabeth the most was a huge revolver in his right hand.

"Out of the buggy. You're coming with me," he ordered, gesturing with the barrel of the pistol. "Bring your bag, Lady Doc. My brother's wounded."

"Put that gun away, Ned," Jenny responded irritably. "You don't need it. I'll come."

"Damn right you'll come. The both of you. Now, out of that buggy. Doc, you ride behind me. Girl, up on that sorrel. And don't try anything stupid, because after what your Mountie friend did to Charlie, I don't mind shooting a woman." Elizabeth looked down the barrel of the revolver and felt cold fear clutching her midsection. But it was not all for her. Paul had obviously been in some sort of dust-up with the Camerons, and it had resulted in a firefight. Was he all right? He had to be, she reasoned, since they had not received a call. Or could he be out somewhere in the woods alone—injured, or worse?

Jenny complied with Ned's orders, though slowly, taking time to put her buggy whip into its socket and loosely knot Jasper's reins around it.

"Ned, I don't understand why you're doing this. You don't need to force me to come on a house call."

"Bloody hell I don't," he spat. "Your husband's buddy shot Charlie. You're damn well going to treat him, and then you're our ticket out of town. Now get up behind me. Girl, hand up her bag." Elizabeth stepped out of the buggy and passed up the medical bag as soon as Jenny had climbed up and settled herself behind the cantle of Ned's saddle. Then she mounted the sorrel gelding, drawing back squeamishly from a blood stain on the apron.

"Ned, you're going to get you and Charlie in a heck of a lot more trouble than you're already in. Whatever made Paul shoot at you, kidnapping is just going to add to it. Let Elizabeth go, and I'll come with you and help Charlie. That way you won't be making a bad situation worse for yourself."

"Shut up," Ned barked. He heeled his gelding,

forcing Jenny to grab the cantle of the saddle to avoid being unseated. Elizabeth, too, had to pull leather as the sorrel lurched out on its lead rope. But as they passed the buggy, she reached out and booted Jasper's rump. Young and coltish enough to react, he tossed his head, and jumped into a canter. She watched over her shoulder as he turned at the end of the alley, and headed for Main Street, the empty buggy rattling behind him. Maybe, just maybe, someone would see him and realize she and Jenny were in trouble.

Ned turned up a wagon path that skirted the skating pond and terminated at the margin of the woods east of the church. Once into the trees, they headed up what looked like one of the million game trails that wove and crisscrossed through the forest.

Eventually Jenny broke the silence. Elizabeth could tell she was trying to ingratiate herself with Ned. "So what kind of wound are we dealing with?" she asked.

"Just below the right elbow. It broke both bones. They're through the skin, and I couldn't make it quit bleeding." Elizabeth heard tension and fear for his brother in his voice.

"You did the right thing, leaving him wherever he is and coming for me. Listen, Ned, put away your gun and let Elizabeth go, and we'll forget you kidnapped us. I'll come and treat Charlie, and we'll make this right."

"Don't try to cozy up to me, Doc. If she goes back to town she'll run squealing to that Mountie, and me and Charlie will be up to our ears in lawmen before we can turn around. No, you two are coming with me. When Charlie can travel, we'll take you with us until we're out of Ontario and nobody can touch us."

"What was this all about?" She tried to keep him

talking.

"We had a still. One of those damn injuns told on us."

"So you made illegal liquor. That might not even get you jail time. If you should be found guilty of kidnapping, you might never see the light of day again."

"Nobody is going to catch us. Your dirty Métis is out of town. His sidekick can't do much by himself. He proved that yesterday."

"I'd say he proved he could do a lot, if he shot Charlie."

"Just blind damn luck," Ned snorted.

"Paul's an expert marksman. Don't sell him short. If he did it once, he could do it again."

"Listen, Doc, I'm through talking to you. You're getting on my nerves. Now shut up." Jenny looked around at Elizabeth with an expression on her face that said she had done all she could.

"It's all right," Elizabeth silently mouthed back.

They traveled seemingly forever; the way to somewhere unknown could always seem many times longer than the return trip. Finally they came upon one of the many trappers' line cabins that dotted the area. Smoke rising from the chimney said that someone waited inside.

"All right. Get down," Ned ordered. Elizabeth dismounted, smoothing her skirt where it had been rucked up around her knees. Then she took Jenny's medical bag and gave her shorter cousin a hand down. Ned grabbed Jenny by a wrist and almost hauled her toward the cabin. She twisted and yanked her arm down, breaking his grip.

"Don't you dare touch me, Ned Cameron!" she spat. "Don't forget your brother's life will be in my hands!"

"And he'd better live, or the two of you will die with him!"

"Now you're talking murder, Ned. You'll hang."

"Not if they don't catch me. Now get inside."

The cabin measured perhaps twelve feet on a side. One bunk, a wood stove, and a small, rough table and stools crowded the interior. Their patient lay on the bunk, wrapped in a blanket, his right arm bandaged crudely in blood-soaked remnants of his shirt. Jenny set her bag down on the table and opened it.

"All right, Charlie, let me look and see what's going on," she said gently, stripping off her coat and handing it to Elizabeth.

Elizabeth hung up their wraps on a rack of deer antlers and came to Jenny's side. Charlie flinched and whimpered as Jenny unwrapped his arm, revealing the travesty Paul's bullet had left behind. Both bones in his forearm had been shattered, and a large hunk of flesh blown away, leaving the wrist and hand attached only by a strip of skin and a little muscle. Jenny shook her head. Then she squeezed the discolored fingertips.

"Dead cold," she murmured. "Charlie, can you feel what I'm doing?"

"No," he choked.

"All right. Move your fingers for me, please."

"I can't. It hurts too much. How bad is it, Doc?"

"Bad. It's going to have to come off. The circulation has been destroyed. It can't be repaired. And to boot, infection is setting in already. I have to operate right now or you'll die, Charlie. Do you understand me?"

Charlie's head twisted. "You're going to cut my arm off?"

"I have to."

"Oh, no, you won't," Ned interrupted, coming to tower over Jenny. "You ain't cuttin' his arm off. You're just saying he needs it because you're on their side. You're going to fix him up..." His voice trailed away as Jenny gave an elaborate shrug.

"Fine. If you won't let me operate, there's nothing I can do but wait, then. The infection will spread. Gangrene will set in, and I promise you by tomorrow it will be way too late." She folded her arms and sat back on the crude stool next to the bed.

Elizabeth swallowed against her knotted stomach. If Jenny could be so brave, how could she do less? Besides, she was now a nurse. She crept in to stand next to her cousin, and when Ned's feral eyes searched hers, she made certain her expression stayed calm and unflinching.

All the fight went out of Ned at once. "Charlie?" he asked, coming to his brother's side. "Charlie? What do you want her to do?"

"I don't want to die, Ned. Please let her operate! I don't want to die!"

"All right, then. There's no time to lose. We need to get started while there's still light." Jenny said. "Elizabeth, I'll need boiling water for my instruments." She indicated the iron teakettle on the stove. The frightened girl retreated and the competent nurse moved to the forefront. Elizabeth removed the burner cover and set the teakettle directly over the flame.

Chapter 14

Paul ate a hurried breakfast, gathered his gear, and made ready to go out after Ned and Charlie. Just as he was pulling on his furs, the telephone rang. He snarled an obscenity under his breath and grabbed up the earpiece.

"Northwest Mounted. Sergeant Weller here," he barked.

"Paul? Angus MacBride."

"Yes, Angus? What seems to be the problem?"

"I just rang off with Maddie at Jenny's house. It seems Jenny and Elizabeth left over an hour ago. Maddie said they told her they were coming directly to the clinic, but they've not arrived here yet. Frankly, I'm becoming concerned."

"I'm just leaving now. I'll check on them. I'm sure they just stopped to talk to Ruth, or went by Tillmans'."

"Jenny never stops on the way to work. She always does all her errands after."

"Well, don't worry, Angus. I'll figure out what's going on."

"Let me know as soon as you can, will you, please? As I said, I'm becoming truly concerned."

"I promise I will. But if I'm to find them, I need to be going."

"Well, then, good luck, Paul."

He rang off, feeling an inexplicable cold in the pit

of his stomach. He checked his weapons, clapped his hat on his head, and strode outside. The first thing he saw was Jenny's empty buggy and a bewildered Jasper standing in the middle of Main Street. He led the horse to the hitching rail, tied him next to Brandy, then backtrailed him through the new snow until he caught up with the second set of tracks behind the clinic. Two horses besides Jasper, he concluded, and by the footprints in the snow, both Jenny and Elizabeth had gone with whoever rode them. It could be nothing more than a house call, but why had they abandoned the buggy without even putting Jasper in the barn or telling anyone where they were going? No, this whole situation did not smell right, especially after yesterday, and the way Charlie had nearly fallen off after his last shot. He sprinted back and picked up Brandy, taking time to ask one of Mrs. Hammill's other boarders to take care of Jasper. Then he picked up the trail that led away from the back of the clinic. He knew he had to move fast before the falling snow covered up the hoof prints.

He shadowed the double set of tracks up the wagon road and into the woods, where the trail became much less distinct. He was able to follow it, though he had to dismount frequently to inspect the sign, much less distinct in the forest than it had been on the wagon path. The hoof prints led up through the woods in the general direction of the still he had destroyed the day before. He remembered Charlie Cameron weaving in the saddle after he had taken a shot, and the more he thought about it, the worse the situation seemed. If he had hit Charlie, it could explain where Jenny and Elizabeth had gone. But he ruled out voluntary cooperation on their part, judging from the precipitous departure. That left only one conclusion. Ned had kidnapped them forcibly, and at this point heaven only knew where he had taken them. If only Shane were here! But he was probably clear up to Castlereigh by now, so the situation had come to rest firmly in Paul's lap.

The tension across his midsection ratcheted up with each step Brandy took. *I have to do this right, and I'll have only one chance. I don't dare make a mistake. Elizabeth's and Jenny's lives may rest on my smallest action. And they have that damned dog.*

He and Brandy plodded through the deepening snow, following the ever fainter trail, until he caught a glimpse of smoke hanging low in the sky some distance ahead, along the ridge. He remembered the trapper's line shack where he and Shane had once taken refuge from a storm. That was it! It had to be!

Once again he tethered Brandy where she could not make a noise and alert anyone, and took a moment to recheck his weapons. He crept toward the cabin, walking quietly as Shane had taught him to do. The snow cushioning his footfalls, he circled around behind the building, finding two horses in the fenced lean-to behind it. They were the same scrubby pair, a big bay and a smaller sorrel, that Ned and Charlie had ridden the day before. If the dog was still with them, it must be indoors. Cutting around the corral, he sneaked up the side of the shack. He paused, took his hat off, and leaned his ear against the chinking, listening for any movement inside. Certain he could hear voices, he listened a moment longer, but could not determine whose they were, much less what they might be saying.

I'm going to have one chance to get this right, and

one chance only. Innocent lives depend on what I do. I don't dare make a mistake. Please, Lord, help me. Deep inside he knew that if Elizabeth or Jenny had so much as a broken fingernail he would kill those two, and he would trust Shane to have his back.

Moving silently through the snow, he rounded the front corner of the cabin. He ducked down below the level of the window, paused, and decided to risk a peek. For a split second he raised his head, then dropped down again, his heart pounding. Inside, Ned sat at the crude table, his rifle over his lap, with Elizabeth off to the side, next to the small wood stove, stirring something in a deep frying pan. Presumably Jenny and Charlie were out of his line of vision, probably against the near cabin wall. He duck-walked under the window until he came to the log stoop. He had hoped no one had drawn the frayed latch string in; he breathed a sigh of relief upon seeing it dangling down the front of the door. Now he only had to make sure he maintained the advantage of surprise. Since a long gun would be useless in such close quarters, he leaned his rifle securely against the door frame, took out his Navy Colt, said a prayer, and grabbed the latch string.

Standing in front of the little stove, Elizabeth stirred the bacon and beans Ned had put together. Her announcement that she did not know how to cook had garnered a few choice curses she had never heard before. Ned's fury would have been amusing were the situation less serious. *Just a few months ago these rough men would have frightened me half out of my wits, but Jenny has been so brave through all of this. How can I do any less? By now someone has to have missed us and told Paul. If he's all right, that is. He has*

243

to be. He's our only hope. Otherwise, Lord knows what this pair will do. She looked back at Charlie on the bed, his truncated arm wrapped and propped over his head to minimize bleeding and pain. At the moment, he slept under a heavy dose of laudanum. As her gaze swung back past the window she saw a head duck down quickly. That blond hair could belong to only one person. Paul was here! He had come for them!

She covered her gasp of surprise with a pretend sneeze. "I beg your pardon," she murmured, digging into her pocket for a handkerchief. She delicately blotted her nose, then decided to distract Ned by gathering the hem of her skirt around the handkerchief for a hot pad. It worked. She felt his eyes on her calf even though she wore utilitarian riding boots laced nearly to her knees. Vigorously she stirred the beans.

In her peripheral vision she saw the latch string wiggle. Then the door flew open, banging back against the wall with a report like a gunshot.

"Hands in the air, Ned. You're both under arrest!" he shouted. An oath on his lips, Ned started to his feet. Elizabeth saw horror paint itself across Paul's features and read the situation right. He could not risk a shot in the confines of the cabin. Jenny, at Charlie's bedside, sat directly in his line of fire. Overpenetration, or God forbid, a clean miss, could doom her.

Instead of taking time to think, Elizabeth reacted. She grabbed up the frying pan and swung it at the side of Ned's face. Some of the boiling contents splattered in an arc across Paul's chest before the weight of the cast iron pan collided solidly with Ned's cheekbone. Ned let out a scream as the scalding liquid coated his face and splashed into his eyes. Nevertheless he rose all the way and tried to aim the rifle from his hip. All the training that had made Paul the high school boxing champion came to the forefront. He stepped forward and drove a vicious left hook to the point of Ned's jaw. The blow, with all Paul's weight behind it, dropped his adversary to the floor. He kicked the rifle out of Ned's reach, and for a moment everyone froze but Ned, who writhed on the packed dirt, trying to wipe the fiery, greasy mess from his face. Paul knelt, planted his knee in the small of Ned's back and handcuffed him. The noise woke Charlie, but the laudanum had rendered him so woozy that Jenny's hand in the middle of his chest pinned him neatly to the bed.

"I'm burning! My face! I'm on fire!" Ned sobbed, trying to shake off Paul's blow.

"I've just the thing for that," Paul grated. He jerked Ned to his feet, marched him outside, and flung him face down in the snow.

Elizabeth glanced from Jenny to the mess on the floor, kicked the frying pan aside, and followed Paul out the door, pulling it closed behind her.

"You came for us," she said rhetorically.

He looked back at her and smiled, and the sun rose in her heart. "Of course I did. Angus missed the two of you, called Maddie, and when she didn't know where you had gone, he called me. I found Jasper in the middle of Main Street, backtracked him, and the sign in the alley told me everything I needed to know."

"I can't thank you enough."

"You're all right, then?" He came to her and took her hands.

"Everyone except Charlie. Jenny had to amputate his hand." Then she caught sight of what appeared to be a burn mark along the left side of his jaw. She dropped a hand and reached toward his face. "Oh, Paul! I'm afraid I hit you when I threw that pan."

"What? Oh, this?" He lifted a gloved hand to touch his cheek. "No. That wasn't you. That's from the gunfight yesterday. If those guys had been better shots, I'd not be here. And if you hadn't done what you did just now I could have been in serious trouble. You're brave, Elizabeth. You're as brave as you are beautiful, and your instincts are right on the money. You pulled my chestnuts out of the fire, and I'm grateful."

Beautiful? He called me beautiful? But he's still wound up from the fight. He'll change his mind when he calms down.

"It was the only thing I could think of to do," she demurred. Then Ned claimed their attention, sitting up with snow dripping from his face. She could see that some of his burns were going to blister.

"My face!' he complained. "You burned me, you…"

"Shut up, Ned," Paul interrupted roughly. "Or on second thought, go ahead. Keep talking. I'd love another excuse to shut your foul mouth for you."

"What are we under arrest for?" Ned whined.

"You must be stupider than I thought, if you have to ask. All right. One, manufacture of illegal liquor. Two, selling that illegal liquor to natives. Three, attempted capital murder of a police officer. Four, kidnapping, two counts. And if that isn't enough, I'm sure I can come up with a few more offenses that ought to keep you and Charlie behind bars for the rest of your lives. Now get up. We need to get out of here if I'm to get us on the train for River Bend this afternoon."

Not half an hour later they were on their way back toward town, a bandage-faced Ned supporting Charlie on the sorrel gelding and Elizabeth riding behind Jenny on the larger bay, the quieter and better of the Camerons' horses. Now that the crisis had resolved, Elizabeth's mood turned into a curious combination of elated and terrified. Her attention fixed itself involuntarily on Paul, riding ahead of them, erect on his big Irish thoroughbred, as glamorous and elegant as any hero from her penny dreadfuls. On second thought, he was much better than any protagonist in what her father had termed her "trashy fiction." He was real and, right now, much larger than life.

When they dropped out of the woods and picked up the wagon path that led past the church, Paul dug out his pocket watch, consulted it, and shook his head.

"We've missed the train," he said with a sigh.

"So what does that mean?" Jenny asked.

"We have to find somewhere to lock these two up for the night. I can't ride through to River Bend with them in this weather, especially with Charlie the way he is."

"I guess we could always put Charlie in the ward upstairs in the clinic," she said after a thoughtful pause.

"And Ned? I need to watch both of them at once. Could I maybe shackle him to a bed, or something like that?"

"The beds are iron, and they're really heavy, I'm sure that would work, as long as it's all right with Angus. The clinic belongs to him. I'm just an associate in his practice."

"I'll clear it with him. Otherwise I'm going to have to take both of these guys and lock them in a closet at

Mrs. Hammill's. We really need to get a jail built here in Elk Gap. It's getting big enough to need one."

"I really need to watch Charlie the rest of the night. If you need to take Ned and lock him up at Mrs. Hammill's, I think Charlie would be all right with us. I'll keep him so full of laudanum he won't know if he's afoot or on horseback."

Paul shook his head. "They're my prisoners. I'm responsible. I have to keep them both where I can watch them until tomorrow afternoon. I'll ask Angus if it's okay to keep them in the clinic."

Jenny nodded, falling silent. Then she turned to Elizabeth. "Well, Bet, it looks like you're stuck at the clinic with me, unless we can figure out what happened to my buggy. If it's around, you can drive home and come back in the morning."

"I'm fine. I'll wait with you."

"Thanks. This is one of the times when three heads are definitely better than two."

They stopped in the alleyway behind the clinic. Paul handcuffed Ned before letting him dismount, then helped Charlie down. Elizabeth and Jenny hazed the horses into the little barn on the far side of the alley and closed the door on them before joining the odd party in Madame DuBois's kitchen.

When Angus came through from the office, his reaction was one of surprise.

"What's going on here?" he asked.

"Long story, Angus," Paul responded. "Yesterday I caught Ned and Charlie with a still, up on the ridge east of North Village. They shot at me, and I hit Charlie. Ned kidnapped Jenny and Elizabeth to treat him. That's why they didn't show up this morning. But now I have two men in custody, one of whom just had surgery, and I need a place to keep them until I can get us on the train tomorrow. Jenny suggested perhaps I could use the ward upstairs, since they both need medical attention."

Angus looked intently at both men, who were decidedly the worse for wear. "It looks like a much longer story than that," he observed.

"Well, yes. But for now, we need to get these men upstairs," Jenny put in.

Elizabeth had not been upstairs before. She followed Jenny to the left at the top of the stairs, into a six-bed ward that appeared rarely used. On the other side of the hall was a smaller room Jenny explained was used occasionally for labor and delivery, and next to it, a bathroom. To the right, through an open door, Elizabeth saw the two-room suite that obviously belonged to the housekeeper.

Paul directed Ned onto the bed at the far end of the ward and handcuffed him to the rail while Jenny settled Charlie in the bed closest to the door. Tiredly Paul pulled off his parka and hat and hung them on shaker pegs near the door. Then he claimed one of the chairs between the windows. "Now we wait," he said with a sigh.

Elizabeth found herself banished to the small room for a nap. Even though she thought she was too keyed up to sleep, she stretched out on the bed, coat and all, and immediately dozed off.

She awoke much later, warm and uncomfortable in the dark. She lay still for a moment, orienting herself and letting the events of the day flood back over her. Suddenly she sat straight up, every hair on her body erect. She smelled smoke! And, to boot, the room that had been bone cold when she lay down had now become unbearably hot. She bolted from the room and around the corner into Madame DuBois's suite, which seemed to be the source of the smoke, since the air was hazy and foul.

"Madame?" she called. "Madame?" But there was no answer. In the gloom she could make out the sitting room and the obviously unoccupied bedroom behind it. She wheeled and ran down the hallway to the ward where Jenny and Paul watched the prisoners. Sparing a glance over her shoulder, she now made out a definite orange glow coming through the doorway behind her.

"Jenny!" she said, opening the door. Her cousin stood next to Charlie's bed, while Paul, sitting on a nearby chair, came to his feet at the alarm in her voice.

"What is it, Bet?" Jenny asked.

"I smell smoke. Something's on fire."

"What?" Paul looked like her words made no sense.

"It's hot in my room and I smell smoke. It looks like there's a fire in Madame DuBois's rooms."

He opened the door, letting in a billow of smoke, and immediately closed it again. Across the room Ned tried to sit up to the limit allowed by the shackling of his hand to the bed rail.

"Fire! Let me go!" he demanded.

"Shut up, Ned. I'm getting everybody out, but you're going to be last." Ned acted as though he had more to say, but discretion won out. He shut his mouth.

"Can we make it down the stairs?" Jenny asked.

"I don't think so. It's really smoky out there. I don't want to risk it. There's a ladder out in the barn we can use. I'll go get it." The window stuck initially, but yielded to a bit of muscle. Jenny came to stand by Elizabeth to watch. Paul crawled over the windowsill, hung briefly by his hands, then dropped the rest of the way to the alley below. His height allowed him to land easily. But instead of going across the alley to the barn, he jogged down and pounded on the office window. Elizabeth heard him shouting to Angus and his housekeeper to get out. A moment later he dragged a heavy painter's ladder out of the barn and leaned it against the wall. By this time Jenny had gathered her medical bag and her hat and had wrapped her coat and Paul's bear parka around them, and now she dropped them down to him. Elizabeth looked back at the door, seeing the glow of fire around the frame.

"We haven't got long. There's fire in the hallway," she said, loud enough that below them, Paul could hear.

"The two of you come down the ladder, quick. I'll come back for Ned and Charlie," he instructed them.

"You first, Jen. You're so short you're going to need me to balance you," Elizabeth said. For once her cousin accepted her direction. She backed out of the window and Elizabeth held her wrists until her feet found the ladder. She scrambled down, into a night heavy with falling snow. Elizabeth followed her much more easily. To her surprise, she felt Paul's hands around her waist as she descended the last few rungs.

"Are you all right?" he asked.

She nodded. "I'm fine, thank you."

"Well, move out of the way. You can go into the barn with Angus and Madame. I'll get Charlie and Ned out."

Elizabeth watched him as he climbed back up the

ladder. She clenched her hands nervously; she could now see the glow of flames reflected in the room, and smoke had begun to seep upward from the window. She retreated to stand between Jenny and Angus in the barn doorway, out of the heavily falling snow. It seemed Paul had been in there forever; she found herself praying.

After a long, tense interval she saw Paul's Red Serge at the window. He took a long-legged step down onto the ladder and helped Charlie back out. He almost lifted the shorter man and walked him down, then across the alley. Charlie stumbled twice even with his good arm drawn over Paul's shoulders. Jenny took Charlie back into the stable and spread Jasper's blanket for him to lie on as Paul went back up the ladder.

Ned. Here was where the danger lay. All the way along he had seemed like the ringleader, the real desperado. It had been hard for Elizabeth not to show her fear of him. However, Paul had been trained to cope with bad characters like Ned. She simply had to trust Paul, the way she would trust Jenny to know what she was doing.

Not soon enough to soothe her anxiety, Paul descended the ladder, then he stood off to one side, pistol drawn.

"All right, Ned. Nice and slow, now," he called. Ned, hands still manacled in front of him, climbed through the window and let himself down from the sill. Once down, Paul herded him into the barn and cuffed him to a thoroughly sedated Charlie. Wisely Ned said nothing. Both men were coughing from the smoke, and Paul's temper had grown decidedly sharp.

By this time the fire had been noticed, and Will

Tillman, taking charge in Shane's absence, organized a bucket brigade from the well at the side of the clinic.

Jenny, leaving her patient handcuffed to his brother, drifted up to watch the men splashing water on the fire, which had evidently begun around the chimney. Between the water and the heavy snow, it appeared they were winning.

"Bet, the excitement is over. I'm sending you home," she said eventually.

"No. I'll stay with you. You may need help."

"Paul's here. I don't know where we're going, but..." Her sentence broke off as Paul came up to her.

"I think we can take them back to Mrs. Hammill's and put them in my room."

"I hope she won't fuss about a woman upstairs. I need to watch Charlie tonight."

"I can do that, for you, lass," Angus volunteered. "Just let me have your bag. I don't know how much of the clinic will be left when this is over."

"That sounds marvelous, Angus, if you don't mind. It's been a long day. I'm exhausted, and I need to get this one home." She indicated Elizabeth.

"I told you I'm all right," Elizabeth grumbled.

Jenny fixed her with a sharp look. "You are going home. Now." Elizabeth wanted to protest, but the baby weighed heavily inside her, and for the last hour she had been running on nerves, nap notwithstanding.

Willing hands helped harness Jasper, and as they made ready to leave, Paul gave her a hand up into the buggy.

"Elizabeth, I wanted to thank you for today. You have a level head. A good part of the credit for the way today turned out is due to you."

"I only did what I had to," she responded, looking down demurely.

"I appreciate it." He held her hand a fraction longer than necessary, letting it go slowly. Then he turned to go back into the barn. Even tired, disheveled, and dirty, he still outstripped any of the fictional heroes in any book she had ever read.

Chapter 15

May 11, 1822

It is said that time heals all wounds. We are making ready to go to Sand Island again, and I am now determined that time shall heal me. True, I spent most of the winter brooding and miserable, and I am much thinner than I was last year. The last of my puppy fat is gone, and when I look in my glass it is a woman's form I see. Though I have never worn it and I probably never will, I still look at my locket and the dear miniature portrait each day, and I still pray for George. However, I realize that if I spend much more time in my self-imposed mourning I shall turn into a bitter old spinster. Every day I see the happiness Mother takes from her marriage and her family, and I above all else want similar happiness for myself. I will soon be of an age to choose, and I do not want to make an impulsive choice. In ways, George may have been a hasty decision I would have regretted later. This time I shall let caution and a cool head rule my woman's heart, and when the time comes to select the man with whom I will spend the rest of my life, I vow I will choose wisely. Until then, I will dance, flirt, be merry when the occasion presents itself, and enjoy the last of my carefree days.

~*~

June 2, 1822.
Once, it seems a century ago, I thought I had met

the man I would marry. He was my first love and will ever have a place in my heart. But two weeks ago I renewed an acquaintance with another. His name is Robert Walker Talbot. I knew Robert in childhood, since he is the eldest son of my parents' friends who own a nearby plantation called Archer's Walk. However, I had not seen him in several years; he has been away at school in England. We met again recently in a rather dramatic way. Pansy and I had driven down to the free blacks' settlement to purchase herbs from Mama Lou, something we do every month or so. I had dreaded that errand the first time after the dramatic visit last fall, but Mama Lou proved to be a woman of discretion. Of course no words would dare pass between us, but even her eyes gave away nothing. I duly paid her the grand sum of thirty-five cents for her medicinals, and then we started back. Along the road a colony of wasps had evidently taken up residence beneath a root or a stone, and my horse disturbed them. Suddenly we were engulfed in a crowd of the angry, stinging demon creatures, and I lost control of my horse. Both it and I panicked at the same time, and suddenly it was galloping blindly, mad with pain. I managed to dislodge the wasps from my clothing and my face, only to find that I had dropped one of the reins. The buggy bounced and twisted beneath us. I shouted to Pansy to hold on, and prayed that the horse would not step on the flapping, loose rein and fall. I remember shouting for help and wondering where it could possibly come from. Then, as the horse left the road and bolted into an unfenced pasture, I stopped screaming and simply prayed, and that was when our salvation came.

At first I only saw the figure of a man on a gray horse overtake us. From the way his mount was running, it was a thoroughbred racehorse. He passed us with offhanded ease, leaned from his saddle, and gathered up my reins, turning my panicked animal in a large and ever-slowing circle until it stood exhausted, lathered, and trembling as though Armageddon had arrived. Then he trotted around to my side of the buggy, rose in his stirrups, doffed his hat, and bowed formally to me.

"Robert Talbot, ma'am. Pleased to be of service to you."

"Thank you so much, Mr. Talbot. I do believe you have saved my life. My horse seemed to have found a wasp nest."

"I don't believe I've had the pleasure of meeting you before. You are?"

His question amused me to no end. Had I changed all that much? "You don't recognize me. Mr. Talbot? I'm Eliza Morgan."

His face split into a lovely laugh. "Miss Eliza, all grown up I see! So much has happened behind my back while I was away in England. I shall have to find an excuse to visit Brookhaven."

He did find an excuse. Immediately. He insisted on escorting me home and telling Mother and Father what had transpired. Of course I was packed off to have my stings properly poulticed, and I only found out later, from Pansy, that he and Father had an apparently satisfying chat, the upshot of which was that he garnered a dinner invitation for the following Sunday. It proved a most edifying visit, the first of many.

~*~

September 19, 1822

Though our summer at Sand Island passed quickly, as all pleasant interludes do, I was more than ready to return to Brookhaven. Of course I missed Pansy, but more than that I yearned for Mr. Talbot's visits. He and I kept up correspondence through the summer, and to my great delight, he rode his gray thoroughbred down our lane not four hours after we arrived home.

Mr. Talbot is quiet and kind yet witty and intelligent, a perfect gentleman, and while my heart will never take wing at the sound of his voice, I realize that is not due to any lack within him, but simply because I have outgrown girlhood.

He is a diametric opposite to George. He is slender and not tall, only just over my own height. He is fair and blond, with hazel eyes, while George, for all that his eyes were blue, was dramatically dark. He is reading for the law in order to join his father and uncle in their practice, and will sit for the bar exam next year. He strikes me as serious and dependable, a complete gentleman upon whom a lady could rely for the rest of her life. He is also well mannered and proper, but in an unassuming way. I know I could count on him to treat me well.

When I think of him as the father of my children and my partner for life, it is a comfortable idea. I have decided, with the concurrence of my parents, to entertain his suit, and we will simply see where the Good Lord leads us. Of course he comes of a good family, so Mother and Father strongly approve of him, but they approved of George, too. They are good enough to allow all their children their heads in the matter of marriage, although they do reserve the right of veto.

Even Nanny Pearl reminded me that life goes on, and she told me over a year ago that I would find another beau. She has even granted her somewhat grudging approval of Mr. Talbot. I say grudging because I have now come to see she would begrudge anyone who bade fair to take away one of her "chilluns," that is to say, one of us, since she never jumped the broom with a man to have children of her own. But I know that in the deepest recesses of her heart she is happy for me.

Elizabeth awoke. Then, remembering it was Saturday, she snuggled down under her covers again. She had been tired ever since the night of the fire, and the opportunity to sleep in felt marvelous. However, a dull pressure in her lower abdomen could not be denied. She sat up, reaching for the dressing gown she had left across the foot board of her bed. But when she thrust her feet into her slippers and stood up, cold horror roared through her.

"Jenny!" she screamed.

It took her cousin only moments to burst through the door, half-dressed, her hair combed but loose and her robe thrown haphazardly over her slip. "What is it, Bet?" she asked.

Wordlessly Elizabeth pointed to the red stain where she had sat on the edge of the mattress. "I'm bleeding!" she breathed, her voice robbed by sheer terror.

"All right. Lie back down and let me look." Jenny went from Cousin Jen to Doctor Weston in a fraction of a second.

"Am I…am I losing it?"

"I can't tell yet," Jenny responded, helping her

back into the bed. As she did, Elizabeth saw there were other stains and spots on the sheet.

Shane paused outside the door. "Do you need help, Jenny?" he asked, his voice calm as always.

"For now, towels," she responded. He disappeared while Jenny turned Elizabeth's gown back and examined her quickly.

"What is it?"

"I can't tell yet. You're bleeding vaginally, though. Sometimes that's significant and sometimes it isn't. Are you cramping at all?"

"No. It just feels…heavy…down there. Is that good or bad?"

"At this point, neither. I need to get my bag so I can listen for a heartbeat. That'll tell me more."

"Oh, Jenny…am I…could it…"

Jenny laid a comforting hand on Elizabeth's shoulder. "Just lie back and be calm now, Bet. Like I said, it could be nothing. Let's not worry unless it's time to worry, all right?" When Shane returned with the requested towels, Jenny spread a double thickness under Elizabeth's hips and tucked a third towel between her legs. "Now I'm going for my bag. Just lie still and take deep breaths, and I'll be right back."

She listened until the pounding of her heart drowned out her cousin's retreating steps, leaving her in the loneliest void she had ever known.

Elizabeth had not considered the baby developing within her as anything other than the center of her shame and an insurmountable obstacle to her life. Now she thought of it for the first time as a person, a child with hands that would grasp hers in love and a face that would smile in response to her. She knew deep down that her body could betray her again, ejecting the life it had initially betrayed her by conceiving. When she felt for its consciousness she encountered only dark emptiness. Lying in the terrifying solitude of her room, she felt tears running backward into her hair. Then a ripping pain, magnitudes worse than she had ever imagined pain could be, rent her body and doubled her up. She bit her tongue against the cry that built up in her throat.

Though Jenny had only gone down the hall to her bedroom, it felt like an eternity before she returned. When she came back, Elizabeth saw why it had taken her some time and felt even more deeply chilled. She had dressed quickly in working clothes, sleeves rolled up, apron on, and her hair tied back in a messy knot. Her stethoscope hung about her neck.

"Okay, Bet. Let's see what's going on." Her voice projected quiet confidence. By now Elizabeth's cramp had abated, but her lower belly burned with grinding pain.

"I'm going to lose the baby. While you were gone I had a cramp, and I'm still hurting," Elizabeth said, her voice flat.

Jenny leaned over her and stroked her hair. "I won't mince words with you, Bet. You've read my texts, and you know what's going on. I think you are going to lose it. That's a lot of blood for anything but real labor. And you said you're in pain?" Elizabeth nodded tightly, not trusting her voice. "All right. Let me examine you, and let me listen."

She tried to contain her fear as her cousin's hands moved knowledgeably over her belly. For a very long time she pressed her stethoscope to Elizabeth's abdomen, her face unreadable. Elizabeth felt the pain mounting again. Evidently Jenny did too, because her hand rested on the small, tense mound of her belly just where the pain had set in.

"That's another contraction," she said matter-of-factly in response to her cousin's whimper. "I'm not hearing a fetal heartbeat anymore, either."

"What does that mean? Is my baby… Is it dead?"

Jenny pulled the covers back into place, took off her stethoscope, and laid it over her medical bag. "I'm going to be frank with you, Bet. I think it is. Usually when these things happen, the fetus is defective and unable to survive on its own. It's nothing you've done, no fault of yours. It's like a lightning strike—it just happens. You'll be able to have other children, just not this one."

In spite of herself, Elizabeth felt the tears come, partly with the new wave of agony and partly in pity for the child that would never know life or love or joy, never know her as its mother. And she also knew in that instant that, in spite of the circumstances of its conception, she wanted that child, wanted to keep it, rear it, and love it. Now all that was gone, swept away as surely as the wind that had swept away her former life.

The pain had not subsided when another contraction slammed into her, submerging her in agony. This time she heard her own voice crying out. Somewhere down the long, dark corridor of pain she also heard Jenny ask Shane to bring Doctor MacBride.

In the next minutes she felt Jenny bathing her face and stroking her hair. "Don't worry, Bet. This will all be over soon. You'll be all right," she said gently.

"The baby?" She looked up into her cousin's face, blurred by her tears. Jenny shook her head slowly.

"I'm sorry, Bet. It's way too early for it to survive. I suspect some profound birth defect. Just let it happen, Bet. Let it be. You'll come out of this just fine. We'll take care of you, all right? Now I'm going to touch you. I just want to see how far along you are, whether or not it's time for you to bear down with your pains." Jenny's calm voice gave her a lifeline in a tempest.

Later she would remember that day as one blaze of nearly unbearable agony. Eventually Angus arrived, and not long afterward, Jenny urged her to push with her contractions. The pain became a living thing that flowed and ebbed and flowed again, leaving her helpless to do anything but yield herself to it. Then with the agony came a terrible pressure that threatened to cleave her in two. She only half heard Jenny encouraging her, telling her one more push, only one more. She did her best to comply, bearing down through the burning between her legs.

Suddenly it was over. The pressure abated and the pain all but stopped. Exhausted, she let herself go limp. She felt them touching her, tending her, heard their murmuring voices, as she concentrated on her next breath.

Jenny's gentle hands bathed her face, then cleaned her body. Refreshed, she fought herself back to the present.

"Jen? What happened?" she breathed. Her cousin laid a comforting hand on her shoulder.

"It couldn't have lived, Bet. It was badly deformed. I'll explain it later, after you've had a chance to rest. Just know that you didn't cause it and it's nothing hereditary. It's just one of those bad things that happen sometimes. Now I'm going to give you something that will make you sleep." Jenny offered her two pills and a glass of water. She swallowed obediently, then sank back against her pillow Not long afterward, a black vortex swallowed her consciousness.

In the long, blank days that followed, she reacquainted herself with Eliza Morgan's diaries, particularly how she had dealt with her profound loss. Elizabeth took heart at the healing in her great-grandmother's life, but her own situation was different. If there were healing out there for her, she could not imagine how or where it would come.

Chapter 16

A fortnight after what Jenny referred to as her "sudden illness" Elizabeth dressed for church. When she decided to put her corset on, she realized it no longer fit. It was slack even when she hitched the laces around her bedpost and drew them in as far as they would go. Resigned, she worked it off and, in chemise and drawers, studied her body in the tall mirror. While her breasts still held their firm fullness, she now had a small waist and a flat belly. Her hips and derriere had lost some of their former roundness, as had her thighs and her upper arms. For the first time in her life she could see dancer's lines in her height and carriage, and definition in her cheeks.

Deciding she could not stand there all day staring at herself, she finished with her underthings and rummaged through her armoire. Then a gentle knock came at her door.

"Bet? Are you dressed? Breakfast will be ready in a few minutes," Jenny called.

"I'm just deciding what to wear. Nothing fits anymore. My corset is even too loose." Jenny's amused laugh surprised her. Then the doorknob turned and her cousin let herself in.

"I'm not surprised, Bet. You've lost a lot of weight. When you get back to the clinic we'll have to weigh you and see."

"That's no help for today."

"Why don't you just wear working clothes? If your skirt doesn't button right, I have one I think you could borrow. It's almost to the floor on me, so it ought to be just about the right length for you."

"Me? Wear your clothes? You have to be joking."

"Not at all. You're within a hair of too thin now."

"Lord! I never thought I'd hear those words as long as I lived!" she exclaimed.

"I smell more of Aunt Rose's nonsense. Find a shirtwaist. I'll go get the skirt." Jenny ducked out. Elizabeth assessed her armoire again and found a lavender silk blouse she had never worn since it had been intended for her to come out of mourning. It had a fashionably high collar with matching lace trim and a softly draped self tie. She had just finished working up the bow when Jenny came back with a black serge skirt over her arm.

"Here. Put this on. It has three sets of buttons. I always wore it on the smallest one, so if you're still a little bigger than I am it should fit you somewhere."

"I should imagine my bare skeleton would be much bigger than you are," Elizabeth said dryly. She dropped the skirt over her head, and to her surprise the middle buttons did up nicely. As she adjusted her blouse, she caught sight of her great-grandmother's wedding ring sitting crookedly on her finger. She held up her hand. "Even this is too big for me now."

"You could always switch it to your other hand. That's proper now, you know."

"No, not until…"

"You're not in the South anymore, Elizabeth," Jenny reminded her ungently. Wordlessly she complied, switching the ring to her right hand and mentally defying Arlington and everybody in it.

"But speaking of the South, I guess I could go back now, couldn't I?"

To her surprise, Jenny crossed the room to sit on the unmade bed and patted the rumpled spread. Elizabeth took the indicated place next to her. "I wanted to talk to you about that. I wasn't going to do it just now, but since you brought it up, yes. You could be in Arlington in time for all the Christmas parties. And if you're considering going home, I'd advise you to do it very soon. That will take care of any rumors that you had to leave for a compromising reason."

"I don't know. I need to give it some thought. I really love what I've been doing with your clinic, and frankly I'm in no hurry to return home to Mother, but I am a guest in your house, after all, and you know the old saying about guests and fish."

Jenny's laugh rippled through the quiet of the room. "You're welcome to live here as long as you like. You're no trouble, you're no intrusion on our privacy, and I like having you working with Angus and me. He's even said he appreciates how you've kept our supplies and patient records in order."

"Well, that's food for thought, isn't it?"

"Yes. It's never wise to make these decisions too quickly. Mull it over for a while. Now let's go to breakfast."

When they went outside for the ride to church, winter had definitely arrived. Their breath clouded about their faces, and even in her seal coat Elizabeth felt the chill in the still air. Low stratus clouds lay in oily rolls across the sky, their dark gray bellies heavy with snow. She felt thankful for Shane's aiding hand into the buggy; she was weaker than she had thought. She hunkered down next to Jenny as her cousin shook the hackney's reins and they started down the lane.

Very soon they arrived at the church. She noticed a blanketed Brandy already striking a bored pose at one of the hitching posts, right hind hoof rested. Shane hitched Midnight next to her and flipped an old three-point Hudson's Bay blanket over him, then came to tether Jasper. He gave Elizabeth a hand down and waited politely while Jenny slid across the seat to allow him the same privilege. He picked Jenny up and swung her down with a laugh that went to the center of Elizabeth's being and brought with it an arctic cold. *Not for me,* she thought for the thousandth time. *Never for me.*

Once inside the church, she left her seal coat with one of the greeters assigned to take people's wraps. The sanctuary felt warm enough, although she could have stood a shawl. Jenny, too, left her sables with Shane's white wolf parka.

Paul already sat in the pew when they came in. She paused to let Jenny and Shane precede her. Paul looked her way and she gave him a proper nod.

"Mrs. Morgan," he acknowledged.

"Sergeant," she responded, feeling his eyes on her waistline.

During the service, his eyes were not the only ones she felt on the waistband of her skirt. But she was not a Southern debutante for nothing. She pretended no one and yet everyone watched her. Each time she stood up, she held her stomach in.

Long before her arrival in Elk Gap, Jenny and

Shane had begun inviting Paul to Sunday dinner, a custom at times difficult for Elizabeth. This Sunday would be no different. She sat beside Jenny, maintaining an aloof dignity suitable for her position, while Shane and Paul rode off for a quick round of the town. After they had parted ways on Main Street, Elizabeth broke her self-imposed silence.

"Jen, I've given this a lot of thought. You know my family will be at Parkfield for New Year's Eve."

"They've done that since I can remember."

"Yes. Well, I thought I'd go meet them."

"Are you going home, then?"

"I still don't know," she demurred. "I only want to go and prove to them—mostly to Mother—that I'm not...compromised. Any longer."

"Mmhmm. I understand."

"Then I will make up my mind whether I will accompany them back to Arlington. I miss Papa and Clara, and even Robbie, for all that."

"Clara is a charming child, and Robbie is a big, bumbling puppy. He's what I would imagine your father was at his age."

"He's a great deal like Papa," Elizabeth concurred. "However, I will have to confess, probably to my discredit, that I don't miss Mother all that much."

A wry smile quirked Jenny's lips. "Why, Bet, I can't fathom that at all."

In spite of herself, Elizabeth gave a small laugh. "But I'll miss Elk Gap, too. You and Shane have been marvelous to me, and I've loved every minute I spent in the clinic. I'm on the horns of a dilemma."

"My advice would be to follow your instincts. Go home, clear your reputation, and then if you want to come back here and resume your position as our nurse, we'll welcome you with open arms."

"I won't really have time to write to Uncle John..."

"Never mind," Jenny responded quickly. "We'll telephone him. That will give Aunt Martha plenty of time to prepare for your arrival. Not that it would matter if you showed up unannounced. There's always plenty of room at Parkfield. You won't mind saying goodbye to Paul, then?"

Oh, my, Elizabeth thought. *Jenny can cut clear to the bone.* "Our relationship has been so troubled that I've given up. I'd certainly rather have maintained a friendship with him, but that was not to be, by his choice, not mine."

"Then it may be time to cut your losses, as gamblers say."

Elizabeth sighed. "Yes, I think it is. I'll spend the holidays at Parkfield, and then I promise I'll write to you and tell you my plans. You're not going home for Christmas, then?"

"This is home to me, Bet. Shane and I decided we want to spend our first Christmas together in our own house. New York will just have to survive without us this year."

"Well, then, I'll have to leave Wednesday, at the latest, to make it all the way there in time. And at that, I'm going to have to pray there will be no weather delays."

"Probably not this early in the season. It takes a lot to disrupt the train schedule." Jenny steered Jasper onto the road that led off toward their farmhouse. Inside herself, Elizabeth felt a curtain going down on a chapter in her life. It felt like the end of the fondest dream she'd ever had. Suddenly a wave of nostalgia hit her, and her eyes blurred with tears. She tried to fish a handkerchief out of her pocket without Jenny knowing, but that was about as possible, as the old adage went, as sneaking dawn past a rooster. She dabbed at her eyes as she sank deeper into the pit of hopelessness that yawned even wider than it had a month ago.

"Want to talk it out, Bet?" Jenny asked.

"I was just thinking...about..."

"About what?"

"The baby. You said you'd tell me about it."

"Oh, dear," Jenny sighed. "Well, it was a girl. The problem was that her brain didn't develop. Sometimes these babies do live a while after birth, but her case was so severe that the brain stem, the part that regulates body functions like heartbeat and so forth, was not able to do its job. She passed away *in utero,* probably two days before you went into labor."

"Could it have had anything to do with the night of the fire?"

Jenny slowly shook her head. "No. It just happens, and it's rather rare. Most doctors see one or two cases, at most, in their entire careers. It's not hereditary, and it's not apt to happen again." Elizabeth digested that for a moment, engulfed in conflict. She ought to feel elated, relieved. The source of her embarrassment and the potential for family scandal had vanished in an afternoon, almost as though a genie had waved a wand over her. But the darkness inside her had not lifted. It yawned before her, a pit even wider and deeper than it had seemed a month ago.

"Then what...what did you do with it? With her?"

"There's a little private graveyard from the first

family that owned this land, before Calvary and the big cemetery in town. It's out in the southwest corner in the middle of the woodlot. We buried her there."

"Could I see? I think if I went there, I'd know it was over. I could go back home and put everything behind me."

"We can do that. We can actually drive most of the way in the buggy, if you'd like to go there now."

"If I don't do it now I'll probably get cold feet."

"All right. And don't worry about how long you take. Shane and Paul are out angling for whatever they can find, and Shane doesn't have much of a sense of time."

Instead of waiting at the barn for Clancy to come and get Jasper, Jenny bounced down and opened the pasture gate while Elizabeth drove through. They repeated this twice more until they came to the wood lot.

Jenny took the horse as far as possible, then tethered him to a tree.

"This is as far as the buggy can go. We'll have to walk the rest of the way, but it's close."

Elizabeth stepped down from the buggy and followed Jenny along a path through the trees. Finally they reached a secluded clearing. To her surprise, the small graveyard had been fenced with hand-wrought iron, the pickets surmounted by arrow points. Jenny unlatched the gate and swung it back. They walked between a double row of grave markers to freshly turned earth at the back corner. Silently she walked past Jenny, tears blurring the scene, before coming to her knees beside the tiny new grave and reaching out to the carved wooden marker. Shane, with his artistic talent, had incised a lamb at the top of the cedar slab, and below it the words *Stillborn Infant.* A rush of gratitude brought the tears again. *Bless Shane*, she thought. *Jenny is so fortunate where he's concerned.*

Then she looked down at the turned earth, so carefully shaped where a small coffin had been interred. She removed a glove and pressed her hand to the cold earth, wordlessly praying for the soul whose journey had never begun. When she finally said goodbye, it was to more than her daughter who would never know life. It was to Elk Gap, to Jenny and Shane, to Paul, and to all her hope.

Chapter 17

In a lightly falling snow, the taxicab pulled up under the *porte cochère* at Parkfield. Elizabeth paid the fare, then allowed the cabbie to give her an aiding hand out. Refusing his help with her one bag, she tiredly mounted the steps to the side door and knocked. Only half a minute or so later, the door opened. Since she expected the Westons' butler, it surprised her to see her Aunt Eleanor instead. With all her senses Elizabeth took in the luxurious ambiance of the Weston family home, exemplified by the heavy Wilton carpet on the floor, the hand-carved furniture, the crystal chandelier that hung in an otherwise utilitarian side entryway, and the ever-present perfume of the lemon oil religiously rubbed into the elaborate walnut wainscoting every month.

"Elizabeth, darling! Do come in!" Eleanor gushed. Seal coat and all, Elizabeth walked into a quintessential Brisbane hug.

"Hello, Aunt Eleanor. It's good to see you again. How have you been?" She dropped back to shed her coat and unpin her hat. Eleanor took them from her and hung them in the guest closet.

"Oh, I've been rubbing along as usual," Eleanor replied, her voice muffled by the rack of coats.

"You've told me that many times before." Elizabeth laughed.

Eleanor shut the closet door and turned around. "Oh, my! I turn my back on a girl and suddenly she becomes a woman! You're shed the last of your baby fat, I see. You look wonderful, my dear. John will absolutely *have* to ask you to be the Snow Queen at the New Year's ball."

After a lifetime she was accustomed to her aunt's gushiness. "Of course that'll be up to Uncle John," she responded.

"I'll simply need to put a bug in his ear, then. Come on in, dear. You have to be tired after such a long train ride. We can go into the front parlor and I'll send for tea. How does that sound? Or would you rather be shown to your room and have a rest before dinner?"

"Tea would be wonderful. Then maybe a rest." She let Eleanor lead her out to the informal front parlor where the Weston family members took their leisure. A coal fire rippled in the marble-faced fireplace, shedding gentle light into the snow-dimmed room. As Elizabeth sat down on one end of the sofa, Martha Weston materialized through the door that led to the luxurious front foyer.

"There you are, Elizabeth! How nice to see you again."

"Hello, Aunt Martha." Though Martha was part of the Weston clan and not really a blood relative, Elizabeth had grown up with the typically Southern custom of addressing all her parents' in-laws as aunt or uncle. They, too, traded an obligatory hug.

"Come and join us for tea, Martha?" Eleanor offered.

"I think I will. Dinner preparations are made, and I've a moment to relax." She claimed a chair next to the sofa.

"Doesn't she look wonderful, Mart?" Eleanor asked as she picked up the small bell to call the maid.

"Quite," Martha agreed. "You do look much more mature now, Elizabeth."

"Thank you, Aunt Martha." She realized just how much attention her slim waist had garnered. No doubt if the Westons did not have direct knowledge of the circumstances that led to her banishment to Canada, they had guessed.

Martha called for the maid to bring tea, and then Eleanor picked up the thread of their conversation again. "Don't you think she'd make a wonderful Snow Queen?" she asked.

"I don't see why not. That's John's choice, though. He's hosting the party."

"Couldn't we influence him a little bit? Put a bug in his ear, so to speak?"

A small smile tugged at Martha's serious features. "I don't see why not," she repeated.

"By the way, have my parents arrived yet?" Elizabeth asked.

"Not yet. They should be here on the twenty-seventh. You'll be with us for Christmas, and we'll have a little respite before we have to face my redoubtable elder sister," Eleanor responded.

"I've had a while to think. When I go home I'm not going to let Mother buffalo me any longer."

"Hear, hear!" Eleanor clapped her hands in delight.

"I didn't tell her I was coming here for Christmas."

"Oh, my," Martha sighed. "That will be a shock, won't it?"

"No worse a shock than when I simply showed up

unannounced at Jenny's door. I thought Mother had written, and I was mortified." Her tone was dour.

"Tit for tat. Rose has it coming," Eleanor sniffed.

Though she thoroughly loved Parkfield, and her aunts could not have been more cordial, this time Elizabeth felt strangely out of place in John Weston's sumptuous mansion. Instead she imagined herself back in Jenny's parlor, sitting on the sofa with her feet pulled up, drinking tea with her cousin and laughing over the foibles of the citizens of Elk Gap. *I know that in spite of what Jen said I couldn't stay there. I imposed on their hospitality long enough, and anyway, she was right. If I want to silence wagging tongues I had to come back and show everyone I wasn't compromised. Had things worked out differently with Paul... But they didn't, and that's that.* She sighed, accepting the cup that Martha handed her. This was a situation to which there was no perfect solution, only the acceptance of the least of evils.

After half a dozen shopping trips with Aunt Eleanor, Christmas came and went quietly. Elizabeth tried not to think of the day her family would arrive, and yet some twisted part of her wanted to see her mother's face at the sight of her slender waist, crammed with a vengeance into the smallest corset she could manage. She stopped on the center landing of the grand staircase, simply considering her circumstances, and as she went deep into thought, a knock came at the front door. Since she was closest, she came down to answer the summons. When she opened the double door, her heart almost stopped at the sight of Jenny, Shane, and Richard on the front porch.

"Jen!" she screeched, launching herself into her

cousin's waiting embrace. "Come in! But I thought you were staying in Elk Gap this year."

"It's a woman's privilege to change her mind," Shane said wryly, gesturing toward Jenny. She cut her eyes at him, then pointedly waited for him to help her with her coat. However, the butler interposed himself and took their wraps.

"I wanted to be here for the New Year's Ball. Father hasn't said anything about who he plans to ask to be the Snow Queen, has he?" Jenny asked, following Elizabeth back to the small parlor. She and Shane claimed the sofa, and Elizabeth and Richard took the chairs that flanked it. "So where are the aunties?" she continued.

"Upstairs, I think. They're going to be surprised to see you."

"Aunt Martha knows. She also knows how to keep a secret."

"Jen, I ought to throttle you."

"I didn't want it to filter down to Aunt Rose. The only way to do that is not to tell anyone. Except Aunt Martha, of course, since she had to make all the room arrangements."

"I'll bet that's why she has me in with Aunt Eleanor. I don't mind that a bit, though. She's good company, even though she's a bit of a butterfly." Jenny giggled. Their scatterbrained aunt had been the family character for as long as Elizabeth could remember.

"No one could ever accuse her of being a Weston, could they?"

Eleanor chose that moment to show up, resplendent in a loose cloud of coral and teal blue silk set off by a long string of pearls, the entire look culminating in henna-red hair. Shane's eyebrows went up with barely concealed surprise.

"Jenny!" she exclaimed. Jenny rose to meet her hug. Respectfully Shane stood up a moment later.

"Aunt Eleanor. You look ravishing this afternoon."

"Thank you, dear. And Shane. How nice to see you again."

"Ma'am," he murmured, obviously a little stunned by the haute couture that had not yet filtered down to Elk Gap. And before they sat down, John and Martha, attracted by the voices in the front parlor, made their way in. Another round of greetings followed, and in spite of herself Elizabeth felt the familiar old excitement welling up inside her. Perhaps this would not be such a harrowing holiday after all.

That night she dressed for dinner, taking extra pains with her hair. She brushed out the luxuriant walnut length: heavy, satiny, and Brisbane wavy. She twisted it up, then pinned a carefully random collection of curls down the back. Pulling a few tresses out at the sides, she used a curling iron to create appealing spirals. Her toilette complete, she turned before her mirror to admire the new frock she and Eleanor had picked out. Garnet suited her well, as did the tiny fitted waist and the overlay of Alençon lace around the neckline. As she had done a hundred times, she waited on the gallery above the grand staircase for Jenny, who emerged from her room only a moment or two later, wearing a chic navy outfit Elizabeth had not seen before.

"I see you and Aunt Eleanor have gone shopping," Jenny observed. "Quite becoming."

"Thank you. Your outfit is new too, isn't it?"

"No. I've actually had it a while. I just haven't

worn it lately. Shall we?" Jenny gestured to the stairs. Together they made their way to the small family dining room, where John, Richard, Martha, and Shane awaited them. Naturally Eleanor breezed in last. John seated his sister, and dinner was under way.

Expectedly Jenny and John talked shop for a while, then coaxed Shane into reciting one of his many adventures. All along, Eleanor and Martha had been trading pointed looks that Elizabeth was certain she understood.

"John, have you made up your mind about this year's Snow Queen?" Martha asked in her usual dispassionate way.

"Not really. Laura Weston was Queen last year, and her sister Marie hasn't come out yet, so there really aren't good candidates in the family. But there's no rule that the Queen has to be a Weston."

"How about Elizabeth?"

John's eyebrows went up. "That would put a knot in a shirttail or two, wouldn't it?" Elizabeth felt her cheeks flush.

"That's the best idea I've heard in months!" Jenny exclaimed. "I know there must be campaigns from some ambitious mothers, but I'd love to see Aunt Rose's face if you made that announcement."

"I would too," Richard agreed.

"It seems I'm in a corner, then, doesn't it? But you haven't weighed in yet, Ellie."

"Of course I'd love to see Elizabeth lead the ball. In case you haven't taken a good look at her lately, she's turned into a real beauty."

"Brisbanes do run to lovely women, don't they, Shane?" Enthusiastically Shane nodded, looking fondly at Jenny.

Then John's eyes slid to Elizabeth. "Would you accept if you were asked?" he inquired.

A flash of her old diffidence made her look down at her plate. But then determination set in. The new, confident Elizabeth raised her head and looked her uncle in the eye. "Of course I'd accept, Uncle John. It's quite an honor. Your New Year's Ball is practically *the* social event of the season. Of course, this might set Mother off like a Roman candle. But if that's what you're after..."

"I'd love to see that," Richard put in on the tail end of Elizabeth's uncompleted thought.

"It would be most entertaining, I should think." John coolly sipped his wine.

"It takes a great deal to put my sister off her feed," Eleanor said at length. "However, that just might do it." Elizabeth smelled a plot hatching among the entire family.

"If you think you're going to shut Mother up..."

"Oh, y'all just watch me," Eleanor interrupted, her Virginia accent deepening for emphasis. "Just watch me and see. She picked on me from the day I was born. A little revenge will be quite sweet."

"She doesn't know what happened, does she?" Jenny asked. Elizabeth knew she referred to the baby and shook her head.

"I haven't written to her in several weeks, and even when I did I never mentioned that."

"Good. Let's convince her the whole thing never happened."

"You mean that she was wrong about..."

"Exactly. You were innocent of any wrongdoing,

and in a blind panic she literally threw you out of the house. And what's more, she convinced your father to write all those embarrassing letters to the Cannings."

"Oh, lovely!" Richard agreed, rubbing his hands like a pawnbroker anticipating a silver dollar. By the time dessert arrived, the final nail had been screwed into Rose's coffin.

The next afternoon the men purposely holed themselves up in the library, while Jenny, Elizabeth, and Eleanor sat in the small parlor. The fire fluttered happily in the fireplace, its warmth eliciting familiar holiday pungence from the fir swag draping the mantelpiece. Jenny adjusted reading glasses and added a stitch or two to her embroidery, while Elizabeth continued reading *A Christmas Carol* aloud.

"From the time I learned to read I used to read while everyone else did handwork," Jenny said.

"I've always been the reader too," Elizabeth replied. At that moment they heard a knock at the front door. Elizabeth started to rise, but Jenny raised a cautioning hand.

"Remember, let her say whatever she will. The more she says, the deeper she digs herself in," she warned quietly. Elizabeth subsided into her chair again. Every ear in the room strained to make out what was going on in the entrance hallway. Smiling sweetly, Eleanor put her needlepoint aside and opened the pocket door leading to the foyer.

"Rose! Tal! How was the trip, then?" Her artificially chirpy voice carried back into the parlor.

"Tiresome, as always," Rose replied, accepting her younger sister's embrace.

"Then come into the parlor and we'll have tea, and

I'm certain you'll feel very refreshed." The calm, proper tones were Martha's, as her brother's hostess. Jenny also carefully parked her needle, then put her embroidery hoop and reading glasses into her work bag, a sly, anticipatory grin on her face. A moment later Martha ushered Elizabeth's family into the parlor. Elizabeth, too, came to her feet as Clara bounced across the room for a hug.

"Bet! I saved your Christmas present! I made it myself!" she said, her voice at least twice as loud as it needed to be. The rest of the greetings flowed around her while she embraced her little sister.

"Thank you, Clara. I have a gift for you too, but it'll have to wait until later."

"Oh, but...can you at least give me one little hint?" She tilted up on her toes, making Barkley's velour hound ears flap.

"Elizabeth! What are you doing here?" Rose demanded. Elizabeth straightened up, using her height advantage over her mother and making certain everyone took in her loose afternoon dress.

"I'm here for the same reason you are: Uncle John's New Year's Ball."

"You can't mean that. Why, Elizabeth, your very presence here threatens us all with the deepest scandal! What are you thinking?" she demanded.

"Sit down, Rose. Tea will be here directly," Martha soothed.

"Scandal? What does that mean?" Clara asked, looking from her mother to her sister.

"Never mind, Clara," Jenny said, slipping her arm around Clara's shoulders. "It's grown-up business. Do you remember the pictures of Barkley that Shane drew for your birthday last June?"

Clara nodded vigorously. "They're on my bedroom wall. I look at them every day."

"Well, he's here now. He just might draw you another if you ask him politely."

"Capital idea," Martha agreed. "I'll go tell the gentlemen our guests have arrived. You can come with me, child. I'll take you to Inspector Adair, and you can ask him if he'll do another picture for you. You come with me too, Robbie, and say hello to Uncle John and Uncle Richard."

Confusion swirled around the parlor, but Rose seemed to ignore it, all her ire focused on her older daughter.

"I can't imagine why you would have the unmitigated gall to show your face here! I told you to stay in Canada until the situation was resolved. I didn't raise you to...to do as you did, nor did I raise you to have such...such execrable taste!"

"I have excellent taste, Mother. You'll find out."

"Just look at yourself! Why, it's obvious to anyone with eyes in their head..."

"What's obvious?"

"Your shameful condition! By next week the whole East Coast will be talking! You need to get on the next train back to Moose Foot or whatever that dreadful place is."

"Rose, let's not jump to conclusions," Tal began as he moved between his wife and his daughter.

"I'm not jumping to conclusions! I've heard rumors aplenty already, and I've done my best to keep the situation under wraps. And now she shows up, bold as brass, and..."

"Rose, nobody's done anything yet. So what if she's here? She's family."

"And she's selfish enough to risk besmirching the entire family. Just look at her, Tal!"

"What am I supposed to see?"

"A fallen woman!" Her words were delivered in a whisper. But the arrival of the maid with the tea cart cut her tirade short; not even Rose would continue family drama in front of a servant.

Martha came in at that moment, shepherding the men, along with Clara, who clung closely to Shane.

"Mother! Inspector Adair said he'd draw another picture of Barkley for me! What a lovely Christmas present!" Clara announced.

"How nice of you, Inspector," Rose responded, a thin smile on her lips.

The confusion settled down, to be replaced by a tension so thick it could have been cut with a butter knife. Ignoring it, Martha poured tea. When she came around to Jenny, she leaned close.

"Tea, Jen? Or only cream?" she pronounced the last sentence just above a whisper. Elizabeth giggled in spite of herself.

"Just pour it in my saucer," Jenny whispered back.

After a stiff, uncomfortable forty-five minutes over tea, everyone adjourned to their respective rooms for a rest and a chance to get ready for dinner. Elizabeth left her little sister with Shane in the family dining room, their heads bent over his sketch pad, and she marveled yet again at his ability to connect with virtually anyone. The only other person she knew with that talent was Paul. And Paul was as far away as the South Pole. She knew deep inside she would never see him again.

Once again she stuffed herself into the tiny corset and tortured her hair into a fashionable pile of curls, smoothing the upswept back with sugar water to keep it in place. Then she opened her armoire and took out the dinner dress she and Aunt Eleanor had picked out earlier, a stunning thing she considered her secret weapon. The dark burgundy crepe held mysterious, deep shadows, especially in the skirt, where an overlay of silver-embroidered silk illusion fell pleated to a handkerchief hem. The same rich fabric lay in a panel over the bustline until an inset around the waist caught it into gently pleated fullness. The inset itself set off her waist, more slender than it had ever been in her life, while the skirt lay flat against her belly and clung to the feminine flare of her hips. She carefully stepped into the dress, drawing it upward and thrusting her arms into the sleeves. The buttons would take help, so she settled in to wait for Jenny.

She had sat at her vanity table only long enough to choose her jewelry when her cousin knocked on the door and then edged in without waiting for an invitation. She wore the silver watered-silk frock Elizabeth remembered from the heady days before her wedding; that seemed at least a millennium ago.

"Ready to beard the lion in its den, Bet?" Jenny asked.

"As soon as you button me up."

"And let me give your corset a little extra tug. We want you to look every bit the fashion plate tonight." She stood still while Jenny rooted around beneath the corset cover and took a hook to the laces. Her cousin's less than gentle ministrations managed to shave perhaps another half an inch off her waist.

"I swear if you tighten that any more I won't be able to breathe," she said as Jenny tucked the corset cover back into the top of her petticoat and firmly retied the ribbon.

"Consider it a sacrifice to the great goddess of fashion. It won't last long, after all."

"No. I'll turn blue if it does."

"Wait until your mother has turned blue first. Now hold still while I button you up." She felt various small tugs and pulls while Jenny applied a button hook to the loops up the back of the dress. "Now take a look at yourself," Jenny urged, turning Elizabeth toward the cheval glass next to the vanity table.

The image the mirror reflected stunned her to the depths of her being. No longer did she see a big, lumpy, shapeless girl afraid of her own shadow. Instead, a beautiful young woman looked back, tall, regal, slender, and confident.

"So what do you think?" Jenny asked.

"I...I don't know what to think."

"A few months have changed you a lot, Bet. Let's go downstairs and show everyone just how much." Elizabeth remained a moment more, gazing into the glass.

"There's no doubt now, is there, Jen?" she asked, stroking the skirt where it lay across the plane of her belly.

In reply, Jenny slowly shook her head. "None whatsoever. Now our job is to convince Aunt Rose that she was wrong all along. Shall we go, then?"

"We may as well," Elizabeth sighed. "I really don't want to embarrass Mother, but..."

"Bet! For all the times she's laid into you in front

of others, she has it coming, in spades. Now let's go downstairs." Jenny took Elizabeth's elbow and firmly propelled her out into the hallway, where Shane waited for them. With exaggerated gallantry he offered them an arm apiece. Once again the Red Serge struck a nostalgic chord in her heart.

"What an honor, to escort the two loveliest ladies in New York," he said with a wicked smile which Jenny returned. Elizabeth took his arm, her touch properly light, and with her heart pounding, she descended the marble staircase to face what suddenly felt like doom.

The family habitually gathered in the small parlor and waited for the butler to announce dinner. She heard her mother's strident voice carrying over the conversation in the room.

"...so surprised to see Elizabeth here. No, not surprised. Shocked. Horrified and offended. Why on *earth* did she think it even remotely proper that she come?"

"I think you'll find out she has every reason to be here," Eleanor replied with a coolness that would have done credit to John Weston. The conversation ceased abruptly when Jenny entered the room, followed by Elizabeth and then Shane. Nervously Elizabeth smoothed her skirt over her hips. She watched her mother's eyes. They met hers for the merest instant, then slid down over the figure-hugging outline of the dinner dress. It took only an instant for the shock to set in. Rose drew a quick, surprised breath.

"Elizabeth..."

"Yes, Mother?"

"What on earth have you…"

"I think what your mother is trying to say is that you look ravishing, darling," her father interrupted, coming to her and planting a kiss on her cheek.

"Thank you, Papa. I'm glad you like the dress. Since I took so little with me, leaving as I did, Aunt Eleanor and I had to go shopping."

"So I see," Rose responded, needing something to say because all the eyes in the room were on her.

"Eleanor certainly helped you pick out a flattering dress," John said, his eyes alight with delicious mischief. "She does have a talent for that sort of thing."

"I have lost a few pounds, after all."

"And it certainly shows. You'll make a spectacular Snow Queen." John waited for that one to settle in.

"John, you're...you're not going to..."

John leaned down to tap the dottle from his pipe, straightening up after a properly dramatic pause. "I certainly am, Rose. After all, it's my decision. Why shouldn't I choose Elizabeth?"

"But she...she had to leave Arlington under a cloud, and if she leads that ball, all the gossip will rage again! There'll be scandal!"

"Scandal?" he echoed. Then he gestured pointedly to Elizabeth with the stem of his pipe. "I see absolutely no reason for scandal there."

"Elizabeth, you didn't have one of those horrid operations, did you?" Her voice dropped to something of a whisper.

"Aunt Rose, are you suggesting *I* did something illegal?" Jenny flared. "Because if you are, you'd best have proof."

"Well, something happened." Rose crossed her arms obstinately, but she had never faced Jenny in full spate.

"Something did happen. You jumped to a smutty-minded conclusion; that's what happened," Jenny rapped out, taking a step closer to her aunt.

"But the constant illness, and the...the...lack of..."

John stood up, pipe in hand. "Rose, let's not deal in obfuscation here." Jenny watched her father go from family patriarch to medical doctor in the space of a heartbeat. His cold, scientific approach had cooled many a hot temper. "Countless conditions besides pregnancy can cause protracted vomiting. Gastroenteritis can be quite long-lasting. Sometimes it drags on for months. And any number of complaints, including gastroenteritis, can disrupt a woman's menses, especially in someone as young as Elizabeth, whose menstrual cycle may not be fully established yet." John's frankly clinical speech made Rose flush to the roots of her hair.

"Well, I...I never..."

"You never what?"

"I'm certainly glad Robbie and Clara are not here to listen to such...such salacious language!"

"It might be better for them if they were," Jenny muttered.

"You mean Elizabeth wasn't..." Tal stepped a fraction closer to John and Jenny.

"What do you think?" Jenny asked, looking pointedly at Elizabeth's corseted waist.

"Rose, you put us through all that family hysteria, and had me write those humiliating letters to the Cannings, and all the time you were wrong about Elizabeth!" Tal sputtered. "Bet, I'm sorry you were subjected to all this unfairness and embarrassment. If you want to come home I'll see there will be no more scenes."

"I haven't made up my mind, Papa. You see, I've been working with Jenny. She's training me to be a nurse. I like it, and I'm not certain I want to give it up. It's gratifying to be able to help people in need, and to do something constructive instead of sitting around doing needlework, uselessly simpering over the latest fashions, living for parties, and wondering whom I will marry." Rose's complexion went from florid to pale. She looked at her husband; his gaze dared her to dig herself in any deeper.

"A nurse! Of all the terrible, disgusting… I don't believe I can join you for dinner after all," she murmured, dabbing a lacy handkerchief over her forehead. "I suddenly have the most raging headache. I'll be all right. I just need to retire."

"I think that is a capital idea, Rose," Tal growled.

"If you still feel bad at bedtime, let me know," John offered. "I'll give you something so you'll sleep."

"Thank you, no, John. Though it's most gracious of you, it just might turn out to be hemlock. I can't believe my own sister would actually have stooped so low as to marry a...a..."

"A what, Rose?" John's tone was as mild as fresh cream.

"A damn Yankee!"

John looked at her as though he could not believe his ears. Then his eyes crinkled and his mouth quirked sideways. He grabbed off his spectacles and nearly bent double with laughter, which Richard echoed wholeheartedly. In the end he had to dig out his handkerchief, wipe his eyes, and blow his nose.

"Well, I never! Tal, we're taking the next train back for Arlington. All of us!" Rose spat.

"No, Rose." He emphasized his words by crossing his arms belligerently.

"What?"

"I said no. You can leave if you want to, but the rest of us are staying as we planned. I, for one, intend to see my daughter crowned Snow Queen, and I want Robbie and Clara here to watch her lead the ball. It'll be Elizabeth's day, and no one is going to rob her of her moment of triumph, especially you."

"You'll stand there and let your own wife be insulted? What kind of man are you?"

"Remember *The Glove and the Lions?* Don't ask me to save you from your own vanity. You brought that on yourself. If you must pay the piper, it's no reflection on me. Now go upstairs before you embarrass yourself further."

Defeated, Rose turned and whisked out of the room as quickly as a woman of her ample girth could whisk. Jenny looked at Elizabeth with an expression of glee, but Tal's face was still as dark as a thundercloud.

"John, please accept my apology for my wife's actions. I'll not try to justify her; there is no excuse for that kind of scene. All I can do is say I regret that it happened. And Bet, I can't tell you how sorry I am about this whole sordid situation. I'll see that your reputation is not damaged. You can come home with us, and I'll personally guarantee that your mother will leave you alone," he said with the grace of a lawyer who has lost a case but knows he will live to argue again another day.

"Thank you, Papa, but you can't guarantee another

person's behavior. I've always taken the brunt of Mother's anger, and I doubt that will ever change. However, I'm used to it, and if I do go home I'm much better able to cope with it now."

At that moment the butler came to the pocket doors to the side hallway and announced dinner. Tal offered his daughter his arm, and she gave him her most charming smile. One huge puzzle piece in her life had just clicked into place. Now if there could only be one more... She shook her head sharply. No. Paul was as far away as the surface of the moon.

Chapter 18

Anticipation of the ball ratcheted up a notch at a time. Early in the morning of New Year's Eve, the caterers and the extra help started arriving, and Elizabeth began to feel the butterflies. Just after lunch, Jenny led her up into the deliciously spooky old attic to hunt up costumes. Generations of clothing had been relegated to storage there, along with family mementos, old furniture, and other oddments too good or too sentimental to throw out.

"What are we looking for, Jen?" Elizabeth asked, surveying the sheet-draped shapes lining the sides of the attic.

"A ball gown for you. There are a lot of them up here. I think I know just the one you need. I really haven't decided what I'll wear. I've been considering going as a gypsy. You know, bare feet, bangles to my elbows, dangling earrings, a bracelet around my ankle, a scarf over loose hair, lots of makeup."

"I like that idea. How about Shane?"

"Oh, you know him. He's as married to that uniform as he is to me. He doesn't even own any civilian clothes to speak of."

"That's close enough to a costume, I guess. At least it's certainly exotic here in New York." Jenny bypassed a long pole hung with oiled silk garment bags, then opened a beetling old armoire.

"Ah! Here!" She pulled out a white garment bag seemingly stuffed to bursting. Enough of a hem protruded for Elizabeth to recognize the dress. She gasped despite herself.

"Isn't that your Grandmother Weston's famous ball gown?"

"The same."

"But I'll never fit into that. To begin with, I'm way too tall."

"I don't think so. She was taller than I am, even when she was in her eighties. Besides, it's actually two separate pieces, and it has an antebellum waist so it'll come low enough in front, and the bow in back will cover the rest. We'll just tie it farther down. And if we can find a narrower crinoline, we can let the tapes down at the top and the length will be just fine."

"But she was so much smaller."

"Not really. She'd already given birth to one strapping son by then, don't forget. I know when I wore it all those years ago I didn't even have to put on a corset. Don't worry. It'll be fine for you."

"But, Jenny, that gown is almost a legend in your family. Your grandmother even had her portrait painted wearing it and she looked so tiny."

"Artists flatter their subjects all the time," Jenny said with an airy shrug.

"I'd feel terrible if something happened to it."

"It won't. But if it does, it's a ball gown. This is a ball. That's what it was made for. Here. You hold the dress. I'll snoop around and see about a crinoline." Jenny shoved the garment bag at Elizabeth and dug through two more armoires until she found what she sought. Then, arms overflowing, the two made their

295

way down the creaky stairs and through the ballroom. Eventually they arrived at the room Elizabeth shared with her Aunt Eleanor.

As they approached, Eleanor opened the door. "So what do we have, girls?" she asked.

"Grandmother Weston's white ball gown. I think it'll fit if we work things right."

"Nothing could be more perfect for a Snow Queen," Eleanor agreed. "So, how about you, Jenny?"

"I just collected some odds and ends. I'll go as a gypsy. But now we have to get Elizabeth dressed, and that'll take a little bit. Everything has to be absolutely perfect."

"Oh, I do *so* agree!" Eleanor clapped her hands together like a little girl. "All right, Bet. Sit down and let us do your hair. We'll use my tiara for your crown."

"Good idea, Aunt Eleanor. Yours is much taller than mine." Jenny took up a comb and began to stroke Elizabeth's hair smooth.

It took them an hour to pile her hair up, weave pearls through it, and set the tiara in just the right position. Inexplicably her stomach tightened as the magic time approached. Jenny had been right about the stunning ball gown. It buttoned easily, and over the substitute crinoline the hem came properly to the floor. Eleanor added a discreet amount of makeup to Elizabeth's face, and before they allowed her a glimpse of herself, Jenny ordered her to close her eyes. As she stood before the glass she felt a warm weight around her throat. She raised her hand to her bosom. Her questing fingertips confirmed her conclusion, counting the three strands of matching graduated pearls caught up in scallops above the large central teardrop.

"Jenny, your pearls!" she whispered without opening her eyes.

"The dress was made to go with that necklace. You'll be the most stunning Snow Queen ever. Ice white looks so much better on you than it ever did on me."

Slowly Elizabeth opened her eyes and allowed them to float into focus. At first she felt overwhelmed by the huge cloud of silk illusion Austrian puffs held in place by hand-embroidered white garlands accented with seed pearls and crystal. The magnificent Weston pearls echoed the sweetheart neckline that merged with insubstantial, off-the-shoulder gathers passing for sleeves. Below the point of the antebellum waist the skirt was divided, the sides caught up in graceful drapes echoing the shape of the necklace. In the gap, a panel of illusion and point d'esprit lace, accented with more of the seed pearls and crystals, came an inch or two shy of the rest of the lace-bordered hem.

"I can't believe it," she whispered, almost incoherent at the sparkling, shimmering vision before her.

"What, Bet?"

"How I look."

Jenny laughed merrily. "You're the loveliest Snow Queen ever. All of New York will be talking about you tomorrow. It'll be in all the newspapers."

"I'm so surprised that the gown fits perfectly, waist and all." Elizabeth stroked her corseted midriff where the delicately embroidered illusion over peau-de-soie lay smooth and perfect against her body.

"You're positively stunning, dear. I think Rose has finally met her match," Eleanor agreed.

"I never wanted to hurt Mother."

"I know you didn't, darling, but sometimes people are their own worst enemies. Now go enjoy your ball and don't give your mother another thought. This is your night, after all."

How can it be my night when the one man I really want to dance with is almost half a world, and certainly a whole lifetime, away? But Miss Eliza found another love after George. Maybe there is hope for me.

The latest in a long line of hired conveyances pulled up at Parkfield's grand front door. One lone passenger stepped out, his brilliant red tunic unremarkable against the fanciful and brightly colored costumes of the other guests. He mounted the steps, then handed his invitation and his hat to the butler, who directed him up the grand staircase. There he joined the line straggling up the stairs to the third floor ballroom, moving slowly in deference to ladies in sometimes voluminous and awkward skirts. Although greeted by several guests, he did no more than reply politely and identify himself as a Canadian friend of Richard Weston's.

The elaborate marble staircase culminated two floors up in a ballroom that reminded him of the one in Adrian Beaufort's grand mansion in River Bend. There he had spent an enchanted night watching Jenny and Shane fall in love. *If it could only be that way for me. But she left Elk Gap to see if she wanted to resume her life in Arlington society. If she's to be persuaded to come back, I have this chance and this one only.*

Inside the ballroom a crowd stirred around in dignified anticipation. He took in the festoons of garlands and bows. Even the great crystal chandeliers had been decorated with balls of mistletoe set off by red velvet ribbons. In its loft a small orchestra tuned discreetly, while the royal blue velvet curtains across the stage-like dais hung motionless, adding to the excitement that preceded the grand appearance of the Snow Queen. He circulated with the crowd until at last he found a familiar face. Jenny, dressed as an appealing gypsy, her tumbled hair loosely tied back by a headscarf, gave him a small wave. Then he saw Shane behind her, wearing full Iroquois regalia: moccasins, leggings, breechclout, and a belted doeskin tunic, all heavy with fringe, elk ivories, and incredibly detailed beadwork.

"Hello, Paul!" Jenny said brightly. Shane merely smiled.

"Good evening, Jenny. God, Shane, I never thought I'd see you dressed like that in a million years."

"Why not? Now everybody knows I have Iroquois blood, I may as well own up to it."

"It certainly caught me off guard."

"This is a costume ball, after all. Nobody thinks twice about what anyone else is wearing," Jenny responded, flashing a bare, braceleted ankle above ballet technique slippers.

"I did notice that nobody stared at me like they did when I came down for your wedding." He combed the crowd with his eyes.

"Before you ask, Paul, yes, she's here. She's the Snow Queen this year, so she'll be on the dais," Jenny said.

"Snow Queen?" he echoed.

"Yes. The Snow Queen and her consort, the Lord of Misrule, who lead the dancing, are a tradition at the

Weston New Year's Ball. This year Father appointed Elizabeth. She'll come down from the dais and choose her partner for the first dance." She glanced at Shane, who looked down at the toes of his elaborately beaded moccasins.

"Don't you think it's about time?" Paul asked.

"Pretty soon. Uncle Richard is playing the Court Jester. He'll come out in a minute." Paul felt his stomach tighten and tried to hide his nerves. To his chagrin, his partner's steel-gray eyes were on him. Then the velvet curtains twitched and began to open, and Richard, dressed in parti-colored hose and tunic and a horned jester's hat, leaped through the breach, danced a little jig, and shook his belled staff until silence fell.

"Oyez! Oyez! Oyez! Ladies and gentlemen, loyal subjects, on this portentous and joyous Yuletide, I give you Prince John, Lord of Misrule, and your sovereign, Her Imperial Majesty, the Snow Queen!"

Paul looked up at the stage, and his breath came in involuntarily. He had never seen such a breathtaking vision as Elizabeth in her cloud of silk and pearls.

Perhaps two hundred guests drew back toward the walls of the ballroom, and all bowed deeply. With great dignity John rose and gave Elizabeth his arm, and amid a fanfare of trumpets they descended carpeted steps leading to the dance floor. Then John bowed to her and backed away, and she was on her own. The orchestra would not even begin until she selected her partner.

Suddenly overwhelmed, Paul stepped backward, almost hiding behind a woman in a huge ostrich-plume headdress. He could still see Elizabeth, regal and graceful, gliding toward the assemblage. All manner of costumes and all manner of masked faces watched her raptly. Musketeers, knights, ladies, magicians, courtiers, fairies, Indians, pirates—seemingly a lifetime of myths and legends materialized before her, and every one stood at her beck and call, at least until midnight and the new year. With proper hauteur she made eye contact with a dozen or so young men whose expressions said they stood willing to die for a mere smile. One rather nondescript Mountie could easily become lost in this crowd. With bated breath he waited and watched as she scanned her gathered subjects. As she progressed down the line, he withdrew even farther behind the tall lady with the feathers in her hair.

To the accompaniment of the tinkling chandeliers, Elizabeth shimmered her way down the ballroom floor, holding her fan as if it were truly a royal scepter. The graceful ball gown dazzled Paul's eyes until watching her regal approach became almost painful. He saw her pause and look his direction.

She thinks I'm Shane. I'm probably the last person she expects here Well, if a case of mistaken identity nets me a dance, I'd be a fool not to make the best of it. He turned so it would be difficult for her to see his face or the sergeant's stripes on his sleeve. She broke off from her path down the line of guests and pointed toward him with her fan. Then when she came close enough to see him fully, a look somewhere between astonishment and fear flashed across her face. He watched her cast a desperate glance around, as though looking for a way out. But when he discreetly looked to his right, where Shane had been standing, his partner had vanished like the Iroquois warrior he really was. Committed, Elizabeth had nowhere else to go. She drew herself up a little taller and indicated him with her fan.

In the spirit of things, he took a knee. "Your Imperial Majesty," he murmured. As one in a dream, she gave him her hand, holding it regally down, forcing his bow even lower. He kissed her gloved fingers, then rose and took her in his arms. He felt her come to him, light as the sparkling cloud she resembled. Then the orchestra began to play, and they stepped out into the swinging rhythm of a waltz, her voluminous skirt breaking like a comber against his ankles. In the fantasy ball gown and unimaginably expensive jewels, with her hair up in a careless, pearl-shot riot of curls, rouge on her lips and cheeks, she looked so beautiful it made his heart ache.

"What are you doing here?" she managed at length.

"I was invited," he replied, feeling a wry grin spread across his face.

"I had thought I was going to ask Shane to lead the ball with me."

"I know. I was watching you. Surprised?"

"Of course. I had no idea…"

"I know you didn't. But Shane would have killed me if I hadn't accepted the invitation."

"It doesn't do to defy one's superior officer, after all." Her frosty voice sent a chill down his backbone.

"Well, you're queen of this ball. You led the dancing with me by mistake. We needn't dance again if you don't want to."

"Well, I do owe everyone the honor of at least one dance."

"Tall order that, what with the number of gentlemen here. So afterward I gather you're going back to Arlington?" He initiated a sweeping turn; she kept up with him with leggy grace.

"I haven't made up my mind. My trip here was mostly to silence wagging tongues. I may just return to Elk Gap."

"Why do that if you don't have to? Life is a lot easier in Arlington."

She shrugged. "In some ways, yes. In most, no. I've grown accustomed to working with Jenny, and I like it. However, you must agree that Elk Gap is somewhat limited."

"Not really. You have Garver Finley trailing after you like a hound on scent and his father is reasonably rich." The bitterness in his voice surprised him.

"You're right, of course. If I'm only after marriage, I should really go back to Arlington. The son of one bank president is truly slim pickings." They lapsed into silence then, and he noticed many couples had joined them on the dance floor, including Jenny and Shane. Once again he reflected on their happiness and felt a flash of regret he and Elizabeth could not share the same thing.

But if it's not to be, it's not to be. I just have to accept that.

After the music ended he thanked her for the dance and handed her off to John, who, dressed in the purple cape and white tunic of the Lord of Misrule, claimed the next one. He drifted around, looking for Jenny and Shane, and because they were still dancing, he found a convenient young woman dressed as a French courtesan and invited her onto the dance floor. He amused himself that way most of the evening, as he did at home when the local timber baron Adrian Beaufort gave his huge galas at which all the River Bend detachment of the Royal Northwest were expected to give command performances: he kept the widows and wallflowers happy. But after explaining ever so many times that no, his uniform was not a costume, and yes, he was really a Royal Northwest Mounted Police officer, the evening began to weigh heavily on him.

Finally the orchestra took a break. He looked around for Elizabeth and found her sitting next to a window, the center of a large circle of admirers. He gave up on that scene and found Jenny not too far away, sipping punch with her Aunt Eleanor.

"So, Paul, are you having a good time?" Jenny asked rhetorically.

He shrugged. "It's an impressive affair, all right."

"And Elizabeth has made a grand Snow Queen," Eleanor put in.

"You'll get no argument from me on that."

"She opened the ball with you, after all," Shane said, taking Paul by an elbow and steering him away from the women so they could talk privately.

Paul shook his head slowly as they walked. "It was a mistake. She thought I was you. She was as cold as ice toward me. I haven't talked to her since."

"Well, you can lead a horse to water, et cetera," Shane said with a sigh.

"Yes. It appears there's nothing between us now, unless she decides to come back to Elk Gap. I'm not holding my breath."

"So are you going home?"

"I think so. Tomorrow's a holiday, so I couldn't get a train, but I think I'll go back the day after and relieve Laurence early. I know you and Richard and Jenny are staying a few more days, but all I'd be doing is using my fingers to count my toes if I waited to go back with you."

"Well, if that's the way you feel…"

"Yes, it is. I'm ready to admit I'm beaten."

"All right. But at least come back here for lunch tomorrow? Jenny says that's a family tradition. No one wants to get up for breakfast after such a late night, so they always have a big buffet at one."

"Why? What's the point?"

"Just to celebrate the holiday among friends."

Paul sighed. He felt genuine fondness for Shane and Jenny; it would go hard with him to disappoint either of them. "Well, since you put it that way…"

"Yes, I do. And what's more, do you remember the lecture you gave me when I was willing to let Jenny go back to New York? You asked me if I'd mislaid my manhood somewhere? I'm going to ask you to take a long look in the mirror and ask the same thing of yourself. If you leave New York, it may be the last you'll ever see of Elizabeth. I know how you feel about her. Are you willing to let her go just because she offended your pride?"

Paul sighed. Shane, as usual, had hit the bull's-eye. All the dancing around each other he and Elizabeth had done for the last three months had its origin in his hurt feelings. "I honestly don't know, Shane. If she wants to go, there's nothing I can do to prevent it."

"Except fight for her. Tell her how you feel, and let her make up her mind. Now, I expect to see you tomorrow, right?" Shane hand gripped his shoulder, an oddly reassuring gesture since they rarely touched each other.

"If that's all, I think I'll thank our host and go back to my hotel room. There are enough people here I won't be missed. If I were a lady I'd have a headache."

"Well, then, if you must. *Á demain, mon vieux.*"

"*Á demain*, partner." He watched Shane go back to Jenny and Eleanor, then wandered toward the door. The orchestra began playing again, a waltz he found familiar. His sisters Lorena and Alicia had learned it on the piano and played and sung it until he thought he would never forget it if he lived to be a hundred.

After the ball is over,
After the break of morn—
After the dancers' leaving;
After the stars are gone;
Many a heart is aching,
If you could read them all;
Many the hopes that have vanished
After the ball.

As he made his way through the crowd, he saw Elizabeth walking toward the center of the floor. She gave him a poignant look, then reluctantly turned to her partner. But half way to the door he was waylaid by Eleanor in her sparkling domino mask, southern belle ball gown, and henna-red hair in barrel curls.

"Oh, Sergeant, you simply *must* ask me to dance," she said with an exaggerated Southern accent that had always meant tongue-in-cheek among the Brisbane clan. "Why, I've been waiting all evening!"

"I had no idea you had aspirations in my direction, Mrs. Hanley," he responded with a smile. Eleanor's euphuistic flirtatiousness excused a lot.

"But of course! You're a handsome gentleman, if a little young for me."

"My goodness, I'd never guess you were *une femme d'une certain age.*"

"We are *all d'une certain age*, Sergeant Weller." She fluttered her fan toward her bosom and batted heavily mascaraed eyelashes at him. In spite of himself he felt his brown study lifting.

"Then, would you grant me the honor of this dance, Mrs. Hanley?" He bowed elaborately and drew a deep curtsey by way of reward.

"The honor is entirely mine, Sergeant." The consummate debutante, Eleanor danced well, and her lightness in his arms lifted his mood, at least for the moment. "So, are you enjoying the evening, then?" she continued at length.

"It's quite the extravaganza, isn't it?"

"Since my brother-in-law is widowed and quite absorbed in his work, he isn't given to entertaining. This is the only party he ever hosts, so in a manner of speaking, every effort goes into it. Martha and I literally plan for it all year."

"You've done very well between the two of you."

"Between us there's very little we can't do."

Except make things right between Elizabeth and me. The abrupt change in his mood must have been evident, because Eleanor cocked her head and gave him a concerned look.

"Is everything all right, Sergeant?" she asked.

"I'm just tired. It was a long, boring train ride from Ontario, and I'm not used to simply sitting around with nothing to do for days on end."

"And you have that long trip to look forward to on the way back. Pity."

"I've brought along a good book. Shane lent me his copy of *By the Grace of God.*"

"You must tell Richard how much you enjoyed it.

As a writer, his worst fear is that his friends won't like his work."

"I read *Milestones* twice because it was so interesting, but it's a history text. I like history. It's real. It's something you can sink your teeth into. I've never been much for made-up stories, but he brings the same scholarship to fiction. So far I feel as if I'm right there in France with the duchess and all her entourage."

"High praise. He'd be gratified to know." Then the orchestra drew out the ending of the piece, and he squired Eleanor back to the sidelines. After turning her over to her next partner, he consulted his pocket watch. It read eleven-fifteen. So instead of locating John and paying his compliments, he decided to hang around until the end, which came and went unremarkably. After the traditional "Auld Lang Syne" at midnight and the kiss from someone he barely knew to herald the new year, he made his way down the grand staircase with the crowd.

He encountered a windless night, cold but not bitter, and had almost made up his mind to walk back to the hotel when the offer of a shared cab intervened. He accepted, but to his almost immediate chagrin it was occupied by the parents of an awkward, chubby wallflower with whom he had danced twice out of charity. Her mother chattered nonstop about wonderful this and perfectly lovely that, and did he not think it the grandest ball he had ever attended? He looked back over a year and a half to a reception for the governor of Ontario. As great and grand as John's party was, it could not hold a candle to one magic night when he had watched his best friend hopelessly in love. He mindlessly agreed here and there, nodding and following the woman's recitation with half his attention, then bade them a happy new year at his hotel and felt glad the whole ordeal had finally ended.

Chapter 19

Elizabeth sat before her bedroom vanity table in her nightgown, deconstructing her elaborate coiffure and winding her hair around kid curlers. There had been tea and some small refreshments in the front parlor after the guests departed, and now she was left face to face with an evening that had further shattered her heart. In retrospect, it seemed a hideous mistake to have accepted John's nomination as Snow Queen. Yes, it indeed had cleared her reputation and paved the way for her to return to Arlington, but now, facing her freshly washed face in the mirror, she also faced how wrong that course of action felt. She combed back over every minute she had spent in Elk Gap, how she had saved Alice Redfield from choking, what had transpired when she and Jenny had been kidnapped, every single routine day in the clinic, and she realized how alive, how vital she had felt. The life of a debutante seemed wasted and sterile, useless when laid against the sense of purpose she had discovered working with Jenny. But one big obstacle loomed in the way of returning to Elk Gap; it had Paul David Weller written all over it. As she saw it, she had two choices: either accept the fact he would never forgive her for what he considered a betrayal and carry on despite, or give up and go cringing back to Arlington like a whipped cur with her tail between her legs. Even though tears blurred her image in the mirror, she drew herself up tall. She was not now, nor would she ever be, a whipped cur. She might even accept the attentions of one of the young men in Elk Gap. Or maybe more than one, if she so chose.

She awoke the next morning to softly falling snow. The Dresden clock on her vanity table read eleven when she hauled herself out of bed. In her mother's absence she decided she could get away with pulling her hair back and tying it with a black velvet ribbon, and wearing her lavender shirtwaist and a black skirt. She looked at herself, then went back to the vanity table, opened her jewelry case, and took out the locket her great-grandmother had never worn. She redid the bow on her blouse into an ascot and arranged the locket over it. Deciding she was pleased with the look, she dabbed on a little lavender water and wandered downstairs. Half way down the grand staircase she heard Clara practicing on the concert grand piano in the formal parlor. To her surprise the rest of the family was there too, in a comfortable tableau that included Martha coaching Clara at the piano, with Barkley beside them on the bench, Shane working with wax pastels, the three Westons sharing the *New York Times,* and Robbie sitting cross-legged on the floor, engaged in a chess game with their father.

"Hello, Bet!" Eleanor caroled. "Coffee? Tea? In deference to our committed Canadian, we have both this morning." It took a moment for her to realize her aunt meant Shane, who disdained coffee. She recalled Paul was just as bad.

"Coffee, please." Eleanor filled a delicate china cup and handed it to her as she claimed a vacant chair. Shane looked over at her with a little moué of distaste, but when she took a sip from her cup, she found both the strength and the temperature perfect.

"It was quite a fête last night, wasn't it?" Eleanor asked.

"Quite," Elizabeth agreed.

"It'll be written up extensively and all over Arlington by tomorrow."

"Then Aunt Rose can quit crying scandal," Jenny responded in an undertone.

"Gossip won't matter if I don't go home."

"I can't imagine you not coming home," Tal said, tearing his attention from the chess game to look up at her.

"I've missed you, Bet." Robbie gave his sister his most appealing look.

"Well, I've missed you and Clara both, but there comes a time when everyone grows up and leaves home. It's the way things are supposed to be." She sipped her coffee again.

"You're unmarried and not of age yet," her father reminded her.

"Close enough to twenty-one that it shouldn't make much difference. You could take me back to Arlington and compel me to stay there for all of, um, two months and three weeks."

"You're right. I may as well declare you emancipated." Tal gave in gracefully. At that moment Martha and Clara changed the song they were practicing. It became *After the Ball.* Elizabeth fell silent. Her own heart was among the casualties the song spoke of. They had almost reached the refrain when the butler ushered a visitor into the formal parlor. Her stomach contracted into a hard knot as Paul came down the four steps between the foyer and the living room.

"Hello, Paul. Tea?" Eleanor caroled.

"Yes, thank you, Mrs. Hanley." But his eyes were on Elizabeth, except for the few moments when shaking hands with the gentlemen and greeting the ladies claimed his attention. Then he drew up a chair between Shane and Tal and leaned over the chessboard.

"Your move," Tal prompted. Robbie's hand wavered over the pieces.

"Castle," Paul whispered. "You'll put him in check." Triumphantly Robbie followed Paul's advice and announced check.

"It's not very often I can best Father."

"You're in a position to mate in three moves."

"Yes, I can see it. Thank you, Sergeant. But I didn't know you played chess."

"In addition to boxing there was a chess club in my high school. They wanted us to use our minds as well as our muscles."

"A sound approach," John agreed absently, pausing as Martha and Clara came to the end of their tune. "I love that song. Would you please sing it for us, Elizabeth? You have a lovely voice. It'll also be good training for Clara to accompany a soloist." It was on the tip of her tongue to refuse, but one does not deny one's host. She set her coffee cup on a convenient occasional table and took up a place next to the piano where she could see the music if she needed it. She nodded to Martha, who gave Clara a count, and they launched into the four-measure introduction. Elizabeth smiled at her sister's competent little hands, still childishly straight-fingered as they moved over the keys.

Elizabeth drew breath, then began the sad,

sentimental little ballad in which a little girl asked her bachelor uncle why he never married. As it came to its denouement, she watched her audience, especially Paul.

That's why I'm lonely, no home at all;
I broke her heart pet, after the ball.
After the ball is over,
After the break of morn—
After the dancers' leaving;
After the stars are gone;
Many a heart is aching,
If you could read them all;
Many the hopes that have vanished
After the ball.

She held her last note out, giving Martha, playing secondo to Clara's primo, a chance for a dramatic plagal cadence, which she accomplished with a flourish.

John was the first to his feet. "Bravo," he called as he applauded. "Bravo!" Elizabeth took her bow, then gestured to Martha and Clara. Her sister wiggled down from the bench, grabbed up Barkley, and all three linked hands and took a second bow. Elizabeth sneaked a discreet peek at Paul, whose expression had gone from neutrally pleasant to introspective.

As she came down from the dais, the butler appeared in the doorway and announced lunch was served. With a poignant look at Paul, Elizabeth accepted her father's arm and allowed him to escort her into the dining room. After John pronounced the blessing, he seated her.

"Are you comfortable?" he asked with his usual punctilious politeness.

"Quite, thank you." Her voice held a debutante's

detachment. She wandered through lunch, eating little and saying less. Outside a gentle, light snow fell, isolating the house and silencing the noises of city streets. It reminded her of the quiet in Elk Gap. She turned her mind loose and let it slip back into the peace and purpose she had known there. Surreptitiously she cut her eyes toward Paul from time to time. He seemed almost as detached as she felt, only speaking when someone addressed him, paying attention to his meal.

So what if he and I have insurmountable differences? I need the life I had in Elk Gap. I need to work with Jenny, help her patients, and go riding on Sundays. I need to walk to Tillman's, chat with Ruth at the post office, and go to the Ladies' Handwork Society. Arlington can go begging. I don't need to be strangled by someone else's false ideas of propriety, to be told I'm too tall, too clumsy, too whatever. I need to be where I'm needed. Whatever Paul does or doesn't do, I'm going back with Jenny and Shane. Perhaps the attraction I felt for him was only puppy love, meant to come to naught. It doesn't matter. I'll be where I can make a positive difference in people's lives. I'll be doing something important, something of value. That of itself can be good and fulfilling.

"You're quiet, Bet," Jenny observed.

"Just thinking."

"Oh?"

"About Arlington and Elk Gap. I'll have to make up my mind soon."

"Not really. If you go home with Uncle Tal you can come back any time. After all, it's a woman's privilege to change her mind."

"Thank you. You've at least made me feel better."

"I meant to, Bet. I know you've felt pressured about your decision."

"Truly, no." Elizabeth hoped she could give her cousin the lie in a convincing manner.

"I'm glad," Jenny replied. "I wouldn't want to add to any burden you may feel."

"Rest assured you haven't."

The table conversation drifted off in a different direction then, leaving her comfortably ensconced in her decision. After the meal ended, the family returned to the formal parlor. Paul hung back until he could step in next to Elizabeth.

"I know it's snowing outside, but would you walk with me a while? Maybe the maze?" His words were tentative, unlike the competent, forceful Paul she knew.

"The weather isn't that severe. I wouldn't mind. But have you a reason?"

"Just to say goodbye. I'm leaving tomorrow. I don't feel I can leave Laurence by himself much longer."

"Well, then...all right. My coat is in the guest closet."

"Paul, if you're going to go running around outside, wear my parka. I told you, you should have brought yours. It gets cold in New York too," Shane said as he passed them.

"Next time I'll know better." Conscious of his presence, she led into the side hall to the *porte cochère* and let Paul help her with her seal coat. While she settled her hat, he shrugged into Shane's bead-trimmed white wolf parka, which left a two-inch margin of red cuff below the sleeves. She took his arm while they negotiated the slippery steps, and then they headed down the path toward the privet maze. The snow still fell, lazy goose feathers from a dirty gray sky. She was glad she had worn boots, because at least three inches of fresh fluff had accumulated overnight. She could even smell the snow, a certain dry tingle at the tip of her nose.

"So you wanted to say goodbye to me?" she asked rhetorically as they approached the maze.

"Yes. As I said, I have a train ticket for tomorrow. So what will you do?"

A lifetime of living with Rose Talbot made Elizabeth cautious. "I'm not certain yet. You know how much I've loved working with Jenny at the clinic." They strolled through the entrance to the maze, leaving tracks in the pristine snow. Overhead the large trees that shaded the yard in summer stretched eerie, skeletal branches skyward, while the ornate gardens lay shrouded in a soft, white blanket that hid winter's dead ugliness.

"Well, whatever you do, I just wanted to say that I wish you all the best. I hope whichever life you choose turns out well for you. And I also want you to know that...that..." He seemed to be gathering his courage, something she had never thought to see.

"That what?" she prompted.

"That..." He paused, swallowing heavily. "I had to come here after you. I could accept it if you rejected me or turned your back on me to go back to your high society life in Arlington. What I can't accept is the coldness, the distance that has grown between us."

"That came about because you accused me of deceiving you." She looked up at him, a thing she still found surprising.

"I did, and I shouldn't have. I'm sorry I said what I did. I was hurt and I just reacted."

Elizabeth considered his words; they touched her in a deep spot she had thought invulnerable. But this was the moment of truth, or, more precisely, the moment for truth. "Well, before this goes any farther, you need to know the truth. I was never married."

"I won't tell you that thought never crossed my mind. People of your social status insist on proper engagements. A whirlwind courtship is simply not done."

"No, it's not. I have to tell you the rest, because by the time I'm through you may change your mind about me altogether. Last summer at Sand Island a man courted me. His father is an impossibly rich railroad baron. Mother was delighted someone like Noah found me attractive. She pushed me at him every chance she had. Just before we were to return to Arlington he maneuvered me into going to a picnic with him, alone. He told me others would join us at the next island, but it was a deception. He gave me something to drink that made me so sleepy I didn't have the strength to resist him, and he...he took advantage of me. Mother sent me to Jenny to hide my shame; she'd have sent me to Europe except that one can't do the Continent when there's a war on. I know there was all kinds of speculation in Elk Gap that I was some sort of erring girl banished by her family. It would have been confirmed had I not lost the baby. Jenny told me it was defective and couldn't have lived. That was a little over a month ago. Now Mother thinks I was never...compromised, as it were. My appearance as Snow Queen will clear my reputation. But now you know the truth, how do you feel about me?"

"What happened to you wasn't your doing, but if I could get my hands around that bastard's neck I can guarantee he'd regret ever touching you. He'd regret it for the rest of his life. All two hours of it." She saw his right hand clench into a gauntleted fist.

Their conversation paused while they rounded a bend in the maze. In spite of the long distance, they neared the center.

"You could forgive me?" she asked at length.

"There's nothing to forgive. What I couldn't forgive is him taking your innocence."

"He's a rakehell, it's true, but what he did to me forced him to join the regular Army instead of waiting for his West Point appointment, so perhaps he'll be repaid in time. At any rate, it's no concern of mine any longer."

"You didn't love him, then?"

She shook her head slowly. "Of course his attention flattered me, but no. I think I was more afraid of him than anything." They rounded another corner and came to the center of the maze, where snow had turned the now dry fountain into a weird abstract sculpture and laid down soft-looking cushions on the marble benches.

He turned to face her, taking her gloved hands in his. "And me? Do you fear me too?"

"No. I trust you, Paul. I always have."

"You trust me? Is that all, then?"

"Should there be more?"

"At one time I had hopes, yes. I still do, for all that." He looked down at her, his gaze locking with hers. She saw such sincerity there she could not tear her eyes away.

319

"Paul..."

"I love you and I want you to marry me. Please? You can give it some thought. I'm not demanding an immediate answer, by any means. I just want you to know that..." His voice bogged down and he swallowed heavily, and in that moment the tears in her eyes blurred the monochrome landscape into a shimmering rainbow.

"That what?"

"That I'm yours. Forever. If you would be the wife of a very ordinary cop, that is."

"Paul..."

"Please, Elizabeth?" Smoothly he dropped to one knee in the snow. "I'm proposing to you formally. Please marry me? Be my wife?"

"What happened to take my time to make up my mind?" she asked with a small laugh. He rose easily, with the often surprising strength of a wiry man. He moved toward her, halving the distance between them. His hands came to her shoulders, drawing her to him as he had after the wedding ball.

"Because I have to go home in two days, and I want nothing more than for you to come with me. We don't have to marry right away..."

"You still want me after what I've told you?"

"I just said I do." She heard the patience in his voice and knew it could wear thin.

"I...I love you too. I have since Jenny's wedding. Thinking you were lost to me broke my heart."

"But I'm not lost to you. I'm right here, and I'll be by your side for the rest of my life if you want me."

"I do want you, Paul. I want to be with you forever. I'd be honored to be your wife." Now she had said the words, a crushing weight dissolved from her soul. She yielded to the pressure of his hands and moved into his arms. Oblivious to the world, they kissed, while around them the curtaining snow fell.

December 26, 1822

Yesterday we had guests at Brookhaven. The entire Talbot family came to celebrate Christmas with us. It was a very happy occasion all around. After supper my mother suggested a stroll in the garden since it was an unusually fine night. However, Robert steered me back into the parlor, wanting a word with me. There he presented me with a lovely little serpentine parquetry box. He instructed me to open it, and when I did, nestled inside in a bed of white velvet I found the most beautiful ring I could imagine: a deep blue sapphire surrounded by small diamonds. Robert dropped to one knee before me and asked me to become his wife. When I accepted his proposal, he placed the ring on my finger and sealed it there with a kiss.

Now I know the direction my life will take. In due course I will be the mistress of his household, and eventually he will inherit Archer's Walk, a plantation every bit as great and grand as Brookhaven. Robert is kind and good and gentle, and when I make my vow to God to love, honor, and obey him and to keep myself only for him, it will be no more than the public reiteration of the pledge my heart has already made. I will bear his children and raise them to be godly men and women, and I will make his home a haven for him. In return I know I can trust him to be the kind of husband the Bible directs, to love me even as he loves himself, to be true to me, and to provide for and protect me to the end of our days.

The rest of the evening passed for me in a sort of sweet fog. Robert's sister played the piano and we all sang carols, and Father proposed a toast to Robert and me, for long life, prosperity, happiness, and children. It was close to midnight when the Talbots left to drive home, after inviting us to Archer's Walk to celebrate the new year. I will be counting the days until I can see Robert again, but I think I will not have to wait the entire week. He promised that if the weather held he would ride over to Brookhaven to visit me.

Of course Mother and I have discussed the wedding. My trousseau has been ready for some time now, and I am going to turn my hand to embroidering the fabric for my wedding dress. I have some lovely pale pink silk that I will sprig with little flowers, well suited for a spring ceremony. It will be the event of the season, uniting two influential landed families into something greater than the sum of their parts.

I see now that all the pain and grief I underwent when George died was only the fire to refine me into gold pure enough to present myself to a man like Robert. It made me sensitive and compassionate, careful of others' hearts. It ablated the last of my adolescent self-centeredness in a forge of loss and sorrow, and it made me realize that life can be short and happiness fleeting, so when times are good, as they are now, I need to enjoy them to the fullest, laying up an account of sorts to give myself strength against life's trials. I pray to God for the grace to enter my new life as Mrs. Robert Talbot with a serene and loving heart, with hands ever ready to serve, with fortitude to do what must be done, and with wisdom to know His will for me.

~*~

June 19, 1823

Yesterday was the happiest day of my life. I consider my prayer for God's grace and His will fulfilled, at least in part, when I came down Brookhaven's grand staircase on Father's arm. My bridegroom awaited me in the formal front parlor with the most beautiful smile I have ever seen. He truly adores me, and I him.

Pansy cried as she did my hair and sent me off with an embrace. Mother's reaction was similar when she crowned me with the pearlin veil under which four generations of brides in her family have been wed. I had thought it destroyed in the fire, but to her relief she discovered it packed away in a cedar chest that came through undamaged. I wore the gown on which I had spent so many hours and carried a bouquet of day lilies from our garden. Pansy, Nanny Pearl, Titus, and Feli, Cicero, and the other house servants watched from the dining room door, and I saw tears in practically every eye. Robert's mother and sisters were even dabbing handkerchiefs to their cheeks.

Our own Reverend Donovan waited for us in front of the fireplace in the formal parlor. It had been festooned with garlands of the same lilies I carried. But I had eyes only for Robert, whose soft, private smile when Father gave me to him felt like enough to warm my heart for the rest of my life. And when I promised God to honor my husband and keep myself only for him, I knew I would never mean anything as much as I meant those words. Then he sealed the wedding band onto my hand and kissed me, and my heart took flight as ecstatically as any bird.

And now a new life begins for Robert and me. Since I have conveniently come to the last leaf in this journal, I shall also start a new volume. I know there will be more endings and beginnings in our lives, and I shall set them down faithfully. The chronicle of my life is my gift to the future. By the grace of God someone else, hopefully a descendant of ours, will come along someday and profit by my experiences. If so, wherever my soul is, I shall rejoice. So I send my blessings and my best wishes to the next eyes that read this memoir. Go bravely into your future, do well, and when the opportunity presents itself, take the path of good and right. May the Lord bless you and keep you ever in health and happiness.

Eliza Regina Morgan Talbot.

A word about the author...

After a long and varied work life that began as an English teacher and ended as a computer support technician, Lael Neill retired to a new career: becoming a full-time author. She began writing somewhere around age eight, studied Creative Writing under (or rather, worshiped at the feet of) Dr. H. L. Anshutz at Central Washington University, and has finally fulfilled her lifelong dream.

A transplant from the Pacific Northwest, she lives on two wooded acres in rural Central Texas with deer, bunnies, armadillos, hawks, the occasional skunk, and a resident roadrunner. In between stints of writing, she decompresses with volunteer work, knitting, and music.

www.ingramcontent.com/pod-product-compliance
Lightning Source LLC
Chambersburg PA
CBHW071527260626
47170CB00002B/535